#STATIC

ERIC LASTER
#STATIC

AUTOMATIC PUBLISHING

9200 Sunset Blvd, PH 22, Los Angeles, CA 90069
automaticpublishing@gmail.com
automaticpublishing.com

Design by Debbie Berne
Daggers and lettering by DoubleMRanch

Manufactured in the United States of America.

Summary: A murder mystery about coming of age and brotherly love, complete with lust, meds, family dysfunction, and an afterlife Walmart.

First edition 2016
9 8 7 6 5 4 3 2 1

ISBN 978-0-9912729-3-8

For Kate

1

It was strange—Wilt calling me when he'd died the week before. Maybe a lot of other people get calls from the spirit world or whatever, but it was a first for me and so I didn't pick up until the fifth or sixth ring.

"It's me."

His voice didn't have that hollow sound you sometimes get on a cell. He could've been in the next room.

"Uh, what're you doing?" I said.

"Not much."

"I'm not going to tell you again," Mom threatened, "I *will* take that thing away from you."

I'd answered the phone in the middle of dinner—a big no-no where I live. No calls, texts, tweets, IMs—no cyber-doings of any kind at the feeding table is Mom's rule. It's supposed to be Family Time.

"Is that what you want?" she said. "You want your social life to be laughable, your friends unable to urgently get in touch with you to say all kinds of things of no importance?"

"But it's Wilt."

The words came out before I could decide if it was a good idea to tell her. Mom's face crumpled like it was made of tissue paper.

"Is that supposed to be funny?"

I thought she was going to cry so I handed her the phone, which I know confused her because she did this little chicken-bob with her head, moving it backwards and forwards like I couldn't be serious, but there I was, acting serious.

"Hello?"

She pinned me with this huge disbelieving stare when she heard his voice. Then she did cry—just the tears, no sound and her whole body shaking while she kept saying "uh huh" into the phone, which she eventually handed back to me.

"He wants to talk to you."

"Hey," my brother said.

"So . . . where are you?"

Soon as I asked, I thought of a better question, like *why* was he calling, but we got cut off.

Mom let tears fall onto her plate while I wondered if maybe Wilt had been calling from his coffin and we'd made a big mistake burying him, but I couldn't remember if we'd buried him with his phone.

"Should I try him back?"

It was the only time Mom didn't tell me what to do. She shook her head, nodded, shrugged. I got Wilt's voicemail:

"If I wanted to talk to you, douceface, I would have answered. Leave a message."

I hung up. No way Wilt was calling from his coffin, not after a whole week and the autopsy and all the stuff they did to his body at the funeral home.

"What'd he say to you?" I asked Mom.

She didn't hear me right away. "I had trouble concentrating. It was about Suzy, I think."

Suzy? Wilt had called to talk about his girlfriend? Why would he do—?

Duh. This was like some movie where he was going to give me clues to prove Suzy'd killed him. Or had hired a hit man to kill him. I'd follow the clues, learn that Wilt had been involved with Suzy in some big scheme to make money but she'd gotten greedy. I'd learn things about Wilt that I'd never known and would probably be better off not knowing.

"You think maybe he wants us to help the police find his . . . I mean, the person who, you know, might have had something to do with—"

"Life isn't a video game!" Mom screamed, getting up from the table and taking my plate even though I wasn't done eating.

Murder, murderer: I should've known better than to go near those words.

2

The night of the crash, a couple detectives drove us to the hospital morgue to ID the body. They watched Mom sob on my brother for a while—watched me too, while I stood there wondering why I didn't feel like bawling. I used to think it'd be pretty cool to see a dead person up close, but when the person's all bruised and cut and swollen and doesn't look the way he's supposed to, it basically just sucks. There are places on the body I didn't know could balloon up so much. Wilt's face looked like the Elephant Man's after being pummeled big-time in a UFC cage match.

The detectives eventually took us out to the hall and asked us questions. Did we know what Wilt was doing on St. Benny Road at eleven p.m.? (No idea.) Had he been particularly depressed or suicidal lately? (Not that we'd noticed.) Did he have anything against telephone poles because the one he'd hit head-on was as dead as he was? (. . .) Mom didn't tell them Wilt shouldn't have been driving the car, that she'd banned him from using it on account of finding this fist-sized wad of cash he kept hidden in a sock under his mattress. He hadn't said where the money came from and so she'd accused him of dealing drugs and banned him from using the car until he admitted to dealing drugs.

Which he never did.

I don't know if Mom was afraid of telling the detectives about the cash or what, especially after they said they couldn't rule anything out—not accident, suicide or murder—and that they'd be holding on to what was left of the car till further notice. All I know is that she didn't say anything about it and flashed me this look like I shouldn't either.

The detectives drove us back to our apartment and one of them gave her his card in case she had questions or remembered anything potentially helpful, and I was all, *What, I don't get a card 'cause I can't be potentially helpful?* They said they'd interview Dad once he was back in town, and then Mom and I were trudging upstairs to our dinky one-bedroom—a ten-floor walk-up ever since Mr. Pappas our landlord decided no way he'd fix the elevators, he wanted us freeloading tenants to move out so he could sell the building to developers for serious money—we were clumping up the stairs when somewhere around the seventh floor I noticed Mom wasn't behind me. I found her crouched on a landing a little ways down, hugging herself while she rocked back and forth, mumbling over and over again, "How do I get through this?"

3

I was at the computer the second time Wilt called, fifty minutes after the first, Mom pressing at the nicotine patch under
her left collarbone, saying that if I had to stare at naked women
on a screen, I could at least check out NatGeo's site and learn
about other cultures while I was at it.

"It's a skate video," I told her.

Then my phone rang and she laid off the nicotine patch
and came over from the couch to watch me answer it.

"Hello?"

"It's me."

I nodded, which was pretty dumb. "Can you see me?"

"Don't be stupid. Wait, you can't help it!" He fake-laughed
at his own joke. "What's Suzy been up to?"

"How should I know?"

I didn't exactly have a VIP pass to Suzy's world and Wilt
knew it, and for a second I wondered if he was just rubbing it
in as usual—that he'd been with a girl like Suzy and I never
would be. But then he didn't say I'd only ever be with inflatable
toys, *if* I was lucky, so I thought maybe dying had made him

more sensitive and he really was asking after Suzy. Unless he was just easing into what he had to verbal by asking about his murderer.

"I've only seen her once," I told him. *At the funeral* I didn't say, to keep Mom from freaking. "Aren't you gonna ask if she's seemed at all suspicious?"

"Why?"

Mom started splashing invisible water on her face, wanting me to give her the phone.

"You're gonna ask if Suzy's showing signs of guilt," I said. "She *should* be acting guilty, right? Because of, you know, criminal behavior? What's the evidence I'm supposed to be looking for?"

"I think there's something wrong with this connection," he said. "You sound like an idiot."

"I'm just saying, since you're calling to help us catch your—"

Mom grabbed the phone from me. "Wilt, honey? Come home. I miss you. Come home. Wilt, baby? Wilt?"

But he was gone, the line already dead.

Somewhere in her stressed-out self Mom had to know Wilt couldn't come home, so I didn't remind her about the morgue. It was obviously a shock—hearing his voice like that. It was a shock for me too, but it didn't seem like I had a choice. I set my phone to vibrate to keep her from hearing it, and Wilt called one more time before I went to bed.

"Hey."

"What was all that crap about Suzy?"

I told him he couldn't rest eternal until his murder was avenged, which was why he was calling—to provide the necessary info that'd help me help the police arrest Suzy for his murder. "Justice served and all that," I said.

"Okay," he said, "I know Mom's smoking while you were in the womb accounts for your mental problems, but no need for you to constantly advertise them. I'm going to clue you in and you should thank me. Say thank you."

"Thank you."

"Okay, so what you're talking about—that only happens in movies."

"Um, until a little while ago I was pretty sure talking to your dead brother on the phone only happened in movies."

There was this long pause and then he was like, "Point taken."

No way he would have admitted I'd made a decent point when he was alive. Dying had definitely made him more sensitive, thoughtful.

"Here's the problem with your scenario, doucheface," he said. "You can't catch my murderer because there wasn't one. I wasn't murdered."

I meant to ask if he'd killed himself, but that wasn't what came out of my mouth. "Not that we can't just talk," I said, "but if there's no murderer, why are you calling?"

His pause this time was longer than the first one and I thought we'd been cut off again, but then in a voice that basically admitted he didn't want to tell me what he was telling me, he was like, "Every new arrival's assigned a counselor because apparently most people had plans in life for doing crap they didn't get around to doing and, being dead, they have a hard time understanding that now they're never going to do that crap."

"Yeah, but you're not—"

"Also, the newly dead, I've been told, tend to get pretty neurotic, worrying that the people they left behind will think less of them since they never accomplished the crap they'd wanted to accomplish."

This being the most Wilt had said to me in years, I was kind of boggled, but he couldn't have been one of the people he'd just described—when he'd actually been a person, I mean, as opposed to a spirit or soul or whatever he'd become. Far as I knew, there hadn't ever been anything he wanted except what he'd had, and he'd never seemed to care what other people thought about him. Which, despite his dickish big-brother routine, had always kind of impressed me.

"So *why* are you calling?" I asked.

"I just told you. It's part of my therapy."

Therapy? WTF?

"And you're where, exactly?"

"What? You dropped out for a sec."

"Where are you?"

"Come again?"

"Where. Are. You?"

"Once more?"

"Forget it."

"I'm just messing with you, doucheface. I don't exactly know where I am. This place is like a cult, everyone not saying what the invisible cult leaders don't want them to say.

Unofficially, it's called Aftermart. But imagine the biggest Walmart you've ever been in, except you can't find an exit, and all the stuff on the shelves is junk you've only heard about either from Mom and Dad or from people even more ancient. Black and white TVs with crappy rotary dials that were around when our supposedly wise elders were kids or even earlier. Eight-track tapes, board games."

"So you're saying . . . ?"

"Yeah, genius. Products nobody makes anymore. Dead stuff."

4

I've always done my best thinking when I'm asleep, and after Wilt's first bunch of calls, between dreams I don't remember, I wondered why my brother had reached out to me. *Only* me, I mean. He hadn't talked to Dad, I knew. He would've called Mom first, but he hadn't done that, so no way he had called Dad. And unless in losing his life he'd also lost his mind— which didn't seem to be the case but was still possible—he obviously hadn't talked to Suzy. Because if he'd talked to Suzy, he wouldn't have kept asking about her, right? Maybe he'd called some of his friends from school, I figured, but then I was all *naw* since he definitely would've called Suzy before he called them. So I had to be the only one. Of everybody he knew, he'd picked me. What does that tell you? I thought. And by *you* I meant *me.*

In the morning I woke up to Mom watching me, sitting on Wilt's bed, her right leg jackhammering up and down.

"I blame the divorce," she said, "the absence of a role model with testes."

Blame it for what? For what'd happened to my brother?

For what was or wasn't happening to me? "You and Dad got divorced over ten years ago," I said.

Her leg stopped jackhammering. "I'm aware of that. You think I could forget the biggest failure of my life?"

I almost said she still had time and there would probably be bigger failures, but I checked myself. I was trying not to blurt everything that came into my head, not only because I thought I should be as considerate as possible in our situation, but also because the things that came into my head were mostly snarks that brought me more trouble than they were worth.

"It's just, I don't even remember you and Dad living together, it was so long ago."

"You've blocked it out. That's what people do when subjected to severe trauma. Ask Dr. Murray."

"Dr. Murray's a loser."

"You're saying that because you don't like when people try to get close to you. And that's *because of the divorce.*"

I saw it coming, the skin of her face twitching like from little electrical shocks: her eye-faucets were about to spill.

"You come from a broken home," she sobbed. "But don't be afraid to let people in, hon. Please don't. Will you let *me* in? Let's let each other in before it's too late."

I did what I always do when she gets like that—played the rag doll while she petted me and sopped me big-time with her tears. She was wrong, though. I wasn't afraid to let people in, whatever that meant. I just didn't want to say anything about anything to Dr. Murray, who was a total loser.

"Where's your phone?" she asked, wiping her nose, her eyes. "I haven't heard it ring."

I pointed to my jeans on the floor and she clawed the phone out of a back pocket. No missed calls. Texts from Lou and Jeremy asking what was up, and since I'd never texted back to say nothing was up, more texts from Lou and Jeremy telling me to check my phone, they wanted to know what was up even if nothing was. Mom scrolled through my messages at least three times to make sure there wasn't anything from Wilt.

"It's as if he knew you were asleep," she said. And then, like she'd brooded over it awhile: "I don't understand how he can be calling."

This was conversational territory we hadn't been in—the whole life-after-death thing. The only religious words I'd ever heard her spew were "Jesus" and some variation of "goddammit." Even with Wilt's calls, I hadn't made up my mind what I believed.

"Curtis," Mom said, "I don't know what this communication with your brother means, but I think it's best you don't say anything to anybody about it until I talk to a few people first."

"You don't want me to talk about it to anyone until you talk to someone about it?"

So much for not being snarky.

Mom huffed to her feet. "Tell you what. You do as I ask and I'll keep slaving away what life I have left to pay for the roof over your head and the food you eat and the internet and your phone and—"

"You're gonna make me late for school."

She stopped and stared, pressed at the nicotine patch under her collarbone. "Is that today?"

She meant was it the day we'd agreed on, when we were both supposed to try and go back about our old familiar routines and act like Wilt's death hadn't happened. The thinking—if that's what we're calling it—was that the sooner we got into our old routines, with me at school and her at work, the faster we'd be absorbed in them attention-wise and would maybe feel as close to Wilt not having died as we'd ever get. The whole thing had been her idea.

"Yeah," I said. "Today's the eighth day of the rest of our lives."

5

That was a lie—what I said about not remembering the parentals living together. I was five years old the morning I went shuffling around the apartment in my pajamas, trying to figure out where this certain weird noise was coming from. I thought Dad or Wilt could tell me about this weird noise, but Dad hadn't been around the night before to say good-night and I couldn't find Wilt. Our apartment back then was probably an average-sized place but it had three bedrooms and I remember it as being huge. It took forever before I puzzled out the noise was coming from the parentals' room. I made it as far as the door. Wilt was sitting hunchbacked and glum on the edge of the bed, with Dad's shirts and socks and shorts and underwear scattered on the carpet, hanging from lamps, mashed into the metal-slatted window blinds—just all over the place, basically. Mom was yanking open the drawers of Dad's dresser and flinging out everything she found. The noise I'd been hearing was her slamming drawers shut.

"Your father will no longer be living with us," she said. "He still loves you. Don't you ever think for a minute that he doesn't."

She heaved a pair of Dad's jeans at her wedding pics and went back to slamming drawers, and Wilt kept staring at the floor like it owed him money.

I didn't know it was called Ritalin until later, knew only that I had to swallow a pill three times a day: when I first woke up, at lunch, and at night before bed.

Because I punched things.

If somebody took my pencil without asking, if I thought a teacher was being unfair—for whatever reason.

I punched desks, lockers, walls, doors. Never people.

Morning and night, Mom would be like, "Open up," and force-finger a pill down my throat. But it was my first grade teacher Miss Darden's job to feed me the lunchtime pill. She never shoved a finger into my mouth or inspected between my cheeks and gums to be sure I swallowed it, the way Mom did, but she'd come up to me in the cafeteria and watch me wash it down with grape juice in front of everybody.

"What was that?" this girl Allison asked after the first time.

"Something *you'll* never get to have," I said.

Pretty soon, before Miss D made a move toward me, I was going over to her and asking loudly if I could please, please take my pill. She'd look kind of confused and give it to me. Other kids wanted to try the pill, but I played like none of them was special enough.

Except I didn't *always* swallow it. Sometimes, with Miss D standing over me, I kept the pill under my tongue. Later, I would spit it into a napkin when no one was paying attention.

It was usually half-dissolved by then and left a bitter grit in my mouth, and I never could decide which was worse—the bitter grit or just swallowing the pill.

Teachers said I had "behavioral difficulties." But once I was popping meds, they stopped giving me bad reports at parent-teacher conferences. Like the Ritalin made them see me differently. Or like *they* felt the effects of the pills even though I was the one taking them. I don't remember the Ritalin making me feel any different, but everyone seemed to think it did, so.

"She's been dressing that way ever since it happened," Jeremy said.

We were in the hall at school, him and me and Lou, waxing lazy before first period and admiring the way Suzy took books out of her locker.

"It's as if she doesn't want anyone to forget she was your brother's girlfriend and she's telling us we're clueless about what she's going through, having been with a dead guy."

"Real sensitive," Lou said.

Jeremy puppy-faced me. "No offense, dude."

"Yeah."

Suzy was dressed completely in black—black leather boots reaching halfway up her calves, black tights, black mini skirt and black short-sleeved fuzzy sweater. She'd always been able to make me feel clumsy and self-conscious just because of who she was and how do-alicious she always looked, but now even her clothes were making me feel clumsy and self-conscious. I had on my usual red All Stars with the soles duct-taped on, the jeans I'd been wearing since the night Wilt died, and this red-and-blue-striped shirt I'd found in my closet. No black, is what I'm saying.

"So you didn't ask your brother where he'd been going or where he was coming from?" Lou asked.

I'd told him and Jeremy about Wilt's calls.

"Uh uh."

"And he was alone in the car?"

"Yeah."

"Skid marks on the road?"

"That's what the cops said."

Lou thought about this, ogling Suzy, which Jeremy had never stopped doing, his hand at his crotch while he made little moaning sounds.

"I could *so* butter that muffin."

"Skid marks don't rule out suicide," Lou said. "He could have chickened at the last second and slammed on the brakes but it was too late."

"I could *definitely* give that beaver some nuts," Jeremy said. "Suzy being the beave in this scenario."

"Beavers don't eat nuts," Lou told him.

"Yeah, right."

"Listen to what I tell you, fool: Beavers. Don't. Eat—"

"Here she comes," I said.

"Bullshit!"

I knew how they felt. Like no way Suzy was coming toward us because when had she ever come toward any one of us except by accident in a hall between classes, in which case she never even noticed us enough to ignore us? But right then— yeah, Suzy was definitely, purposely, walking toward us.

Lou started raking at the floppy front part of his hair, pushing it one way and then the other and back again. Jeremy cupped a hand in front of his mouth to check his breath and tried out various poses, which were probably supposed to seem nonchalant but just made him look like a guy trying to fart.

"Hey," Suzy said.

Jeremy squeaked and Lou was all, "Hello!" in the kind of super-husky, overloud voice you hear in monster truck-a-thon commercials.

"Hey," I waved.

Suzy stared at me real intense. "How've you been?"

I shrugged, which I guess she took for a sign that we were both having a seriously hard time dealing with the trauma of Wilt's death, going through the motions of life, not feeling anything but pain and loss.

"You remind me of him so much," she said.

She pulled me against her and I breathed in a good whiff of the girly soap she used and the talcum powder and the I don't know what. I got an instant boner and was afraid she could feel it pressing up against her.

"Is that yours or mine?"

She stepped away from me and started digging in her bag. Lou and Jeremy had gone off somewhere and the screen on my phone, as always when my brother called, showed *Wilt* but no number.

"It's mine," I said. And then, into the phone, "Hey. I'm at school. With Suzy."

"Let me talk to her."

Suzy had the same reaction as Mom, the same doll eyes of disbelief while she probably didn't hear a word Wilt said. Then she handed the phone back to me and walked off zombie-style.

"What'd you say to her?" I asked Wilt.

"That long-distance relationships never work and that I'll understand if she wants to see other people."

It's not the easiest thing to suddenly talk to your older brother the way you talk to a friend. Especially when you're not used to doing it because he's pretty much talked *at* you your whole life—whenever he wasn't using you as a punching bag. But I figured I had to try since I didn't know how many more chances I'd get.

"Your therapy with that counselor?" I said.

"What about it?"

"Is that something that people—ex-people, I mean—something they have to do if, you know, they kill themselves? They have to see a counselor?"

"Try to remember, doucheface, of the two of us, I got the brains while you got the usual complement of limbs. You want to ask me if I killed myself, just ask."

"Did you?"

"Why would I? Is Suzy still there?"

"Uh uh. You freaked her out."

"What time is it where you are?"

"Not even first period."

"Her homeroom's 312. Go to it."

"You could be a little more polite."

"Go to it, *please*. 312."

He didn't have to tell me where Suzy's homeroom was. I might not've had a VIP pass to her world, but I knew as much about it as anybody could who suffered through life two grades below her. Like not only where she had homeroom, but also that she ate these weird deep-fried tofu cubes every day for lunch, and that she and her friends smoked Marlboro Lights behind the school's humongoid HVAC unit before first bell and during afternoon free period. From overhearing her with Wilt, I knew she was insecure about the size of her earlobes—ear-loogeys, she called them—and that she sometimes woke up in the night afraid she'd already lived the best days of her life. I even knew the kind of yelpy sounds she made having sex, since when you live in a dinky apartment, it doesn't matter if your brother kicks you out of the closet you share with him or he uses the fold-out couch in the living room and orders you to be elsewhere. Why it doesn't matter is because so long as you don't leave the apartment altogether—and I never did if I could help it—you'll hear your brother and his girlfriend going at it.

"Wilt, what were you doing on St. Benny?"

"Exercising my right to privacy. You see her yet?"

"Uh uh. So you were exercising this right to privacy and you just . . . crashed?"

"That sounds an adequate summary. What about now? See her yet?"

"Yeah. She's in the hall outside class, talking to Rick Calvados, and he seems pretty willing to comfort her now that you're—"

"Forget him. What I need you to do, please, is go up and smell her. And describe to me what you smell."

Weird, his wanting me to do that. I could've already told him about Suzy's personal aroma that a.m., but then I wouldn't have had an excuse to get close to her again. And I definitely wanted to get close to her again.

Which I couldn't decide if that was sick or not.

Like psycho-sick—me wanting to get another hard-on from the girl who might've killed my brother.

I wasn't sure I believed what Wilt had said about not being murdered. I still couldn't help thinking Suzy had something to do with him dying or at least knew stuff about it no one else did. I even thought Wilt might've been pretending otherwise, because—and maybe this was why he kept calling—he planned ultimate revenge on Suzy instead of just having her busted. He wanted to haunt her first was all, toy with her a little, and he'd tell me the deal when the time was right, not before, to keep me from screwing things up.

Except if he wanted to haunt her, why didn't he just call her directly? Was the afterlife like being arrested, where you got only a single phone call? Or where you could only ever call the same one person?

Suzy leaned against the lockers, hugging her three-ring binder and books the way I've seen kids do in movies and TV shows but nowhere else. Rick was the kind of guy who looked thirty years old when he was seventeen, with a chest that could've blocked out the sun. He had his lacrosse stick in hand as always and was leaning toward Suzy with one arm propped against the lockers and his back to the hall like he was using his body to shield her from the rest of us. "Us" being what he'd call wannabes, losers, dorks, dweebs, uglies, nerds, mental cases, botched abortions.

When Rick saw me coming, I got the feeling he wouldn't have minded if there'd been another dead Brooks in the world. With crazy unnatural speed his lacrosse stick swooshed down past my head and up under my shirt. He led me off to where he could hiss in my face without Suzy hearing.

"Think you're hot shit because of what happened to your bro?"

"Why'd I ever want to be *hot shit*?"

I heard Wilt laugh in my ear, but Rick didn't get it.

"You got that right," he said. "Don't fuck this up for me."

His lacrosse stick feeling me up, he led me back to Suzy and stood shifting his weight from one leg to the other, wanting me to say what I had to say and get lost. I pretended to be interested in a scab of rust on a locker. No way I was going to smell Suzy with him around.

"I'll see you later, Rick," she said.

He deflated for a second, bummed, but it was the quickest second ever because then he puffed himself up, all high-school-senior-lacrosse-captain confidence again, except his voice had this tenderness in it I hadn't expected.

"You sure that you'll be okay?" he said. "You'll text me if you need anything?"

"Asshole," Wilt said in my ear. He and Rick used to hang out together. "See other people, Suze, but *come on*."

"I'll text you," Suzy promised, and if she was just being nice to get rid of him, she did a good job of faking it.

Before he caveman'd off to I-didn't-care-wheresville, Rick gave me the evil eye, which I guess was supposed to be a warning but I was like, *Whatever. There's a reason the sport you're good at involves playing with sticks and balls.*

"I don't know how you did it," Suzy said after he'd gone, "but if that was a joke, it wasn't close to funny."

"Wasn't a joke." I wagged my phone. "I'm supposed to . . . smell." I moved in close, my cheek practically against hers and my mouth at her ear. "Soap," I said to Wilt. "A perfumey soap. And shampoo. Kind of fruity."

"Organic apples," Suzy whispered.

"Also cigarettes and coffee."

I eased back to give Suzy her space. She was breathing fast, her chest rising and falling like she'd just run the 440 or something, and she stared at me with this mash-up of an expression—all unbelievable hurt and sadness and confusion. Then the bell rang and she slid sideways away from me into class.

I thought my brother had hung up or we'd been disconnected. Silence was coming through the phone.

"Wilt?"

"Yeah."

"Is what I just did, what you asked me to do, was that part of your therapy?"

"Yeah. No. I guess."

It was the first time I totally understood what people mean when they say they can hear tears in somebody's voice.

7

"We've got to figure out what we know we don't know. To do that, we've got to confirm what we know we know. But there's always a chance, once we figure out what we know we know *and* what we know we don't know, that we won't know what we don't know, which could be a problem."

Lou was at the desk behind me in Mrs. Jensen's history class, Mrs. J handing back some test I'd missed while absent.

"You're saying we have to check out St. Benny?" Jeremy said, swiveled in the desk next to mine, the better to scope Shoshana.

"I'm saying, Jer, we have to examine the scene of the incident, learn what we can learn. There might be reasons why Wilt doesn't want to explain what really happened."

"I've kinda been thinking the same," I said.

"Man." Jeremy's hand eased down to his crotch. He pushed his chin out at Shoshana in a *What's up?* kind of way, not taking it as a bad thing when she gave him the finger. "That girl ignites a room."

"Curtis?"

Mrs. J was looming over me, Mrs. J with her mothball-stink

and her wooly hair that always reminded me of those powdered wigs George Washington's people used to wear.

"How are you?" Her hagginess had none of the usual dictator's wrinkles about it, was trying to smooth itself into the expression of a shy, caring great-grandma.

I shrugged, puppy-faced her.

"It's the hardest thing in life, to lose somebody you love. I hope I don't have to tell you that everyone here is extremely sorry for your loss?"

I super-relaxed the muscles in my cheeks and forehead for maximum puppy-face effect.

"You can make up the test whenever you think you're ready, okay? No rush."

"Dude? Mrs. Jensen?" Jeremy said. "I hope you're well today?"

"Watch yourself, Mr. Hopper."

Mrs. J dropped Jeremy's test in front of him, kept on with her teacherly business.

"Robbed!" Jeremy shouted, and showed me his grade: 9%.

"Could be," Lou said at my back, "Wilt's trying to protect you and your mom from somebody. Anyway, why shouldn't we check out the scene of the incident? What else we have to do?"

"I don't know."

"Exactly."

Just then, this annoying seventh grader Todd Winkleman came into the room and everyone started winging paper clips, erasers, pens, and wadded up tests at him.

"Yes, Mr. Winkleman?" Mrs. J said. "Why are you disrupting my class?"

"I have a note from Dr. Murray."

Still getting beaned by school supplies, Weasel-Winkleman handed Mrs. J a folded piece of paper, and I was like *crap* because I knew what a note from Dr. Murray meant. Mrs. J gave the scrawl a quick once over.

"Curtis," she said, and I got up and followed weasel-boy out to the hall.

"You're the one whose brother died?"

"Yeah."

"DEATH GERMS!"

Weasel-boy sprinted off toward Principal Chu's office, his laughter ping-ponging between the lockers, and I figured I'd deal with him later since I wanted to get my torture with Dr. M over with and his office was at the opposite end of the building from Principal C's. Opposite as in like Principal C knew what a loser Dr. M was and didn't want the guy too close to him. Which it was pretty cool to realize—that adults didn't want to socialize with losers any more than I did. I've never been able to figure out why some people are always flaunting their authority, as if acting all Nazi's supposed to make up for a loserness they can no way get rid of except by offing themselves.

Anyway.

I used to think Dr. M was gay, that he yanked me out of class so much because he wanted the two of us to get to yanking of another kind. Thing is, it probably would've been better if he *had* been gay, since what started his whole power-tripping-yanking-me-out-of-class routine was Mom having dropped a verbal load on him at a parent-teacher conference. She'd told him I was growing up without a dad, after which the all too frequent visits to his office started, and I had to listen to him vomit up conclusions about me based on garbage he'd read in psych books or online or wherever.

I showed up at his door and saw him hunched roly-polyish in front of his computer.

"What up, C?"

The other thing about Dr. M: he was a cliché, thinking wannabe-gangsta speak gave him a special connection with students when it only made him more of a joke. He was the whitest guy around—a mostly bald white guy forever in this turd-brown blazer who looked like he'd been taller and thinner at some point, but then a giant hand had pressed down on his head, flattening and swelling every part of him sideways a couple inches.

"Park yourself," he said, his pudgy finger pointing me to the plastic chair next to his desk. "You been maintaining?"

"I guess."

"Must be hard. Real hard."

" . . . "

"Anywaze, it's good to peep you back."

"Uh huh."

Dr. M had too many leisure hours—like, clearly pestering students didn't fill up all his time because he'd used some of it to mess with a bunch of Murphy's Law posters and wall calendars, the kind that had pics of cats with feathers in their mouths and captions saying *Anything that can go wrong, will go wrong*. He'd taken a bunch of those and glued a laser-printed "Murray" over every "Murphy" and tacked them up around his office.

"Check it, C. I thought I should tell you that your moms gave me the 411 on your brother's phone calls."

"What?" I couldn't believe it. Dr. M was the person Mom had meant? She'd wanted me to keep quiet about Wilt's calling until she'd talked to him?

37

"Me and your moms, C, we worry 'boutcha."

There was just no way. Whoever Mom had really wanted to talk to about Wilt must have said something to make her think of Dr. M, mistakenly believing like always that the guy was actually helping me deal with my life.

Except—and I have no idea why I didn't wonder this before—who'd Mom know that could possibly give advice about calls from beyond the grave? She worked at a UPS distribution center. Did UPS have employees good with that kind of stuff?

"Must have tripped your dome the first time Wilton called," Dr. M said.

"I guess."

"It's okay to be tripped out once in a while, C. Feel yourself."

"Uh, I don't want to."

He bobbled his head like I'd uttered something deep, and I realized what I had to do to get out of there.

"It's just, Wilt's accident was only last week," I said, "and I'm too . . . you know, it's all still too raw to talk about. But I mean, when I'm ready to talk . . . it's like you're always saying, I've gotta be on a first-name basis with my feelings, Al is anger and all that, and like maybe George is grief—"

"Grief has many names."

"—yeah, but I'm not ready to talk to George, you know? Not yet. Except when I *am* ready? I definitely want you to listen in on our conversation. Yeah, I'd totally appreciate that, and your door's always open, right? I mean, I know it's always open, so."

"Canine, I am feeling what you've just said, absolutely."

Go figure: I spat back a little of Dr. M's nonsense and he got misty-eyed with self-congrats and couldn't recognize BS pelting him in the face. But that's when he gave me the ghoulies, breaking with the wannabe-gangsta and talking like the old white loser he was, which I'd never heard him do before.

"Your mother told me Wilton phones not infrequently?"

I nodded.

"Tragedies can affect people in surprising ways. I want you to know, Curtis, that you needn't be ashamed of anything you admit to me in this office. Losing a brother—I can't imagine what that must be like. I'm not in the least surprised that you think you're talking to him."

I flushed hot and was going to punch the moron. "Mom talked to him too," I said.

"Did she?" He thought he was clever. "Should the opportunity arise, I wouldn't mind having a word with Wilton myself."

I shot to my feet, about to knock everything off his desk and rip his stupid posters and calendars off the walls. But because he eyed me like that's exactly what he expected me to do, I sat back down.

"I'm not asking you to go out of your way," he said. "But if it's possible, I would really love to talk with him."

"Okay."

"Yeah, boy-ar-deeee. Peace out."

Even though I generally tried not to touch the guy, I bumped fists with him, the sooner to escape back out to the hall.

The day clocked its hours and I don't know if it was because I'd nosed Suzy or what, but I didn't hear from Wilt again. I figured if his getting all emotional had been the point, therapy-wise, of my Suzy sniff-a-thon, then maybe he was busy talking through his feelings with his counselor. Which I tried to picture.

And the hardest thing about it wasn't imagining a Walmart so big you couldn't escape or the black-and-white-rotary-dial-Morse-code stuff clogging the shelves. The hardest thing was trying to imagine Wilt sitting on some dead lawn furniture, gushing to a counselor. I could count on half a hand the number of times I'd seen evidence of my brother's mushy feelings.

Suzy didn't avoid me so much as keep her distance, but she was noticing me more than she used to. In the halls, during lunch and free period, I caught her staring like she was trying to figure me out. Or like she was trying to figure out how much I might know about her involvement in Wilt's murder. And while part of me still thought wanting to get into her pants was probably psycho-sick, I was kind of hoping she'd come on to me, that she'd tickle my ear with whispers of how she'd always liked me and would prove it in the janitor's closet, using sex to find out what I knew, the way people are always doing in movies.

Or.

More like I *would have been* hoping she'd use sex the way people do in movies if Rick Calvados hadn't been such a major case of herpes, infecting her personal space every chance he got. The curious eye Suzy kept flicking my way definitely didn't fill him with glee. Twice when I was dumping books into my locker, he swatted me with his lacrosse stick as he passed in the hall. And in the cafeteria at lunch, I was pushing my tray past unidentifiable food sludge when he slammed into me and said, "Best stay out of my way, Brooks." And just before final period, when I was taking a leak in the bathroom, he stepped up to the urinal next to mine.

"Think your bro's dying gives you an opening with Suzy?"

"Don't be an ass, Rick."

"You calling me an ass?"

I made a show of looking around to see if there was anyone else named Rick I could've been calling an ass. There wasn't.

"Doesn't seem like my brother being dead's been bad for you either, Suzy-wise," I said.

I'd finished my business at the urinal but didn't move. I had a better chance of not getting pummeled if Rick was afraid of being pissed on.

"Look, dude," he said. "I don't completely dislike you. I know it sucks about your bro, but he's gone. He's gone but I'm not and neither is Suzy and I'm warning you: do not cock-block me. Suzy wants to cry on your shoulder, you send her my way. If you don't, you *will* regret it. Fair warning."

He walked off in that way of his that always made me wonder how he could be good at lacrosse or any sport at all really—kind of stiff in the hips, with not a lot of lift in his step, like he had a perfectly formed turd in his jeans he didn't want to squish.

The bathroom door swung shut behind him, which was when I had my seriously duh moment: that I'd had it all wrong, that Suzy was innocent and Rick Calvados had offed my brother for the most obvious reason there was.

To get into her pants.

"It goes against everything I believe, Jer, but I think we're gonna have to face facts."

"What facts are those, Lou?"

"That being in mourning has its benefits."

"You read a study, Lou?"

"Yes, Jer. Yes, I did. But I didn't have to. Our friend Curtis has proven it. Consider: not only has Mrs. Jensen essentially given him a pass on that last test we took—"

"Culturally biased, that test was."

"Might have been, Jer. But focus. Mourning. Benefits. Not just with regard to tests, but also—and I say this intending no offense, it's just an observation—to possibly getting play from the most luscious girl in school."

"Why does everybody think that?" I said. "I'm not trying to get 'play.'"

Both Lou and Jeremy snorted.

It'd taken us three long, boring bus rides to get to St. Benny—this half-mile stretch of broken blacktop canyonned between industrial ruins. Squat, rectangular cinder-block warehouses with bricked over windows, rusted security gates, and loading docks for trucks. Buildings with stucco flaking so bad you could see the metal mesh underneath. Big steel shipping containers with their locks busted and their doors wagging loose, graffiti covering everything like some kind of urban mold.

The street's north end, where I was standing with Lou and Jeremy, teed into Carnova Way, but the south end just stopped. A stop so abrupt and inexplicable I'd always assumed that the workers laying the blacktop had taken their first real snoop around one day and, not enjoying it much, said *screw this* and vacated the scene forever. Past the dead-end blacktop was an overgrown field—all six-foot stalks of whatever, supposed to be off-limits except that the chain link fence with its barbed wire and No Dumping signs had slumped to the ground so you could easily walk over it if you wanted.

Which no way I wanted.

Everyone knew escaped mental patients lived in that field, feeding off dead bodies dumped by gangs and mafia-types. If you were scoping out a place where you could indulge in some nasty illegal activity, St. Benny was perfect. Too perfect.

"Why would anybody ever want to be here at night?" Jeremy whispered.

I could think of a lot of reasons. None of them good. And none of them having to do with what people might want.

"Just one way in and out unless you count that field," Lou said. "Probably take a machete to hack through that stuff."

The knocked-over telephone pole was in front of a crumbling Wholesale Electric building. It'd cracked in two at about the height where Mom's car bumper would have made impact. Skid marks started maybe ten feet back. Splinters of wood and glittery glass crumbs were everywhere. I figured the pole had been out of commission before Wilt crashed into it, since I didn't see loose wires linking together the poles still standing upright. And there definitely weren't any wires lying in wait to electrocute us, so.

Jouncing along on those buses, I'd thought I knew what I wanted to find at St. Benny: evidence of Rick Calvados's guilt, evidence that'd explain exactly what had happened to my brother and why. But standing in the shadow of that abandoned Wholesale Electric building, the wind carrying echoes of the dead, what little wreckage there was looked like nothing but the leftovers of an anonymous tragedy and I wondered if it'd be better not to find evidence of anybody's guilt. Because what'd happen if I found it? Would Wilt stop calling? I didn't want that. I definitely didn't want that.

"The skid marks are on the north side of the telephone pole," Lou said.

I knew what he was getting at: Wilt had been driving south, toward the dead end, when he crashed.

I went off to be on my own, was looking down at this stain in the dried-out weeds roadside, not liking to think what it might be, when Lou and Jeremy came up next to me.

"Could be oil?" Jeremy said after a while.

"Yeah," I said, but I knew it wasn't.

10

The name of that detective who gave Mom his card, saying she should call if she remembered anything relevant to Wilt's case? His name was Abrams and I'd been home from St. Benny half an hour when he beat on the door.

"Elevators don't work," I told him.

He was wheezing hard, bent double in the hall with his hands on his knees, and I guess I hadn't paid much attention to him that night at the morgue because it was like I was seeing him for the first time—the soggy-dough skin, the wrinkles spoking out from the corners of his eyes.

"Your mom here?"

"Uh uh."

"Any idea when she'll be back?"

"Uh uh."

I don't know why, but I got the feeling he hadn't come just to talk about Wilt and was using it as an excuse to see Mom. Maybe because he reeked of Lonely Old Guy, the kind with no life outside his job who spent nights swigging coffee alone at some diner, then alone in his apartment sucking down beers and watching black-and-white movies on TV or black-and-white porn on his outdated computer. Besides, Mom had given him her cell number the night of Wilt's crash and he could have just called if he hadn't been needing an excuse to see her.

"If it's something about my brother's case," I said, "you can tell me."

"Is that right?" He shook a cigarette from a pack of unfiltered Camels and jammed it between his lips, thumbed open a Zippo and lit up, exhaling a long funnel of smoke. Technically, smoking wasn't allowed in the halls or any of the building's shared spaces, but who was going to stop him? "I noticed you weren't too upset at the morgue the other night."

Where'd he get off? Like there was a right way and a wrong way to show how I felt? I nearly slammed the door in his face.

"Except that I don't cry when you think I should," I said, "you accusing me of something?"

He pinched out his cigarette and put it back in the pack, which Mom used to do, not wanting to smoke whole cigarettes whenever she lit up, so I knew he was trying to quit.

"We've reason to believe the car your brother was driving had been tampered with."

He might've been scoping my response, checking to see if it jibed with how he thought I should react. I can't say for sure. I was far away from him, huddled up in my own head, like, *I knew it. Wilt was murdered.*

"You understand what I'm saying? That we suspect foul play?"

"Tampered with how?"

He handed me his card. "Have your mom call me as soon as you hear from her."

47

I waited till he was in the stairway before closing the door, wondering if Wilt didn't know he'd been murdered. I'd never thought of it before, probably because I'd assumed he was all-knowing, that as consolation or whatever for dying, he'd been given awareness of everything Mom and I were doing, even if he couldn't literally "see" us. But he'd asked me what time it was that morning, right? He hadn't known. Which obviously meant he couldn't have been all-knowing.

So I figured—yeah, it was possible for Wilt to think he'd died by accident when he'd been murdered. And what I wondered then was if his counselor knew.

I put Detective Abrams' card on the kitchen counter with his other one and left a note for Mom: *We need to talk.* Which was a switch, since she always wrote notes like that when I didn't come home by curfew.

11

A drama queen, Mom used to tell anyone who'd listen—not just Dr. M—that Wilt and I had grown up without a dad, and she lugged the single-parent thing around like it was this heavy backpack she had to show everybody and couldn't shrug off. Not that I think my life's been very different from other kids' whose parents split. Wilt and I were supposed to see Dad on alternate weekends and holidays, spend a couple weeks with him in summer. There were the occasional scenes, yeah, especially those first months after Dad moved out. Young as I was, I could always tell when the parentals were hashing through stuff on the phone because Mom's voice would get tight and smoldery, and I remember this one time, after Dad didn't show up for a court-approved visit, I heard that tight, smoldery voice coming from the kitchen.

"Were you going to call? You have certain responsibilities . . . you can't just . . . *you* tell them!"

I stomped into the kitchen and swung my arm as hard as I could, knocking unwashed dishes off the counter and watching them crash all over the place. Grease from leftover chicken streaked the wall and cabinets, and in the second before Mom's anger blew over me, I thought I heard Dad's voice eking "Hello? Hello? Hello?" from the phone.

Another time, Dad had just dropped me and Wilt off at home when Mom started chasing him around the apartment complex, swatting at him with a rolled-up magazine. It sounded like bird wings beating against cardboard—that mag hitting his back and arms and head. Dad wasn't able to get into his car and lock the doors without giving her a push that sent her stumbling back, after which she totally lost it, kicking at the car's windows and screaming so loud I figured everyone in the complex would step out of their apartments to eye and pity the parentals, looking down on them like they were characters in a stupid reality show—the kind who made gawkers feel okay about themselves for a minute, since whatever their problems, at least they weren't that bad off. But lucky me, no neighbors rubbernecked, and Dad's car pig-squealed out of the parking lot, the rear running lights streaking around a corner when Mom flared:

"What are you looking at? Get back inside!"

I was like *Huh?* because I hadn't realized that I'd followed her from the apartment.

So yeah, there have been scenes. Big whoop. Whose family doesn't have scenes? Nothing was ever as bad as Mom made things sound, is what I'm saying, and telling people I'd grown up without a dad was just her way of playing for sympathy.

Which she's always seemed to need a lot of.

Except it's true that, right up till Wilt's murder, Dad would cancel visits for reasons he never explained and a month could pass without our laying a retina on him. Still, he was *around.* Wilt and I knew *who* he was, if not always *where.* And besides, after the funeral, he tried a little harder, calling to say we should meet for dinner even though it wasn't required by any visitation rights agreement.

Which was how I ended up at Chili's after Detective Abrams' surprise interrogation—Dad and some woman I'd never seen before already at a table when I got there, the woman not bad-looking if you didn't mind geriatrics, and except for where most of us have hair on our head, she had this shellacked tower that might've housed gophers.

"Hey, kiddo."

It was Dad's usual greeting but without the exclamation point, the lack of enthusiastic punctuation, I figured, his way of acknowledging what we'd lost.

"Hey," I said.

We shook hands and his arm levered out toward the gopher-lodge-hairdo lady. "This is Diane."

"I was devastated to hear about Wilton," she said. "It must be terribly hard for you."

Dad gave me this wincing, apologetic look. "How you been holding up?"

I don't know. Fine. Lousy. I've been better. Everything sounded wrong, so I didn't answer. I would've asked how *he* was holding up, though, if it hadn't been obvious. He and Gopher Lady were drinking margaritas, and from their wobbliness, I guessed were on their third or fourth round.

I dropped into a chair next to Dad and went stealth behind my menu. "Where's Maria?" I asked, Maria being stepmom number three.

"Some sort of historical architectural tour," he said. "I wanted you and Diane to meet. Diane's been my other significant other for how long now?"

"Almost a year," Gopher Lady said. "Can you believe it?"

Dad was all, uh uh, he couldn't believe it, and before he downed what was in his glass, the waiter showed up with a couple more margaritas, as if he'd been instructed to bring a round every X number of minutes.

"We ready?"

Diane ordered a salad, asking for all kinds of extra stuff on it like cauliflower and sprouts and other weirdness. Dad said he'd have a margarita for his appetizer, which he'd follow up with a main course of margarita, and he thought he'd probably have something special for dessert, like a margarita. I ordered a bacon cheeseburger and root beer.

"Has Curt seen the pictures you and Maria took in New Mexico?" Diane asked, cracking the silence the waiter left behind.

"Who's Curt?"

"You are," Dad said.

"Has he seen the pictures?" Diane asked again, and you'd have thought the parental had been invited to solve an impossible math problem, the way he sat with his head tilted like a confused dog.

"Dunno," he said finally.

"I'll show him mine."

She scooted her chair close to me, stinging my nostrils with perfume as bad as one of those pine tree air ruiners that hang off a cabbie's rearview. She pulled her phone out of her purse and started scrolling through pics.

"This was taken at the Taos Pueblo, where people have lived for the past 2,000 years."

Dad and Maria were grinning in front of a bonfire, with guys in the background wearing beads and feathers, performing some kind of ceremonial dance.

"This was in the White Sands Desert."

"I might have figured that one out, what with all the white sand," I said.

"Curt," Dad's voice had weary threat in it, "I told Diane you were a polite youth."

"Whose fault is that?"

"They were gone for three weeks," Diane said, slideshowing pics of Dad and my stepmom at museums and cactus gardens and old-timey saloons.

I was like, Three weeks? Because even though most adults still don't think my overall awareness is a done deal, for a long time now I've been *aware* of Dad being able to take these lengthy vacations while everyone else has to sweat it out at UPS distribution centers, begging their bosses for even a couple sick days. He was employed as an account exec at some advertising agency when Wilt was born. Around the time I came into the picture, he was selling TVs at Best Buy. He's worked as a real estate agent, EMT, investment advisor, and jewelry appraiser, but it was after his vague job for an insurance broker that Wilt and I lost track of what he did to make money. Wilt asked him once, but all Dad said was, Anything I have to. Wilt was like, Yeah, it's just, you get to take so much time off, I'm wondering what specifically you do for a living because that's the kind of job *I* want. Dad got mad and said he didn't ask where we went and what we did every day, and Wilt was like, Uh, I go to school and supposedly learn things. But Dad had shut down by that point, and from then on, if we asked him what he did for work, his answer was always the same: anything he had to.

It's kind of funny, though, now that I think about it. The way Dad sidestepped Wilt's question of how he made money, then Wilt refusing to say where that cash under his mattress had come from when Mom quizzed him about it.

"I'm interested in your life, Curtis," Dad said at Chili's.

"Yeah? That why, instead of spending alone-time with me, you brought a stranger along?"

Diane became fascinated with the tablecloth. Dad's eyes seemed to shrink back into his head.

"N-No," he said. "I thought . . . this might be . . . easier. If there were three of us. Since we're used to being at least three at dinner."

He picked at the salt on the rim of his glass, not looking at me, and I felt like a complete jerk.

"Sorry."

He reached out and squeezed the back of my neck but still didn't look at me. "It's all right. Things are impossibly difficult."

Our food came and I was pretty sure I'd seen the wind blowing the stuff on Diane's plate across the parking lot a little while before. We ate in silence till Dad let out this breathy "so," as if superhero strength was needed for basic chitchat. "Anything even close to 'normal' been happening?" he asked.

I chomped a french fry. "Not really. An hour ago this detective came to the apartment, this guy Abrams, and he said they've got evidence Wilt was murdered, except Wilt says he wasn't, that he just crashed by accident, and so—"

"Hold on a minute. What do you mean, 'Wilt says'?"

"Mom didn't tell you?"

"Your mother and I haven't talked since the funeral."

"No, yeah, okay. But I thought maybe since . . . it's just that Wilt's been calling me."

Dad and Diane swapped glances, after which she turned to me with this look I couldn't believe. *She* was full-on puppy-facing *me*. The only adult who'd done that to me before was Mom.

"Did you recently change your meds?" Dad asked.

Yeah, I still take meds. Big deal.

"Uh uh," I said.

"So I'm going to have to talk to your mom and Dr. Polk about changing the meds you're on is what you're saying?"

I checked the time on my phone. "He'll probably call soon. You'll see. He used to call every fifty minutes."

The rest of dinner, Diane covered over the silences by blathering on about Dad's New Mexico trip, and he'd egg her on, which bugged me till I realized he was trying to keep things light, not wanting to give me the chance to talk about conversations I was having with dead people.

Wilt didn't call till I was eyeing my sneakers in the Chili's parking lot—Dad and I pretending not to feel awkward while we said our goodbyes. I handed my phone to Dad and he made an expression like, *I'll definitely be speaking to Dr. Polk about the meds you're taking.*

"Hello?"

His reaction was a lot different than Mom's or Suzy's. His face didn't flatten in disbelief. He didn't burp out any distracted monosyllables in answer to whatever Wilt was saying.

Instead, he got mad and kept asking, "Where *are* you?" But after a while he mellowed, saddened. "It's awful. But answer me, Wilt. Where are you?" He listened a few seconds and said, "Bullshit."

Diane hung on Dad's arm, which I guess was supposed to help him get through a surprising phone gab, and I stared at a banner underneath the Chili's sign. Some of the banner's letters were facing the wrong way, but basically it said REVILED EW. I didn't get why Chili's would hang the thing up, and by the time I figured out it was supposed to say WE DELIVER, Dad was off the phone.

"First things first," he said. "I'm going to have a few words with those funeral home people."

12

Mom and some kid were waiting for me at the apartment, standing formal like a welcoming committee.

"Curtis," Mom said, in that voice she used with babies and small animals, "I want you to meet Okafur."

"Why?"

"It's not official yet, but he's going to be living with us."

"You're kidding, right?"

"I'm not, no."

I stared at the kid. He was about two inches taller than me and thin—I'm talking, Guinness-World-Record thin. His hair poofed out from his head like black foam.

"Where's he from?"

"Namibia."

"That's not what I mean. Does he speak English?"

The parental palsied her hand, which I took as *Kind of, but not really*, then turned to Okafur with an encouraging vibe, pointing at me and speaking real slow and distinct, as if to a mental case. "Cur-tis."

"I am not so excited to meet you," the kid said, and bowed.

I was like, "Yeah. I feel the same."

I went to my room and slammed the door. Okafur's suit-case was yawned open on Wilt's bed, his clothes folded neater than they'd be at Old Navy or someplace. I grabbed the suitcase and flung it out of the room and slammed the door a second time. I texted Lou and Jeremy to see if either of them wanted to meet up. I didn't care what time it was or if the parental had her lame curfews, I definitely didn't feel like staying home. Except Lou texted back to say no way he could sneak out and Jeremy texted that he was reading a cool article at Hustler.com, so I just sat on my bed with my back against the wall and my knees up, phone in hand, hoping Wilt would call again and thinking I'd rather wait anywhere but the apartment. Before I made a move, though, the door creaked and Mom's head put in an appearance.

"Knock, knock."

She came in and closed the door and sat facing me on Wilt's bed. "You okay?"

"Compared to what?"

" . . . "

"I'm not too old for you to screw up, you know?" I said.

"Babe, you never outgrow the capacity to be screwed up by anyone."

"Thanks. I feel tons better."

Her shirtsleeve was accordion-scrunched above her elbow. She pressed at a nicotine patch like she doubted it was working and needed to be juiced with a fresh dose.

"It's been too quiet without Wilt," she said in a voice that seemed to be hauled from somewhere deep inside her.

Maybe it was her tone or the kind of pitiful way she toyed with her nicotine patch, but the whole thing got to me, never mind that it'd barely been a week since Wilt's death. People sometimes overcompensated for a devastating loss, I knew, and this Okafur kid being in our apartment, as wrong as it was, probably couldn't be permanent, so.

That stuff about still being young enough to screw up? I'd said it to guilt her, but all of a sudden I didn't want her to feel bad, not because of me. And anyway, whatever else happens, I've decided I'm not going to be one of those adults who turns out a loser and blames a parent for it.

Not that I'm planning on being a loser.

It's just, I'm saying maybe it's because I've had to deal with people like Dr. Polk and Dr. Murray ever since I was six years old, but when I'm creaking around in my 40s, there's no way I'm going to sit in some therapist's office whining about my childhood. I mean, yeah, Mom repeatedly does things that annoy. Yeah, she pisses me off and is sometimes pretty excellent at making me feel like an afterthought by living her life however she wants—going out with friends every chance she gets, bringing guys home and in general just pretending she's not a mom. But so what? I don't think she's ever purposely trying to hurt me. People screw up no matter how hard they try not to, and she's just doing what she has to do to get through her days. A parent sometimes treating you like crap doesn't mean she doesn't love you.

Still, I didn't figure I had to be all mushy with her just after she'd sprung Okafur on me.

"Have you heard from Wilt recently?" she asked.

Which reminded me. "You didn't have to tell loser Murray he's been calling."

"But Peter—"

"Who?"

"Dr. Murray cares about you and I thought he should know."

"You didn't say *you'd* talked to Wilt, though, did you? Did you get my note?"

"What do we need to discuss?"

"Detective Abrams came by. He's the one who gave you his card. He wants you to get in touch about Wilt's case." I figured if I told her more, she might not do it. "Maybe you can ask him to give you a ride to work."

"Why would I do that?"

"Uh, I don't know. 'Cause you don't have a rental car yet?" I didn't owe Abrams any favors. I just thought it might be good for Mom to go on a date. It'd been a while. "This morning," I said, "when you told me not to tell anyone about Wilt's calls until you talked to someone about them? Who'd you mean? No way did you mean Dr. Murray."

But Mom was already heading out the door. "Okafur's being here doesn't mean I love Wilt any less. I hope you understand that. Please give him a chance."

People are always talking at each other, talking at each other all the time, but is anybody ever listening?

13

Fifty minutes after I handed Dad the phone at Chili's, Wilt called. I probably should've asked how he was holding up emotionally and all that kind of stuff, but I just started in about Okafur and how I thought Mom should go back to smoking because trying to quit was messing with her brain, and also never mind that I didn't feel like teaching Okafur the proper way to use a toilet or whatever a kid from Namibia needed to learn, how and where did Mom find him so fast?

"That, I couldn't tell you," Wilt said, "but be patient with her. People cope with trauma in lots of different ways and Okafur is probably her way of coping. Or at least part of it."

I was like, "Be *what*? Who am I talking to? Since when'd you start preaching *patience*?" And then an inexplicable thing happened: Wilt sighed. Which, how could he sigh if he didn't have lungs, a body? How could he *talk* if he didn't have a body?

"Oblivious to the obvious without being attuned to the profound, as always," he said. "Listen, doucheface. Don't make the mistake of thinking I'm the same guy I was when I had a physical form and shared a room with you. Dying gives you a mature perspective on things. The level of maturity it might

have taken me decades to reach in life, *if* I'd reached it at all—
once I died, I reached it. If I wasn't this mature, would I think
to tell you not to take your frustrations out on Okafur, since
none of this is his fault?"

"Probably not."

"*Definitely* not."

"You do talk more than you used to," I said. "To me
anyway."

"What's that got to do with anything? Don't confuse maturity with being well-adjusted. If I was well-adjusted, I wouldn't
be in counseling, would I?"

He must've been paying attention in his afterlife therapy,
because "don't confuse maturity with being well-adjusted"?
His increased favoring of the verbal in general? Dr. Polk, loser
Dr. Murray—they would've called it progress.

"For the record," Wilt said, "a mature perspective means
I can give reasonable advice to others without being able to
follow it myself."

"Tons of people have a mature perspective then," I said.
"Do you actually enjoy talking to your counselor?"

"Doesn't matter if I do or not. If I don't go, I don't earn my
required quota of credits."

"Your what? What're you—"

"Don't have a cow and I'll explain. The bulky old tube
TVs in the Electronics Department broadcast only canceled
shows. Most of the shows are from a long time ago, like *Leave
It to Beaver* or *Miami Vice*. Others are more recent like *Ren
& Stimpy*. Every time a show is canceled where you are, it's
added here. Shows from all over the world. I'm supposed to
earn my required quota of credits by the time an episode of

All in the Family airs in the Electronics Department. The way I earn credits is by going to therapy. I don't know how it is for anyone else, but my quota's 132 and I get twelve credits for every sit-down with my counselor."

"I don't understand. What do you do with the credits?"

"I told you the shelves here are stocked with dead crap?"

"Yeah."

"I use my credits to buy that crap. Because as boring as it can be walking up and down aisles stocked with yesteryear's garbage, let me tell you, it's exponentially more boring to walk up and down aisles, not buying any of it. I keep what I buy in a locker. You wouldn't believe the size of the locker room."

I wouldn't have believed a lot of things if I wasn't actually hearing his voice. "That has to be one humongoid Aftermart," I said.

"My counselor says it's forever expanding, like the universe."

"I guess it'd have to be, right? Because of all the clothes and games and whatever constantly going out of production and people dying every second? But since people are constantly dying, don't there have to be more and more counselors for them to talk to? Where do the new counselors come from? Do you ever graduate from therapy and become one yourself?"

"Unclear. But that's not a bad question. You surprise me."

"And your counselor: Who is he? Or she?"

"He says his name's Sean, but his face is smeared as if it's behind a fogged window. The powers that be—all their faces are like that. I've asked Sean if I'm in heaven, hell or limbo, but he always answers me in the most annoying way possible, by asking me which I think it is. You at home?"

"Uh huh."

"There any ice cream in the freezer?"

"Some chocolate chip, I think."

"Humor the deceased. Get hold of it and a spoon. Please."

The vacuum had started up a little while before and I figured Mom was in one of those cleaning jags she'd been falling into every day since her last cigarette.

Wrong-o.

Okafur was pushing the Hoover around the living room like he thought it might bite him. "That's it! Perfect!" Mom gushed, and since Wilt hadn't said he wanted to talk to her and I still had questions to ask, I held the phone down at my waist so she wouldn't see it. I made it to the kitchen no problem, snagged the Breyer's and a spoon, loped back to my room—"You're a natural!" Mom was yelling at Okafur—and closed the door.

"Okay," I said to Wilt.

He asked me to spoon ice cream into my mouth and describe its taste, which I thought would be easy until I tried.

"Cngolg," I said.

"Don't talk with your mouth full, idiot."

I swallowed and said, "Cold. And creamy." But *cold? Creamy?* How exactly did you describe these things? "When I say 'cold,' I mean that I feel this quick tingling sensation, like, I don't know, a sharp feeling against the warmth of my mouth? And when I say 'creamy,' I mean soft and smooth and kind of . . . buttery? The chocolate chips taste like dried smoke and are a little chalky in a good way."

"Man, to taste what you taste right now."

Before his crash, Wilt had basically been a walking, talking cardboard cutout. I'd known only his lordly big brother side for so long, I'd forgotten he had any other.

"The police don't think you died by accident," I told him. "They suspect foul play."

"They weren't there. They don't know."

"They say it's something about the car, that it was tampered with. Plus you're calling every fifty minutes again and I really think that's a clue."

"I didn't know I was calling every fifty minutes. We don't have Time here, not as you understand it."

"Yeah, well at first you called every fifty minutes, then you stopped. Now you're doing it again. Don't you remember anything about the crash? Anything that might've caused you to wreck? Like you tried to stomp on the brakes but they didn't work or—"

"Actually, I don't. And I've been told that it's not uncommon. Who wants to be stuck in eternity, the last memory of their life being of what unexpectedly killed them? Especially if it was an *unfortunate accident.*"

"Um, how do you know it was an accident if you don't remember it?"

Silence answered me.

"But so you and your counselor Sean have talked about the night you died?" I said. "Maybe he knows what happened."

"How are you for money?"

I didn't understand why he was asking, not right off. "I don't have jack, as usual."

"Pull the drawer of Mom's nightstand out all the way and check the outer side of its rear panel. Tell me about the ice cream again."

"It's soupier," I said, remembering how, when we were real young, Wilt and I used to squeeze Hershey's syrup into bowls of vanilla ice cream and whip our spoons around till the ice cream became like a shake. I loaded a spoonful of soupy chocolate chip into my mouth. "A slug of melty goodness," I said.

"Know what?" He had tears in his voice again. "From now on I should ask you to describe things I hated. This is just too hard."

After Wilt's funeral I'd hunted every day for the cash Mom found under his mattress. Because even though she'd given him the third degree and banned him from using the car till he admitted he was dealing drugs, she'd let him keep the money, handing it back to him with this look like she was a woman serious about discipline. Maybe she figured if she let him hold on to it, he'd rate her as a pretty cool mom and so would want to tell her where he'd gotten it? And maybe he would've told her, if he hadn't wrecked the car before he got the chance.

Or before the car wrecked him.

Anyway.

I'd checked everywhere I could think of—not only under Wilt's mattress, but in our closet and in every drawer of our dresser and just everywhere. I never found the cash, though, and one time when he called and I was about to ask where it was, I assumed he'd probably had the money on him the night he died and there was no point asking about it.

It didn't hit me what I might find in the nightstand till after we hung up.

Mom was in the kitchen showing Okafur how to soap and rinse a plate, tongue-wagging about how we couldn't afford an automatic dishwasher even if we had space for it, which obviously we didn't, because as the kid could see, our kitchen was just this short little aisle so narrow she could touch its opposite walls when she stretched out her arms.

I hurried into the living room and pulled the drawer from the side table she used as a nightstand, found a sealed envelope duct-taped to the outside of the drawer's rear panel. I took the envelope and slid the drawer back into place and locked myself in the bathroom.

$1,635. That's what the envelope had in it. All the fives together, all the tens, twenties, $100s. But only one $50 in the whole stack.

Which I figured right off wasn't a coincidence. I mean, Wilt calling every fifty minutes? One $50?

I found a phone number written on the back of the bill.

I didn't get why Wilt was pretending things weren't clues when they were. But if he was pretending not to give clues, he must've also been pretending not to know he'd been murdered. Either that or maybe he wasn't pretending and the clues were coming from his counselor Sean and the other blurry-faced powers that be in the Aftermart. Sean provided the clues through my brother, who really was calling me because it was somehow supposed to help him cope with being dead.

I needed to get my thoughts together before I dialed the number, so I made some lists:

WHAT I KNOW I KNOW

Wilt says he died by accident

Cops say Wilt was murdered _and_ somebody messed with the car

Wilt had a lot of $

Rick Calvados is making a play for Suzy

WHAT I KNOW I DON'T KNOW

How Wilt's car was tampered with and made him crash.

Where Wilt got all his $

If Rick C. is involved with whatever Wilt was doing to make $

If Rick C. knows how to cut brakes on cars.

Why Wilt pretends not to give clues when he _is_ giving them.

If Wilt is _pretending_ not to give clues or he's actually clueless.

How much counselor Sean knows about what happened the night Wilt died.

WHAT I KNOW I DON'T KNOW

???

WHAT I KNOW that I DON'T KNOW I KNOW

???

The last list was because I figured I already knew stuff that could help me bust Rick C, I just didn't know what exactly that stuff was.

I didn't plan on being an ignoramus for long.

14

I see Dr. Polk every few months for so-called Pharmacologic Management. He asks me questions and writes down my answers, which is supposed to prove whether or not my meds are working. We used to meet more often. In the early days, I didn't know what I was supposed to say to him, so I said nothing and would sit droopy in his office, thumbing my phone, waiting for our boring, pointless thirty-minute session to end. He'd sometimes ask how things were going at home or at school, what apps I had on my phone or what sports I liked. "Fine," I'd say, after which he'd always be as silent as I was.

One session, though, I don't know what happened: my mouth started going, blathering about how I was in his office only because the parentals didn't know what to think of me unless somebody with a fancy degree told them, and why had I been branded the messed-up one and not Wilt? It was suddenly like I had only thirty minutes to get out as much as I could. I said there were weeks, whole months even, when nothing particularly crappy happened, nothing stand-outish crappy, but on any given day I might be walking down a street, passing newsstands and fruit vendors, and in my head I'd be all, *Shut up! Everyone just shut up and go away!* It'd be overwhelming—the feeling that everything sucks—and both the suckiness of everything and that I couldn't stop feeling put out by everything's suckiness would piss me off. It was hard, I said to Dr. P, slogging through the days one after another—so hard that sometimes I wished it would stop. I didn't want to think things were hard. I wanted to lighten up, take a deep breath and shake loose of all this anger, except it didn't seem to be up to me.

Dr. P scribbled while I talked on and on. I knew he was taking down what I said to study me like I was some lab specimen, but it was more attention than my words usually got.

"Don't you think you'd be fine seeing Dr. Polk once a month?" Dad asked, not long after my session of emotional diarrhea.

That was new: a parental wanting me to spend less time with a shrink. But Dad pays Dr. P's bills, which aren't fully covered by insurance.

So once every two weeks with Dr. P turned into once a month, which turned into once every six weeks and then once every two months. We've been on our current schedule of once every three months for a while.

Sometimes I have emotional diarrhea. Other times I don't.

There's the kind of person who lets disappointment make him weak and angry, the kind who lets it beat him down to the point where he doesn't think he deserves anything else. Then there's the person disappointment makes stronger. He fights as hard as he can against it to get what he needs from this world. I've always wanted to be the second kind of person. I can't help it if too often I feel like the first.

15

I spent a lot of the night staring into the dark of my room, Okafur in Wilt's bed making gurgling noises. I was trying to figure out the best way of playing things when I called the number on the $50. And right when I was like, *Okay, no way am I going to get any sleep,* I woke up and Okafur wasn't in Wilt's bed anymore and clinky-clanky noises were hassling my ears from the kitchen.

"Sit," Mom said.

I'd stepped from my room to see her at the feeding table.

I slid into the seat next to her. "This is different."

We never had sit-down breakfasts, but two place settings were laid out: knives, forks, spoons, coffee mugs, glasses for OJ and water, paper towels folded into triangles for napkins.

"Who're we pretending to be?"

"We're a family," Mom said. "Not the same as before, but a family."

She had this look like she was auditioning for some cheesy Hallmark movie. Okafur came out of the kitchen wearing an apron, which was when I lightbulbed: there wasn't any place for him to sit because the other chairs had OCD-neat piles of newspapers, magazines, and unopened mail on them. Okafur poured me coffee and went back into the kitchen and came out again with two plates of scrambled eggs. Then he went over and stood at the edge of the kitchen, waiting. Mom held up her empty OJ glass. Okafur stepped forward with the Tropicana and poured her a refill.

I forked egg into my mouth till I remembered Wilt's cash in my pocket. I was rich. I could eat elsewhere and didn't need to stuff my face in an insane environment brought on by mourning.

"But you haven't finished," Mom said when I got up.

"This isn't right," I said, figuring she knew what I meant.

I bowed my thanks to Okafur and cut out of the apartment, pulling the $50 from my pocket before I even made it down to the building's first floor. Sucking air like I was prepping for something big that had to be done no matter how it ended, I dialed the number on the back of the bill.

"Who's this?" a guy's voice said.

"Brooks."

"Brooks? Where the hell've you been? What phone are you using? You're needed at the Tudor immediately. We've got some new prospects."

I was like, "I need a tutor?" and the voice was all, "Hilarious," then spat out an address and hung up.

I texted Lou and Jeremy to tell them I wouldn't be at school and I'd explain why later, and I made sure Location Tracker was on so that as long as I kept my phone with me, they'd see where I was.

Whatever I found at the address the voice had given me, I knew it'd be something Wilt hadn't wanted anyone to know about, the kind of thing that if you got on the wrong side of, it could get you killed.

16

I didn't usually go to the bird streets since being surrounded by gazillionaires and their mansions always makes me feel like a nobody. Also, the security guards patrolling the bird streets are major dicks. If they catch anyone on Oriole or Nightingale or wherever who doesn't have a certain minimum net worth, they beat on him before tossing him from the area.

I couldn't see any part of 2452 Sparrow Lane from the street. It was fronted by hedges three stories high and I don't know how thick. A solid wood-and-iron gate blocked the driveway. I pressed a button on the intercom, assuming I was being scoped and maybe even x-rayed by umpteen security cams.

"No soliciting," a voice said.

"I was told to come. I'm Curtis Brooks. Wilt's brother."

There was a pause and then the voice was all, "Look directly into the camera at the upper left corner of the gate. Your left."

I did as I was told.

"You got ID?"

"Yeah."

All I had was my school laminate with the pic I hated because my ears looked like busted shells taped to the sides of my head, but I held it up for the cam. The gate unlatched and I walked the long curving drive to where a guy was waiting outside the closed front door. A guy with his hair shaved short who could've been ex-special forces or a white supremacist or maybe both. He was blocky—like weightlifter blocky, I'm talking—with muscles that even under his slick black suit looked to be made of brick. I was pretty sure he could beat the crap out of me just by flexing his biceps.

"Let's see that ID again," he said.

I don't know if he wanted to check that my school ID was legit or what. I handed it over.

"Wilt didn't say he was sending you to cover for him."

I figured that in general I should probably speak as little as possible, give away nothing about what I was thinking, but I wanted to see how the guy'd react. "That's 'cause my brother's dead," I said.

He didn't ask how or when Wilt died. He just had this sort of non-reaction, like people he knew were dying all the time, which maybe wasn't great but there was jack he could do about it.

He handed back my ID. "Sorry to hear it. Wilt was a good man. Trustworthy." That last word seemed to remind him. "How'd you get my number?"

"I found it in Wilt's stuff."

"Uh huh."

He scoped me for a good minute and it was one of the hardest things I ever had to do—scope him right back like I wasn't afraid.

"Wait here," he said. He left me on the front steps awhile. When he opened the door again, he didn't come outside. "You want a job?"

I shrugged, trying not to gawk at what I could see of the house behind him—the wrought-iron chandelier that had probably needed a crane to hoist to the rafters, the front hall as big as my whole apartment.

"It'll take an hour a day max," the guy said. "You'd get $250 a week."

I shrugged.

"Don't get too enthusiastic on me. Go around to the back and I'll meet you. My name's Nuñez."

The house was the size of an entire apartment complex, the side of it landscaped like a jungle at an amusement park, with ferns and palms and other leafy things perfectly arranged. The backyard was the same except about fifty-times bigger and it had a pool that must've cost a ton of cash. It was pretending to be a pond, with a little stream that looped around at one end and a waterfall and a rock-ringed part that I guess was supposed to be a hot spring but was really just a Jacuzzi. The yard could've come straight out of one of those magazines I sometimes flip through in Dr. Polk's waiting room—the kind of yard I can't believe people actually call their own. Except this yard had something I'd never seen in any fancy mag, and which was completely out of place in that money-scape. Like a guy had been paid a truckload to arrange the plants and trees and flowerbeds and then some-one from my neighborhood came and wrecked it by putting a chain link dog run in the center of everything. The run was maybe half the size of a basketball court, the chain link about eight feet high. Which I wasn't sure was high enough the way three dogs inside the run were barking and growling and thrashing around. All three were tethered to stakes in the ground with what might've been anchor chains, the stakes far enough apart that the beasties couldn't fang one another. The closer I got to them, the more they raged.

"Those are mastiffs, in case you didn't know," Nuñez said, waiting for me.

I waved to the dogs and they strained against their chains to get at me like I'd insulted their mother.

"They might be as bad as they look," Nuñez said. "You'll be fine. Come on."

I followed him to a mini version of the main house, all white stucco and dark wood and with a roof shaped like an elf's hat. Inside was a cross between a kitchen and a walk-in pantry. A counter with a sink ran along a wall. There was this fridge and then another sink big and deep enough for me to sit in, if I wanted. A couple car tires were leaning against a wall, beneath shelves stocked with different types of canned dog food. Muzzles, chains, thick leather collars, and pooper scoopers hung on hooks where other people might have hung pots.

"You'll need those," Nuñez said, meaning the scoopers. "You put their shit in plastic bags, which are in this drawer here, and you toss it all into the garbage cans in the alley." The regular sink had two faucets: one big and one small. "Always get their water from the small one," he told me. "It's filtered water. Reverse osmosis." He showed me the forty-pound bags of Science Diet. "Always fill their bowls with an even mix of dry and wet foods. The wet's in the cans here. Half a cup each. But this is the good stuff." He opened the fridge. "Grass-fed sirloin. You give them four ounces each in the morning, before school, and then again at night around five/five-thirty. I'll make sure it's here. The scale's on the counter. Four ounces exactly. And you write down what and when you feed them in this notebook—every time. The key to the dog run's in this drawer here, and that . . . " he pushed shut the front door so that I could see the life-sized Michelin Man costume hanging on the back of it, " . . . is what you wear when you go into the run."

"Are you serious?" I said.

"Do I look like I have a sense of humor?"

He didn't. Nuñez didn't look like he'd ever laughed in his life. He pulled a $50 from a money clip and set it on the counter.

"It's your choice. We good or not?"

I almost bolted. But I'd gone that far, and how was I supposed to find out what happened to my brother if I ran?

"We're good," I said.

I pocketed the $50 and tried to play it cool while I reached for Michelin Man. The costume was heavier than it looked and plunked to the floor, nearly taking me with it.

"I would help you, but you've got to learn to do it on your own," Nuñez said, watching me struggle to put the thing on over my clothes.

I asked where he'd found a one-size-fits-all Michelin Man costume, but he didn't understand the question.

"Wilt wore this, right?" I said. "And now me? And I mean, we weren't exactly the same size, so."

Nuñez tapped an index finger against his UFC fighter's skull. "More wise and less ass," he said.

Being Michelin Man took getting used to. Moving my arms and legs, I felt, I don't know, like Frankenstein on the moon or something. And it turned out I was too big to fit through the door, because leaving the shed, I got stuck.

Nuñez was already outside. He grabbed one of my arms and pulled while I pushed with my feet and sucked in my breath to make myself as thin as possible. I was wedged in good, though. And since I didn't figure Nuñez for the kind of guy who'd call the fire department to help free me, I was starting to think I'd be stuck in that door all day unless he had a crowbar, but that's when I popped loose and we both went sprawling into the grass.

For the next five minutes Nuñez let out a spew of nastiness that was like speed rap—ordinary curse words mashed into these totally extraordinary combos without the slightest hesitation. If I could've reached my phone, I would've recorded him.

"You put the gear on outside the shed next time," he warned, brushing at his suit. "Got it?"

"Got it," I said, except I was thinking he should've known Michelin Man wouldn't fit through the door. Hadn't he been through this routine with Wilt? But not saying everything I thought, that was the new me: more wise, less ass.

The mastiffs were snarling and doing their frothy thing in the dog run. Nuñez had to shout over them to be heard.

"Two of them can reach the gate! If you want to shorten their chains—excellent! Leave all the meat here except one filet!" He motioned for me to grab a steak and set down the rest. "Bring that around this way!"

The deranged mastiffs tracked us to a kind of mail slot in the fence.

"Drop it through here! And while they're trying to get to it, you hurry back to the gate and let yourself in! GO! GO! GO!"

The mastiffs barked it out over the steak and I Franken-walked fast as I could to the gate. Meat-plate and poop-scoop in my big white mitts, I barely made it into the run before the dog-beasties came at me. I panicked. The meat went flying and the beasties had at it like it was them or the meat, the world wasn't big enough for both.

Nuñez shook his head at me from the safety of the outside yard. "I've got to check on some things! I'll be back!"

"How am I supposed to get out?" I shouted, but he'd already gone into the house and I was all *What should I do now?* because the last thing I wanted was to go around scooping poop and have a dog-beastie tackle me, and me either getting covered with the poop as it went flying or having to scoop it all up again.

So I made a decision before the dog-beasties finished chowing, and maybe it was a bigger risk than I knew, but it's what I did, so.

I lay on the ground inside the gate, flat on my stomach, hoping the two beasties who could get at me wouldn't attack, they'd just sniff me or whatever, because I looked like less of a threat.

And it worked.

Finished mauling their meal, the two beasties were like, *Hey, what's this big white lump in our territory?* and trotted over to check me out. One tugged and gnawed on my foot, the other lifted a leg against my shoulder, but it could've been a whole lot worse and maybe would've been except that they started to mellow, like their after-chow digestion period had kicked in or something. They settled in their corners with their heads on their paws, blinking at me while I worked my way onto my feet and went and flopped facedown on the ground within reach of the third beastie, who had this beige spot on his nose and actually let me pet him a little. But by the time I'd gone around and collected a couple pounds' worth of turds and the poop-scoop was hanging heavy in my mitt, they all had their rabid mojo back. The only way I could escape the run was to kick at them.

Nuñez came out of the house as I was hosing down Michelin man. He handed me a burner.

"I'll call you on this," he said. "And if you ever need to call me, this is what you use. Nothing else. My new number's already programmed in."

"Why're you giving it to me?"

"Consider yourself hired on a trial basis. There might be some weeks you're not needed, but you'll be on call and still get paid. I wouldn't screw this up, if I were you. He's plugging you into the system early."

I was like, What system? *Whose* system? Nuñez wasn't the boss?

17

I made it out of the bird streets without being hassled by security guards, early enough I could have still gone to school if I felt like it. Which maybe I would've done, if I hadn't passed the cemetery on the way.

I'd been spending time in Forest Lawn even before we buried Wilt there. The gravestones were mostly granite rectangles lying flat in the grass, so when I stood anywhere in the place, all I saw were hills and trees and big open spaces and it was easy to trick myself into thinking I was far away from everyone and everything I knew instead of in a too-small city where I'd lived for too long.

Plus the gravestones told stories.

Like Beloved Husband Harvey Dobb, who died in 1919, and his Beloved Wife Marlene Dobb, who died early in 1920 and I figured probably kicked it from grief. I used to try and imagine Mom and Dad as the Dobbs—staying together for decades, Mom being so busted up about Dad's death that she gave up living herself. Even in my imagination, though, it seemed bogus and I stopped.

There was Arthur and Rebecca Lindhurst's son Malcolm

who died in 1941. His grave always made me think of parents having to watch their only kid get shipped off to fight in World War II with a backpack full of ammo, and the leftover bits of him coming back in a box, which must've sucked all around.

Except the Millers of the 1800s had it worse. Their four daughters died as teens, between like fifteen and seventeen years old. No way Robert and Irma Miller could've been the same afterwards, but they toughed life out for another three decades.

There were babies' graves—stories that might've been, not even a sentence long—and also graves of people who'd lived to be over ninety years old. Which I used to think was beyond ancient—and in a way, yeah, it is—but whenever I was in that wide open cemetery where trees had been nodding in breezes forever and I looked down at a gravestone showing the dates some old geezer-lady lived—1910–2004 maybe—then ninety-plus years didn't seem so long. It seemed like hardly any time at all.

Being in Forest Lawn gave me a kind of pleasantly sad feeling. Avoiding Wilt's plot, hanging out with the Dobbs and Lindhursts and Millers, I told myself I was just one person in a world with billions of other people and that this world floated in space with trillions of other planets, and I was like, *Maybe hundreds of years from now some kid'll stand over my grave, sweating whatever family problems he has, maybe he'll see Wilt buried next to me and also that Wilt didn't even live to be nineteen years old and he'll make up stories about how it felt for me to go on living without a big brother and for Mom to be reminded of her lost firstborn every time she glanced my way. And maybe, filling in the stories of me and Mom and Wilt—and of the people in the graves*

*around ours—maybe this future kid'll have an easier time dealing
with his own problems because they won't seem so big to him anymore in the scheme of things.*

"I've been thinking," I said, answering my phone when
it buzzed.

"Careful," Wilt said.

"Ha. No, really. They have camera phones in that
Aftermart, right? Dead discontinued camera phones? Could
you buy one with some of your credits and send me a picture
of where you are?"

"I can't photograph what has no corporeal manifestation,
genius. But to prove that I have greater respect for you as an
individual than I've ever had before, I will try what you sug-
gest. Hold on."

Sappy music funneled into my ear till he came back online.

"Okay, I'm taking a picture. Sending it your way."

I put him on speaker and checked out the pic. "It looks like
the inside of a cloud," I complained.

"Told you."

I guess I was annoyed that I couldn't see anything. What I
said next, I said like the cloud was his fault.

"I've started working for Nuñez."

There was this really long pause, the longest in one of
our phone gabs. Then he was all, "A Pet Rock? You believe
people used to buy this stuff? But it *is* only three credits. Think
I'll get one."

"Did you hear me? I said I'm working for Nuñez."

"I heard. Which house did you go to?"

Which house? "The Tudor," I said.

"What kind of dogs?"

"Mastiffs."

"Wilton Brooks," he said to someone or something else. "No, that's it for now." He must have been at a register, paying for his Pet Rock and maybe the dead discontinued camera phone. "They always tell me to 'come again,' as if I've got a choice," he said to me. "Listen, Curtis. Your working for Nuñez? Not a good idea."

It was the first time I remember him ever calling me by my actual name.

"Why?" I said. "You worked for him. You don't think I can handle it?"

Neither of us said that *he* hadn't exactly handled it, being dead, and I was thinking that if he didn't ask how my working for Nuñez came about, then I'd know for sure he'd been giving me clues without admitting it, that I'd been supposed to find the number on the $50 and he'd known all along he was murdered. And then I thought, But maybe his not admitting it was itself a clue I was failing to see? Except that was stupid. Why'd he have to be so mysterious? Why couldn't he just come out and tell me straight-up what he needed? Which question I was about to ask when I figured, Uh, that might be what he was having trouble with: he'd never needed anything from me before and relying on little bro was a come-down that took some getting used to.

"Are there mirrors where you are?" I asked. "I'm wondering what you see when you look in one."

"I see myself as I was when alive. It isn't real. Just a kind of metaphor that my residual consciousness understands, or so I've been told. It sounds like new-age bullcrap to me. But you know those badass characters you watch on TV and elsewhere?

Nuñez is worse. You don't get to be people like Nuñez and Yang without—"

"Who? Yang? Is that Nuñez's boss?"

He realized he'd screwed up because he started to go intermittent, parts of his words dropping out like we had a bad connection. Except the timing was too perfect and I knew he was faking.

"I—nt—ryou," he said, and hung up.

That call was a gold mine: not just the name Yang but there being other houses besides the Tudor and probably other dogs at the other houses.

18

Okafur was treading a path from the kitchen to the table and back again. It was dinner's new usual—Mom and I eating while Okafur served us, except she was less interested in her Hamburger Helper than in smashing her plate with her fork.

Her typical way of letting me know I'd done something wrong: she banged stuff around until I asked what was up. But I didn't feel like playing stupid games.

I moved a stack of magazines to free up a chair. "Why don't you sit down?" I said to Okafur.

He shook his head, his eyes sliding toward the angry parental, who heaved like she was blowing out invisible candles.

"Is there anything you want to tell me, Curtis?"

If there was, I didn't know what, but Okafur took his cue from her and eyed me all, *Yes, sadly there is something you want to tell your mother.*

"No," I said.

More invisible candles got blown out—the parental putting on like she couldn't believe the amount of pain I caused her, I was a bigger disappointment than she ever could've guessed.

"Why weren't you at school today?"

"What? Who said I wasn't?"

I knew Principal Chu hadn't ratted on me. Principal Chu never ratted on anyone. If he spent his time ratting on kids who cut classes, he'd never have had time to do anything else.

"It doesn't matter who I heard it from," the parental said.

But then she seemed to get popped with a pin. Her anger whooshed out of her, leaving her slumped and shrivel-skinned. She aged ten years in ten seconds.

"Just tell me the truth and I won't be upset. Is it too much to take, too soon? Going back to school after only a week? I can understand that. I know it's too soon for me to go back to work and I wouldn't be doing it if we didn't have so many bills. We can get you help."

Yeah, help. I was tired of that kind of help. Dr. Murray with his lame gangsta psycho-babble. Dr. Polk with his Effexor and Fluoxetine.

I handed her a twenty-dollar bill. What with Wilt's cash in my pocket and the $50 from Nuñez, I could've given her a lot more, but I figured she'd take small amounts without much hassle. Large amounts could lead to too many questions.

"What's this?"

"I did some work for a guy," I told her.

"What guy?"

"Just a guy. You don't know him."

Quiet and thoughtful, she seemed to forget about me cutting school. Okafur cleared the table and I heard him doing dishes at the kitchen sink.

"Did you call Detective Abrams?" I asked. "Did he tell you how the car'd been tampered with?"

She scratched the nicotine patch on her left shoulder blade.

"C'mon, Mom. Wilt was *murdered*. You can't pretend this isn't happening."

"I can try." She unpocketed a couple nicotine lozenges, unwrapped them and pushed them into her mouth. "I spoke to Detective Abrams," she said. "He found a device of some kind attached to the car and he's having it analyzed to find out what it did and how it worked. He asked if I know anyone who might've wanted to hurt Wilton. I couldn't think of anyone. Everybody liked him, didn't they?"

Yeah, as opposed to the rest of us, Wilt never had any of that awkward-in-his-own-skin way about him. When I was in elementary school, his popularity/coolness/whatever used to make me proud, but by junior high, when none of it had rubbed off on me, it bugged me no-end.

"Everybody liked him and still does," I said, all of a sudden questioning how the murderer had known Wilt would be driving Mom's car, that he'd borrow it in the middle of the night after she'd banned him from using it. And then I was like, *No way. Just no way.* Because the murderer couldn't have known that stuff.

Which meant Mom must've been the target, not Wilt.

Except Mom was just this exhausted single lady with a nicotine problem who worked the graveyard shift at UPS. Why would anyone bother to hurt her? I mean, yeah, she and Dad had their problems, but nothing too bad, I didn't think. Possibly Yang or Nuñez had been keeping tabs on Wilt, one of their goons following him, waiting for an opportunity, and my brother had stopped at a 7-11 or somewhere before driving to St. Benny, which was when the goon stuck the death-gadget on the car.

Whatever Wilt had done to make Yang want him dead, I didn't know. But how much did I need to know to prove motive?

I was so deep in my own head, sifting through all this, that I didn't hear my phone. Mom had it pressed against her ear.

"Wilt, babe," she was saying, "I'm not asking you to tell me if you don't want to, because it's okay if you were involved in questionable activities—adolescence is about experimentation—but I've always done the best I could raising you. I'll understand if you didn't *want* to talk to me about problems you had, but I hope you don't feel that you *couldn't* have talked to me. Wilt? Babe?"

I didn't like listening to her and went into the kitchen.

"You don't have to do all that," I said to Okafur, meaning the dishes in the sink.

He nodded as if I'd just verballed something he couldn't have agreed with more. Except he kept on washing dishes. I stuck my hand in the cold water streaming from the faucet.

"Haven't had any hot water for a while," I said. "Landlord turned off the gas. Part of his plan to make us so uncomfortable we'll move out."

Okafur's head bobbled up and down like, *Oh yes, you are absolutely correct, we are of the same opinion, yes.*

"You sure you don't speak English?"

He shook his head. I was trying not to hate on the kid. Like Wilt said, he hadn't personally done anything wrong. I knew his life couldn't have been easy because where was his family? It was just hard not to hate on a guy when you hated all the reasons he was in your life in the first place.

"Wait till it gets cold out and we have no heat," I said. "That'll be real fun."

I picked up the towel that hung from the fridge and dried the dishes leaning in the rack next to the sink. Both of us noticed the silence beyond the kitchen at the same time.

Mom was still at the table, her face in her hands, my phone abandoned in front of her and its screen gaping at the ceiling. Seeing her, Okafur got this expression like he was going to start crying any second. I went over and put a hand on Mom's shoulder, Okafur came up and put a hand on her other shoulder, and we stayed that way for maybe a minute before she shook free of us.

"I have to get ready for work. Will you please take the rent check to Mr. Pappas?" She was talking to me.

"Do I have to?"

"No, you don't have to. Of course nobody has to do anything except complain, skip school, and flout their mother at every turn."

"Why don't I take the rent check down to Pappas?"

Okafur was supposed to have made us a family again, she'd said. But with Wilt not being physically around, it was the parental's moods—not the pseudo-bro—that had filled up the space he used to occupy. And then some.

Landlord Pappas was this hairy, overweight troll whose skanky T-shirts never fully covered his gut, which meant if you had the bad luck to be cornered by him, you always got this vomitous peep at the cruddy wormhole of his belly button, the worm's head sticking out all, "Hi there!" He lived in apartment 1A and I generally tried to avoid him, using the stairs farthest from his place and being super quiet whenever I crossed through the lobby, because if he heard me, he'd lurch out from his cave and rail about us freeloading tenants who were ruining his life, keeping him from his American dream of selling a crumbling old building to developers for a ton of cash.

"What's that?"

Whenever I didn't want something to happen, that's exactly what happened: the troll's door had swung open as I was shoving Mom's rent check under it, and there was Pappas in one of his skanky T-shirts—which, what with the way it hung off the shag covering his back and shoulders, didn't seem to touch his skin.

"It wasn't a rhetorical question," he said. "Or don't you know what that means?"

"It's the rent."

"Pick it up."

"Yeah, right."

His belly button worm looked like it was gearing up to attack me. "You heard the Thomases moved out?" he said. "That means only five apartments to go, including yours."

"That's a real interesting story, Mr. Pappas. Tell me more."

I was backing away from him when he kicked Mom's check into the lobby. "How many times do I have to say it? Your tenancy is terminated."

He shut his door and I tried to slide the envelope under it but he'd somehow blocked the opening, and since it probably wasn't a good idea to leave the check where a drug-addicted squatter might steal it, I folded it into my pocket.

I didn't want to rush back upstairs to the dinky apartment. It was just a cubbyhole where I dealt with the grunt work of my life—all the basic upkeep stuff like feeding my face, showering, changing clothes—and more often than not I'd be left counting how many times I winked in an hour, thinking, *Now what?*

The scene out front of the building was almost as dead as on St. Benny. Used to be, lights from people's apartments would angle down so that Wilt and I could throw a tennis ball around at night, but the windows of the building were dark because the few of us holdout tenants who were left, we lived in the back. I started thinking about Wilt's locker in the Aftermart. What'd he buy with his store credits besides a Pet Rock? Would any of the dead discontinued merch he stowed in his locker be the same as what I'd put in mine, if I had one? Did he remember our old Creepy Crawly Maker—how we broke it one day after manufacturing a bunch of squishy bugs that we flopped around, playing ringmasters in a Little Monster Circus? Or the Earthworm Jim action-figure with its detachable head that we immediately lost and so recruited real worms to stuff into the doll's neck hole? Had he bought himself another Mr. Mouth game, like the one we used to have, or a Nintendo 64, which we'd lost on a move to a new apartment, and which Mom had promised to replace but never did?

I stood in the dark of the street, staring at where I lived as if maybe I could stand outside my life and get a better view of it. Except there was this old car repair shop across the street from our building—a black hole of slumminess sucking the rest of the block into its vortex. Wilt and I had snuck into the place once, crawling through a rotted hole in the stucco and wood on the garage's south side, the rot caused by damp. Wilt had said the shop could be our clubhouse. To hide the opening after we left, he pushed a dumpster in front of it, which nobody ever used. The place never became our clubhouse, though. Wilt was too busy doing older brother things.

Anyway.

After a few minutes Mom came out of our building. I dropped deeper into the shadows and watched her, trying to imagine her as just some lady and not my parent, which was impossible even though I hadn't quit trying when a car I didn't recognize rolled down the street and stopped to pick her up. And what with the passenger door open and the car's interior light on, I got a good look at the driver.

Dr. Murray from school. Loser Dr. M.

Mom kissed him on the mouth and I nearly gagged.

19

I expected the knock at the door to be Detective Abrams, that I'd open the door and see him huffing and puffing in the hall after having dragged his rickety self up ten flights of stairs, but it was Suzy. If I still thought she had something to do with Wilt's murder, I would've understood why she was there: to flirt and find out what I knew about her crime. Except I'd pretty much ruled her out as a suspect, so.

"I should've called first, huh?" she said.

"Naw, that's cool."

I was trying to act as if her showing up at a Wilt-free place was no biggie, but my voice sounded stupid. Behind me, Okafur laid off swiffering the TV to watch us.

"You weren't at school today."

She said it like maybe I hadn't known. I stepped back to let her into the apartment, but she shook her head.

"Too much has happened in there. With him."

I could understand that. She waited in the hall while I got Mrs. Holt's keys from a kitchen drawer. Landlord Pappas had been leaving apartments to rot, probably figuring developers would gut the building or just knock it down altogether. He'd forced our next-door neighbor Mrs. Holt to move out a couple months before, but she and Mom had exchanged keys in case of emergencies and her key still worked.

"Going out," I said to Okafur.

I didn't enjoy spending time in Mrs. H's place any more than in my own, but at least I could put the chain on the door and Suzy and I could be alone. Not like in the building's stairwell, which Pappas sometimes patrolled, or even outside, where there were no guarantees about anything.

"Only one light switch works," I said, leading Suzy into Mrs. H's. "Either all of them should work or none of them. Electrical in this building's messed up."

I flipped on the living room's overhead. The place wasn't any more romantic than the street. The carpet was ratty, spotted with bright patches where furniture used to be, the walls grimy gray except for the white rectangles where pictures had hung, nails and hooks still poking out here and there.

"Who's that kid in your apartment?" Suzy asked.

I explained how Mom had sprung Okafur on me. I said that I didn't know if she was really trying to adopt him or what, that he was Namibian but I had no clue where he'd come from locally, and Wilt thought that his being around meant the parental was going through a difficult time and I shouldn't make things more difficult by having a freakout.

"But I don't know," I said, "most people seem to have a difficult time *most of the time* and they don't . . . do what she did."

"Yeah," Suzy said, except she didn't think it was the easiest thing to adopt a kid, not even one from Africa, because wasn't adoption this lengthy, involved process and how could my mom qualify since she was single and didn't make much money? She said maybe my mom was foster-parenting Okafur since that would bring in some money, but still, becoming a foster parent took months and how had my mom found him so fast? Which yeah, was a question I also had, only I didn't say it because I was too busy shifting around to keep Suzy from seeing my hard-on. I swear, the girl only had to breathe to send blood rushing to my nethers, but there we were, sitting close enough I could feel the body heat coming off her. And the sound of her voice—all wet and delicate, with her tongue and teeth and lips having a three-way? And her crossed legs in those super-skinny black jeans, her ankles naked above new pink-and-purple Converse Allstars? And the way she leaned forward to spread her hands flat on the carpet, her fingers decked with black glitter nail polish? All of it was totally serious boner tease.

"The cops think Wilt was murdered," I told her.

"Yeah?" She suddenly got real intense with her bag, beating up its insides.

"They said his car had been messed with. I don't know how exactly, but I'm supposed to find out who's responsible. That's why Wilt's calling, even if he doesn't admit it. He can't rest eternal till I figure it out."

Suzy wrestled matches and a pack of Marlboro Lights from her bag. "Do you think you might be focusing on the murder aspect of things because it's hard to deal with losing your brother?"

"Why does everyone around me sound like a shrink?"

My voice had come out angrier than I expected, my boner'd gone the way of the dodo, and Suzy sat smoking, not looking at me. I couldn't tell if she was pissed or what. Yeah, *I* was kind of annoyed with her, but I didn't want her to feel that way toward me.

"The woman who used to live in this apartment?" I said. "She lived here for thirty years, but you wouldn't know it from looking around, right? Everything she'd ever felt while living here—depression, anger, happiness, whatever? Nothing's left except these patterns on the walls and in the carpet."

Suzy still didn't look at me.

"Want to hear something funny?" I said. "At first I thought you were involved with my brother's murder, that the two of you had like a profitable illegal scheme going and you'd gotten greedy and offed him. Or had him offed by a killer for hire."

She didn't seem surprised or offended. Real quiet, she said, "The police questioned me."

"They did? When?"

"They recovered Wilt's phone from the crash. I was the last person to talk to him alive."

"Did you know he had a job feeding rich people's dogs?"

"Yeah."

"Did you tell the cops?"

"Uh uh."

"Because you're scared. Wilt's murder was a warning to you, right? A warning not to do what?"

I realized only after I had asked: by telling me, she might be putting herself in as much danger as if she did whatever she'd been warned not to do. But the question was out, so.

She sat there, smoking, not answering, and I started to get jealous of the cigarette in her mouth—that little tube of tobacco feeling the kiss of her lips. My nethers throbbed.

"How'd Wilt first start working for them?" I asked.

"He only ever told me that 'a friend' had hooked him up."

"Who exactly is 'them'?"

"Can we talk about something else?"

"Sure, yeah."

It was stupid of me to expect all the info I needed in one go. I'd question Suzy a little every day till I knew exactly what she knew. It'd help me solve Wilt's murder, sure, but it'd also be an excuse to spend time with her.

"How's Rick Calvados?" I asked, unable to keep the snark from my voice.

"Rick's sweet."

"*Sweet*? Have you seen the guy play lacrosse?"

"He's passionate about what he loves. That's a good thing."

"Not if what he's passionate about is smashing other people's faces," I said.

"There are things about him you don't know. He's not as big of a jerk as he pretends to be."

Like she wanted off the Rick subject asap, she started telling me about how she and Wilt had decided to break up after high school, how they'd known they wouldn't end up at the same college and so had figured there was no point staying together once they weren't living in the same city.

"I don't care where I go to college as long as it's far away from this place," she said. "I only applied to schools on the other side of the country."

That Wilt had ever talked about going to college was news to me. He would've needed a lot more money than he'd hidden in Mom's nightstand to pay for it.

"I've thought about moving somewhere else after high school," I said. "Except what if wherever I go turns out to be the same as here, just with different scenery?"

Suzy mashed her cigarette against the wall. "You sound like Wilt. But don't you hate seeing people you used to hang out with in elementary school because they always treat you the way they did back then, like you're the same person you were in kindergarten?"

"I switched schools in second grade."

"I've been here my entire life. Everyone I know, I've known since I was a year old. There's too much history here and it makes me claustrophobic."

"You didn't notice some of us till this week," I said.

"That's not true."

I don't know if I was delusional or dreaming or what, but the way Suzy looked at me right then, I thought something was actually about to happen between us. She brushed ash I hadn't noticed off my thigh. My instant boner was like someone suffocating with a bag over his head, fighting to get to open air.

My phone buzzed and I was all, *Don't look at it. Don't look at it and you won't know for sure it's Wilt and won't have to answer it.*

"You gonna get that?" Suzy asked. "What if it's . . . ?"

"Hey," I said, answering my phone. "Guess who I'm with?"

"I'll talk to her in a sec. First: your job for Nuñez. I don't think you should do it, Curtis, I really don't. But it's good money. If you ever find yourself in trouble, any kind of trouble, you say as little as possible, because talking always makes things worse. You might see some things that are hard to stomach. If you can't ignore them, you get out. You don't make a stink about anything you see. You don't complain. You just quit. They'll want you to swear on your life that you won't say anything, but there's nothing to worry about if you don't ever say anything. Which you won't. Correct? You won't?"

I hardly knew what he was talking about. "Yeah, I won't."

"Good. Don't tell Mom. And be careful."

"I will."

"Now let me talk to Suze, doucheface."

I passed the phone to Suzy, but before I could get up to give her privacy, she grabbed my hand. I sat with her while she listened to Wilt, her head down so that I was sure she saw the wood in my pants. After a while, she let go of me and stood up. Still listening to Wilt, she wandered into what used to be Mrs. H's bedroom, and I stared at the patterns in the carpet till she came back and handed me the phone.

"What'd he say?" I asked, because Wilt had hung up.

"He told me to be careful."

"Me too."

She didn't want me to walk her down to the street. Saying our goodbyes in the stairwell, she kissed me on the lips—just this darting little kiss, which I pretended was no biggie, that as far as kissing a girl of Suzy's caliber went, I did it all the time.

"Maybe we should exchange numbers," I said. "In case, you know, there's anything about Wilt?"

"What's your number?"

I told her, and she thumbed me a text right off. "Hi!" it said.

Even her texts looked different from other people's. Like there was sex in them.

20

Word had gotten around at school that I was talking to Wilt. Most people figured I was lying, using it as an excuse to get out of homework and beg off tests, since how could I be expected to perform decently on a test or anything when I was so boggled by grief that I thought I was getting calls from a dead brother? Other people figured I wasn't lying so much as pretending as part of some kind of therapeutic exercise. Teachers went in big for that one, assuming Dr. M had light-bulbed it to help me get over the hump of mourning. Clearly, Dr. M didn't tell the geezers he'd diagnosed Wilt's phone gabs as hallucinations caused by emotional shock. More than a few people tagged me as insane—permanently or just temporarily, they said it was still too early to tell.

"Impressive, you sticking to that bullshit as long as you have," this kid Chris said, stopping me in the hall. "I wish a distant cousin of mine would croak. I could use it to get out of quizzes without having to lie."

Some disbelievers grilled me about all kinds of nonsense, hoping to trick me into confessing I'd made the whole thing up. They'd ask things like, "What exactly is the entity you're talking to on a molecular level?" and then, without waiting for an answer—not that I'd be about to give one—they'd be, "If we assume that energy is constant throughout the universe, and the energy that physically constituted your brother has taken on other forms, are we supposed to believe the 'Wilt' you're talking to is simultaneously both your brother and not your brother?"

"I guess," I'd say, clueless.

From his sneers, it was obvious Calvados thought the calls were bogus, part of my play for Suzy, except he couldn't come out and say it because Suzy had told him she'd talked to Wilt herself.

Dr. M and the rest of the disbelievers annoyed me no-end. If I put Wilt on the phone with every doubter, they'd hear his voice and probably just think he'd faked his own death. No amount of DNA evidence would convince them otherwise and they'd go on not believing. And it wasn't as if the believers made it easier to tolerate the non-believers. Religious wackadoos threw holy water on me whenever I passed in the hall or else tried to recruit me into their cults. Non-religious near-wackadoos assumed I could put in a call to any dead person I wanted and bugged me to ring up Elliot Smith, Heath Ledger, Corey Monteith.

"The line's busy," I'd say to get them to leave me alone.

Wilt's popularity had finally rubbed off on me. Not that I started hanging out with jocks or any of the supposedly cool kids. Except for Suzy, nothing in my social life had changed much, but I no longer ghosted around unnoticed between classes, and there were times I thought I'd get a concussion from having to nod *What's up?* to so many people.

"My brother died and left me with the rest of my life," I'd say out loud sometimes when I was alone.

One night after watching a bunch of skate videos, I googled "phone calls dead relatives" and in 0.27 seconds had 1,153,000 results. Sites with "angels" or "devils" in their URLs. Blogs about spirit worlds, telepathy, souls needing to say goodbye to loved ones. Sites like Psychology R Us that delved into "crisis apparitions" and "auditory hallucinations." Reviews of some novel with "heaven" in its title about townspeople getting calls from their dead relatives, and which sounded like feel-good Hollywood BS. Even CNN had posted an article on After-Death Communication or ADC.

Some of the results—I guess when you put the word "dead" into a search engine, it's going to happen—had nothing to do with ADC but were news bulletins about mutilated bodies found in public parks, mummified remains discovered in Detroit-area homes, murders solved after a decade. Or else they were sites about funeral etiquette that advised people to turn off their cell phones during services.

But search result number two, after The Center for Paranormal Research's website? It was this blog called How to Survive A Phone Call from the Dead. The thing hadn't been updated in a couple years, but on the right side of the home-page was an ad:

Trouble with After-Death Communication?
You're Not Alone! Talk It Out with OTHERS JUST LIKE YOU!
8pm Wednesdays!!!

So happened, it was Wednesday, not quite seven o'clock. Too bad the address was this old YMCA that'd been torn down to make room for condos. Not that I'd have scurried to the meet even if it'd been happening. Yeah, right: me volunteering for a group shrink session when I'd been forced to go to one-on-ones for almost as long as I could remember.

21

"No way," Lou said. "Calvados wouldn't do it."

"But the guy practically kills people on the lacrosse field all the time," I said.

"That's why I know he wouldn't do it. It'd blow his chances of getting a scholarship."

We were at 7-11 during lunch period, me and Lou and Jeremy, stepping up to the counter with Slurpees.

"I got this," I said, slapping down a ten.

Jeremy's eyes bugged out like I'd just done a cool magic trick, and Lou was all, "To what do we owe this unexpected generosity?"

"I got a job. You guys might want to try it."

"I'm too focused on my studies," Jeremy said.

"This job you speak of, it's the reason you were at the bird streets yesterday?" Lou asked.

"Yeah." I was glad to hear that he'd kept tabs on me through Location Tracker. I explained about Wilt's wad of cash and the phone number on the $50. I explained about the Tudor mansion and Nuñez and the psycho dog-beasties and Michelin Man and Yang.

"It's a dogfighting ring," Lou decided. "There's real money in that. Let me see those lists of yours."

I'd rewritten them since meeting Nuñez.

WHAT I KNOW I KNOW

Wilt says he died by accident but was definitely murdered.

Wilt had a job feeding rich people's dogs. (NUÑEZ. YANG.)

The $ Wilt had when he died he made feeding the rich people's dogs.

~~THE DOGS are scary.~~

the car Wilt died in had been rigged with some kind of device.

WHAT I KNOW I DON'T KNOW

WHY the rich people (NUÑEZ, YANG) wanted Wilt dead

If YANG is definitely NUÑEZ's boss

If/how Rick C. is involved with the rich people.

How exactly the murderer knew Wilt would be driving Mom's car.

How Wilt first started working for NUÑEZ and YANG.

WHAT I DON'T KNOW I DON'T KNOW

???

WHat I know that I didn't KNOW I KNEW

???

"Under 'what you know you don't know,'" Lou said, "you need to add 'if the rich people are running a dogfight op.' But after our next trip to St. Benny, you'll be moving it to the 'what I know' list."

"Dude," Jeremy said, "what're you talking, our 'next' trip to St. Benny? I'm not going there again, and Curtis can figure if it's dogfighting by how much they call in a vegetirarian."

Lou snotted up some of his Slurpee. "A *what*? Is that a doctor who works on sick vegetables?"

"You know what it is, dude."

"It's almost too easy," Lou said to me. "They took out your brother because he was somehow going to sabotage their entire operation. Now you just have to prove it."

"Maybe," I said, "but if Wilt was going to sabotage it, why'd he decide it's okay for me to work for them?"

"Because he has evidence stowed away somewhere and you need to be in the mix to get it."

"Stoo-pid," Jeremy said. "He could've just gone to the cops and let them deal. What I think is Curtis's bro sees the error of his ways: the best thing to do would've been to keep getting paid, and since he can't keep getting paid, Curtis might as well."

We were back at school, sucking down the last of our Slurpees before heading to class. Jeremy pointed his chin toward the flag-pole, where Calvados was hogging Suzy all to himself.

"Rick lives in the bird streets," he said.

Suzy saw me and waved. I did the same, and even from that distance I could see Calvados slit his eyes at me.

"Actually," Lou said, "he lives bird street adjacent."

Jeremy gave him a look.

"Adjacent," Lou said. "As in 'immediately next to.'"

Adjacent or not, with Calvados always going around like whatever he wanted from the world was his to take, he definitely had bird-street swagger.

Lou was right that I needed to go back to St. Benny for a more thorough scope. It'd have to wait till another day, though, because after school I had to be at the morgue for a family reunion.

22

Post-split, the parentals spent a couple years badmouthing each other on a daily basis, as if arguments over child-support and the slinging of blame for my having to pop meds weren't annoying enough. It took that long for them to settle into mostly ignoring each other, talking only when school or doctor visits needed them to coordinate for my or Wilt's supposed benefit. But then Dad started the process of having Wilt's body dug up, and after that I swear they wanted to fight. It didn't matter where they were, in a hallway or just any public place, they'd argue like they were alone in some soundproof room and weren't embarrassing themselves and me.

"I still don't understand the point of this."

"Lucky for us, *I* do."

"Don't give me attitude. Not now. Not—"

"What if there's been a mistake?"

At the morgue, I was a little ways down the hall from this scene of parental bonding, trying not to give a crap. Dad's third wife Maria was in the chair next to me, staring pigeon-eyed at the cinder block wall like one of those women who's had too much plastic surgery and so can't look anything except surprised. Detective Abrams and his partner sat across from us, Abrams watching me more than I was comfortable with.

Mom started yelling. "But it's morbid! It's disgusting!"

"I'll take your opinion under advisement!" Dad snarked.

Not for the first time, I wondered if I'd been born to the wrong parentals, if cosmic genetics had gotten screwed up somehow. Except whenever people had seen Wilt and me together, they said that anyone could tell by looking at us we were brothers. So unless Wilt had been born to the same wrong parentals . . . ?

"You should question this senior at my school," I said to Abrams. "Rick Calvados."

"Really? Why's that?"

I shrugged.

"Did you say something?" Dad shouted. "Because if you've been speaking, I can't hear you!"

"Do you think," I said to Abrams, "I don't know, that maybe it's possible my mom could've been the target and was supposed to have been killed and not my brother?"

Maria's head turned my way, and I could tell by Abrams' crumpled lips he didn't like my question.

"Why would anyone want to hurt your mother?" he asked.

Both his partner and Maria looked at him, then his partner squinted at me. "Why would this Rick Calvados you speak of want to hurt your mom?"

"No, that's not what I—"

"You're on medication, aren't you?" Abrams said.

"He is," Maria nodded. "Forty milligrams of Fluoxetine. And he was on Effexor for a time, in addition to Celexa, Wellbutrin, Venla—"

"It's none of your business," I said.

I usually didn't feel one way or another about Maria. I'd never thought about her enough to decide if I liked her or not, figuring she wouldn't be Dad's third wife forever. But she should've kept her mouth shut.

"How'd you know I take meds?" I asked Abrams.

"He's asking how I know," Abrams said to his partner.

"Tell the boy you're a detective. It's your job to detect things."

The parentals were nearing the end of their fight, sticking to the new pattern: snarky shouting, then the quieter back-and-forth of two tired people sick of themselves almost as much as each other, wanting to come to a temporary truce as fast as possible.

"Can I talk to you a sec?" I asked Abrams. "In private?"

I didn't feel like having the conference in front of Maria. Let her tell Dad I asked to speak to the detective alone. The third degree I might get about that would be easier to deal with than what I'd get if she actually heard me with the guy.

At the opposite end of the hall from the parentals, alone with Abrams, I was all, "Dogfighting's illegal, right? Having people bet on two dogs in a ring and which of them's going to kill the other? It's animal cruelty?"

"Why're you asking?"

"No reason."

"Uh huh."

He kept thumbing the round little gear-thing on his Zippo lighter. *Chk chk chk chk.* "You're getting calls from your deceased brother, aren't you?"

"How'd you . . . right, you're a detective. And we wouldn't

be here if my dad hadn't said why he wanted to check that Wilt was actually buried in his coffin."

Dad could've still been in denial about Wilt's death, I didn't say. Out of town the night it happened, Dad hadn't seen Wilt's bruised and broken body slabbed out on a table.

"Yeah, my brother calls me sometimes," I said.

"I don't believe in an afterlife."

"Guess you're going to have to reassess."

Chk chk chk chk went the Zippo.

"He doesn't think he was murdered," I said.

"No? Tell him to give me a call so we can discuss it."

"How about I'll do what I can if you keep me in the loop with your investigation?"

I expected him to be, *Who're you to make demands? You'd best improve your attitude or I'll fiction-up charges against you and toss you in juvie.* But instead he said, "Maybe it's better I tell you and not your mother. She doesn't seem to want to know and I'd rather not make things harder on her, if I can help it. We're still waiting to hear about the device we found attached to the car's undercarriage. Of the two phones recovered from the scene, one's intact, but its call history hasn't provided a single lead. The other phone's too smashed to do anything with, but we're reasonably certain it was a disposable. My partner and I've been asking ourselves why your brother would have two phones. You wouldn't be able to answer that question, I don't suppose?"

I shook my head.

"Might it have to do with Rick Calvados and your sudden curiosity about the illegality of dogfights?"

"I don't know. That's why you should question Rick," I said. "He's the one trying to get with my brother's girlfriend."

"C homes."

The elevator doors had opened, and I was so surprised to see Dr. M stepping toward me that I bumped fists with him before I realized it.

"Who's this?" Abrams asked me.

"A friend of Ms. Brooks, come by her invitation to offer emotional support," Dr. M said in his doofy-white-guy voice, his natural voice. "And you are?"

Abrams looked like he'd just been force fed a prune or some other gross thing. "Detective Abrams. Homicide." He didn't offer to shake Dr. M's hand.

"This is wack," Dr. M said to me. "Stay strong."

He continued on down the hall. The parentals were done fighting, each of them stewing in a kind of private aftermath, and when Mom saw Dr. Doof-Face, she reached for him like he was a flotation device that'd keep her from drowning. Because of which, crime-solving suddenly seemed the last thing on Abrams' mind—his gravelly eyes focused on Mom, his mouth slack with disgust, as if it'd just lost a battle with a whole bagful of prunes.

A crypt keeper in white lab coat pushed open the metal swing doors and said we should all follow him. Nobody had asked me if I wanted to be at the morgue and I didn't figure I'd be asked for my input that late in the proceedings. Part of me wanted to see what was physically left of my brother, part of me didn't. I knew from the night of the crash there was nothing cool about scoping a dead person up close. Still, when was I going to get another chance to see a body after it'd been in the ground awhile? So I let the parentals decide for me, not only showing up at the morgue as they'd asked me to but also following them into the steel-and-tile room I'd been in once before, and which could've come right out of those forensics shows on TV, with its wall of refrigerated cabinets that stored dead people and its carts of surgical equipment and whatever, some of which—the equipment, I'm talking— was steeping in jars of blue liquid like things I used to see at a haircutter's.

Me, the parentals and their insignificant others, Abrams and his partner—the crypt keeper led us over to this waxy man- nequin of a blue and blistered Elephant Man dressed in jeans and Cramps T-shirt. Wilt's funeral hadn't been open-casket for obvious reasons. Maria veered off to the nearest sink and barfed. Dr. M's arm slithered around Mom, which I guess was somehow supposed to be emotionally supportive. I reminded myself that the body on the table wasn't Wilt—not because someone else had been buried in his place like Dad thought, but more because whatever had made Wilt the guy he was— uniquely him, I mean—it wasn't there in the leftover bones and muscles and other stuff.

"How can I tell for sure who that is?" Dad complained with impressive denial. "It doesn't look real."

"We'll run DNA," Abrams' partner said.

The crypt keeper tweezered a sliver of something off the body and bagged it. Mom started to cry and popped a nicotine lozenge into her mouth, Dr. M copping a feel while "comfort- ing" her, which Abrams tried to ignore by eyeing some mur- der suspect in the air above all our heads. Meantime Maria seemed afraid to let go of the sink, as if she didn't want to leave her barf unattended, and even Dad dropped a few tears, which was more than I'd seen him do at the funeral, where he'd just stared clench-faced at Wilt's coffin.

When my phone buzzed, Mom and Dad turned to me with hopeful looks.

"It's Lou," I lied, and stepped to the hall before answering it. "You won't believe where I am," I said to Wilt, and told him.

"Can't the living leave the dead in peace?" he asked.

"How's it going?"

"It's not. I've never been so bored in my life—and yes, I'm fully aware of the paradox in that statement. But bored beyond belief. I miss Suzy's body against mine. I miss going to the movies. I miss the smell of wet pavement. I miss feeling breezes, sun on my face, standing in the rain. I miss taking showers, *especially* showers with Suzy. I miss hanging out with friends between classes and I even miss sitting in classes, if you can believe it."

It was a long list, especially since I'd never heard my brother say he missed anything before. "And you're not saying you miss me or Mom 'cause we still talk to you, right?" I asked.

"Nothing here has any smell," he said. "Nothing has any feeling or texture to it. All I can do is remember how things smelled and felt and tasted, and it sucks. And now when I ask my counselor Sean where I am, instead of asking where do I think I am or saying, 'This is what there is,' he says, 'For some this is heaven, for others it's hell, and for a third bunch it's limbo.' Which is not an answer."

"What about other ex-people? Shoppers or whatever you're called? You making any friends?"

"There's a guy Elliot I walk the aisles with sometimes, but

I can only take so much of him. He just *browses* and the crap on the shelves inevitably reminds him of things he did with his wife, who's still alive. Then there's Tricia. She's all right. We tried to kiss but our faces went right through each other. If not for these calls of ours, I would've gone insane already."

This was the nicest thing my brother had ever said to me. I welled up without expecting to.

"Hey, so. Wilt? At first I thought you were pretending not to give clues, that like you *knew* you'd been murdered and were using me to carry out your revenge plan without my realizing it—that way I wouldn't screw it up, you know? Except now . . ." I'd decided that asking point-blank questions about dogfight ops, about whether he had been scheming to bust Nuñez and Yang, would get me nowhere, " . . . but now," I said, "I'm not sure. I think maybe your counselor . . . I mean, if you really don't believe you were murdered, then I think Sean's the one giving me clues. Like whatever the two of you talk about at your therapy sessions, it leads you to say things to me that turn out to be clues. Except you don't know they're clues. I don't get why Sean can't just tell you or me outright what's—"

"Not sure *he* can tell *you* anything since you're not the relative he chose to call when he first got here. If he ever 'first' got here. It's not clear to me if Sean was ever alive or if assistant managers and up are angels or devil's helpers who've *always* been here."

"Huh," I said.

"Know what else I'm unclear on? Where are the Romans? The ancient Romans? Where's all the merchandise from antiquity? Where are people from the middle ages and the eighteenth century? Where's everybody who *ever existed before there were stores like Walmart* and what happened when *they* died? Did they come here too? Because that's just odd."

"Okay, yeah, besides that you could try putting me on the phone with Sean, that's kind of interesting. But Wilt? Do you know if the other shoppers there are murder victims or anything like that?"

"No. Did I happen to mention this place has layaway?"

"Because what I'm saying is, maybe your murder needs to be solved for you to leave the Aftermart. Or for you to get promoted to employee or something. And so maybe we need to lure Sean out. What happens if you don't go to therapy? If you refuse to earn your required credits?"

"Everyone always earns their quota."

"So don't and see what happens. Bag therapy. Ignore your quota."

After a pause he said, "You know what? I'll do it. It'll at least be a change."

I pinched the skin on my forearm—pinched and twisted it hard. "Hot," I said. "Stinging, like I'm being stabbed with a dull knife. And underneath the stinging, an itchy feeling."

"What's up with you?"

"I'm trying to describe physical pain, something you didn't like, so you won't miss life so much."

I know people can sometimes do a 180 after a relative dies—Jeremy, for example, who never got along with his dad and bitched about him nonstop right up until the guy croaked from a heart attack. After that, though, Jer started complaining about how he and his dad had lost the chance to ever be friends. And all his dad's nagging and criticism that used to be totally annoying? Jer said he even missed *that* and he wished he hadn't been so stubbornly angry, hadn't let himself be psychically stunted by his dad and had tried harder to get along with him while they were both alive. Not in those words obviously, because Jeremy doesn't talk like that, but what I'm saying is, in a way, I guess I was lucky with Wilt.

"When you're first trying to win a girl over," he said out of nowhere—which, everything from him was kind of coming out of nowhere, but still—"when you're first trying to get a girl," he said, "a certain girl in particular, you don't want to talk too much. The less you say, the more mysterious and interesting she'll think you. By the time she finds out you're not that mysterious or interesting, it'll be too late."

Too late? "Why are you telling me this?" I asked.

"No reason."

More like I wouldn't understand the reason till later.

After our call, I peeked in through the morgue's metal swing doors. The crypt keeper, the detectives, Maria and Dr. M—they'd all stepped away to let Mom and Dad have a moment alone over my brother's body. I watched as Dad took Mom's hand, and even though they kept their wet eyes lowered to Wilt and didn't look at each other, it was the tenderest moment I'd witnessed between them . . . maybe ever. Still, it was a pretty tense scene and I was afraid they would start fighting again. Most of the time when they fought, they'd be too busy going at each other to pay attention to me, even if they were fighting *about* me. Because they could argue about what was allegedly best for me while ignoring the me jumping up and down and waving my arms right next to them. Every now and then, though, their fights had the opposite effect and they'd both start impersonating major disciplinarians, not letting me do the slightest thing without a game of Twenty Questions, like it'd prove who was the better parent. And because I still had to make my late afternoon stop at the Tudor and didn't want to risk explaining where I was going and why, I decided to just skip out—left them at the morgue and caught a bus to the bird streets.

23

It's weird how certain things stay with you and others don't, the way memory leaves gaps: I have this scene in my head, then nothing, then another scene from around the same time as the first, then nothing.

Like when Dad moved his stuff out of our apartment before the official divorce. He and Mom coordinated so he could do it while Wilt and I weren't home. One afternoon Mom made us go with her to some animated movie about talking penguins, except in the theater she was too jumpy to let us stay till the Happier Ever After. When we got home, the living room seemed bigger than it used to because Dad had taken the black leather recliner and also a couple lamps and tables. Shelves around the apartment were emptier too, Dad having hoarded off with books and framed pictures of me and Wilt. But I mean, books? I'd never in my life seen Dad read a book.

What I remember next, though, I don't think it was the same night—Mom stepping into my and Wilt's room as we were going to bed. She reeked of cigarettes, sat on my mattress and said she had to get a job, that we couldn't afford to live in our big apartment anymore, we'd have to find a smaller one in a different school district and Wilt and I'd have to change schools.

Wilt stayed quiet but I was like, "I don't want to go to a new school."

"We don't have a choice," Mom said. "You'll still be able to see your friends here on weekends. We're not moving thousands of miles away."

"I can take a bus. If I get up early enough—"

She jerked to her feet. "You think I want to move? You think I wanted all this?"

Wilt still didn't say anything and I don't remember him talking again till the day our toys and junk were piled in the parking lot, waiting to be loaded into a yellow truck by men wearing wide leather belts. He glared at it all with this expression like he'd lost some game he was supposed to've won.

"It looks so small and dumb," he said.

Over the next six years we moved five times. Not to different school districts, but we both got pretty used to seeing the little-everything we owned heaped pathetic at curbs and in parking lots.

But our first day at Paradise Hills Elementary? It might have been during lunch or recess. I remember walking up to Wilt and Rick Calvados and other fourth graders who were in a circle by the bike racks, passing around a black plastic comb.

"What're you guys doing?"

"None of your beeswax, butt-for-brains," Wilt said, but Rick was like, "We're playing Bloody Knuckles. You wanna play?"

I didn't know how. One of the kids made a fist and dragged the comb teethside-down across his knuckles. Blood bubbled up on his pinkie. He passed the comb to another kid, who dragged it across his knuckles, except there wasn't any blood, just a white scratch mark.

"Wuss," Rick laughed, and punched the kid in the arm.

Wilt took a turn with the comb, bled two of his knuckles. He made sure everyone saw, then held the comb out to me. I pretended not to notice the way they were all smiling, as if they thought it was a joke, me thinking I could play, and they figured I'd wuss out and were just waiting to make fun of me.

I didn't watch what I was doing, didn't wince or anything. I dragged the comb hard over my fist and felt blood on all four knuckles but still didn't look. I handed the comb to Rick. No one was smiling anymore.

"I have to go," I said.

I didn't check my hand till I was maybe a football field away from them. The smeary blood, the shredded skin—it didn't hurt as much as I'd thought it would.

At dinner, Mom asked what happened and I said I'd fallen on the blacktop during recess. Wilt stopped eating for a second and lowered his hand under the table, not wanting her to see his two cut knuckles.

Weirder than certain things staying with you while other stuff doesn't? I remember what I thought weren't good times, except now I realize they kind of were because I shared them with Wilt.

24

No voice came over the Tudor's intercom. The security cameras fixed on me and the front gate unlatched, swinging back slow and smooth. I walked up the long curving drive and through the jungle shade at the side of the house to the backyard, the dog-beasties going ape the second they caught a whiff of me—more because they knew I was about to feed them than because they wanted to tear my limbs off, I like to think.

I figured that if Lou was right about the kind of operation Nuñez and Yang were running, there should be fight-training prods somewhere in the elf shed. I'd read about it online, and also how owners/trainers sometimes have blood transfusion setups on site along with other vet supplies like syringes, surgical scissors, anti-inflammatory and antibiotic injectables, vitamins, steroids, hormone and weight-gain supplements.

Keeping the shed door open enough that I could see anyone coming, I snooped in drawers and cabinets and carefully scoped the stuff hanging on the wall. No prods anywhere. Just those noose-on-a-stick things I've seen animal cops use—the kind where if they have to catch a dangerous mutt or wolf, they stand back at a safe distance, telescoping the noose out and looping it around the beastie's neck. The car tires lean-ing against a wall had more teeth marks on them than I remembered, but according to the web could be used either for jaw-strengthening exercises or as innocent chew toys. I moved the tires and found a locked cabinet. No key.

If I was being supervised from a distance, I was taking too long.

I hustled the steaks and dry/wet food together and filled a plastic gallon jug with water at the reverse osmosis fau-cet. I dragged Michelin Man out to the yard and suited up, Franken-walked to the mail slot in the side of the dog run and dropped a steak through. And while the dog-beasties strained to reach that meat-tease, I lugged everything and myself into the run, immediately tossed the rest of the steaks at the beast-ies, and made like a white lump on the ground where at least one of them could get to me.

Not finding prods wasn't the biggest deal. I didn't think it blew Lou's theory, which had also become mine. It just meant the dog-beasties were aggressive enough without sometimes needing to be electrocuted. Facedown in the grass, I hoped I hadn't picked a go-to toilet spot. Because waiting for a beastie to come over and pee on Michelin Man before mellowing into after-chow digestion was one thing, but pushing my face into piss-wet grass was totally another.

After lying there for I don't know how long, I felt a snuf-fling at the side of my head. I turned slightly and saw this black-and-beige nose going *sniff sniff, sniff sniff.*

It was the beastie who'd let me pet him on an earlier visit.

I shifted onto my side a little, probably a moronic thing to do since it left my face exposed, but I was doing a lot of moronic things back then. Except the beastie? He just set his head in the grass next to mine, his eyes like wet marbles. One of his ears had been shredded and what was left of it glued back together.

Real slow so as not to alarm him, I got up on my knees. "It's okay, I'm not going to hurt you," I kept saying, which was pretty ridiculous since the beastie could've easily fanged open my face. I shook off the Michelin Man mitts and touched him with my actual hands. "It's all right, it's all good," I said. He had hashtag cuts on his legs. Patches of fur were missing on his right side, and down near his belly he had what might have been scrapes from sliding on cement or rocky ground.

"How about I call you Manson? Huh? You like that, Manson?"

The beastie pushed himself against me and wagged his tail, so Manson it was, and while I went around scooping up turds, he barked for me to come back and pet him. The other beasties digesting in their corners kept suspicious eyes on us. But probably I should've said my body went around collecting turds. In my head I was somewhere else—living with Suzy and Manson in Mrs. Holt's apartment, which wasn't in Pappas's lame building and wasn't really Mrs. Holt's apartment but just laid out the same. And Manson never acted rabid but was this friendly, mellow dog, and what Suzy and I liked best about him was how obvious he always was in what he felt. When we came home from elsewhere, Manson'd be wagging his tail a hundred times a minute and we'd swear no beastie alive could be happier to see us. When Manson wanted a munch of our dinner, he'd sit between us with his tongue hanging out and this look in his eyes like, *I'm the saddest beastie in the world without a bite of your tasty food. Please give me a bite of your tasty food.* And a dog being so obvious in his feelings? I think maybe he's got a kind of honesty people don't have unless they're really young kids or else mental. When you can't help being so straight-up with your feelings, your needs and wants and dislikes and whatever out there for everybody to see because everything you are is what you feel at every particular moment? That's a good thing, right? So Manson was showing Suzy and me how to live: like if the whole of us was how we felt in the here and now, then maybe we'd whine less about the present because there wouldn't be any (better) past to compare it to, the same as there wouldn't be any future to sweat over. There'd just be what there was at that exact moment, every moment.

"Percentage," a voice said, bringing me back to my body and the dog run.

The door to one of the Tudor's second floor balconies was flung wide. The angle of the sun made everything misty. I could see Nuñez and another guy in the house, but both of them were kind of blurry, smudged the way I imagined Wilt's counselor Sean and the other Aftermart employees looked. Nuñez was listening, nodding while the other guy talked. The guy must've felt me staring, though. He turned to look at me, his mouth still spitting words at Nuñez, whose head kept bobbing like it was on a spring *boing, boing, boing.*

I crowded empty bowls, turd-bags, poop-scoop, and the water jug by the gate. I had one chance to get safely out of the run with everything, because I couldn't trust my ability to open the gate twice without riling the beasties. Once was hard enough. Except this time the beasties didn't even wait for the gate to squeak on its hinges. Soon as they sensed I was *getting ready* to leave, they went rabid, but not with the typical foaming-at-the-mouth insanity aimed at gnashing their way to freedom. No, this time it was like they were trying to keep me from leaving—like well-padded or not, I was the only succulent meat around and they weren't about to let me get away.

Manson was the biggest bummer, though—as rabid as the other beasties, demon-possessed. I guess he couldn't help but freak when the others freaked. Which maybe was one of the problems with living always in the present like he did.

Anyway.

I trashed the poop and hosed down Michelin Man and was about to head out when I noticed a door to the house lolling open—a door servants or kitchen workers might use. I couldn't remember if it'd been open when I first got there, but if it hadn't, and this was supposed to be a test of my trustworthiness, I was going to fail.

I serpentined toward the door, pretending to hunt for something that had fallen out of my pocket. I took a quick look around. Not seeing anybody, I stepped into the house.

"Hello?"

The kitchen was easily twice the size of my entire apartment, all copper and wood and shiny-cloud countertops.

"Hello-o?"

The only answer was a rhythmic sound—*thung thung, thung thung*—which took me a second to realize was my heart beating in my ears.

"I'm looking for a bathroom," I said out loud, in case someone was listening.

The front way out of the kitchen led to this humongous

atrium or gallery or whatever—a hall as wide as a three-car garage and as long as a bowling alley, with a dark wood floor and a faraway ceiling, wrought-iron chandeliers hanging from it like giant spiders. Two massive staircases with frilly black and gold railings curved up to the second floor, and opening out from both sides of the atrium/gallery/whatever were living rooms that didn't look like they had hosted much life, both of them decorated with the whitest furniture I'd ever seen.

The back way out of the kitchen was just this regular-sized hall with rooms on either side of it and a narrow carpeted staircase to the second floor. The first room I came to had nothing in it but mannequin heads on pedestals—a bunch of blank-faced heads wearing the same thick and bushy brown toupee with a part on the side.

The next room was creepier.

Against every wall: floor-to-ceiling, glass-fronted display cases filled with dolls. And not the kind of dolls little kids drag around by a raggedy arm. I'm talking stiff-limbed things, real-looking, their round eyes with mechanical lids staring at nothing. They reminded me of contestants in some children's beauty pageant, dressed up in ways no kids should ever be, adult-like. They seemed to be waiting for a command to come to life and go on a murder spree.

I backed slowly out of the room, all, *Where're the maids and butlers?* because the Tudor was definitely the kind of house that should've had maids and butlers. I made it up the carpeted staircase before I heard anyone.

"He's going to tell *me* about customer metrics?"

I'd passed three bathrooms and so couldn't use the need to empty my bladder as an excuse for being where I was.

"If his numbers don't improve, I'll disembowel him myself."

I stood in an alcove off the hall, in front of a chair and a small table with a phone on it, not pretending to hide but waiting for the wrath to come, my heart thundering in my chest. Nuñez walked right past me, blocking my view of the guy he was with, his head going *boing boing boing.* "Let's do it at wholesale tomorrow night. Send out the word at the usual time," the guy said as they went clumping down the stairs. Their footsteps faded and I heard a distant door close.

I didn't realize till right then, but I'd been holding my breath. I'm pretty sure that if I'd tried to be stealth and play the master spy instead of standing in the open the way I did, I would've been busted, maybe even disemboweled and fed to the dog-beasties. I'd been lucky.

I counted twenty Mississippi before soft-footing it out to the backyard. What with the whole dogfight thing, I had to acknowledge that Rick Calvados probably hadn't murdered my brother or been involved in his death in any way. Was it more likely that Wilt had been killed on account of his own problems with Nuñez and Yang? Or that b) Calvados had offed my brother so that he'd have an easier time getting into Suzy's pants *and* he just happened to know the same dogfight money-makers Wilt was working for? Or c) that not only did Calvados know Nuñez and Yang, he knew them well enough to make a deal with them, getting *them* to kill Wilt for him, in exchange for whatever?

I left the Tudor and walked fast-but-not-too-fast out of the bird streets, not wanting to attract attention. Nothing would've brought neighborhood patrol down on me more than if I speedwalked down the blocks. Or worse, ran. Security cams were bolted to stop signs, mounted high up in trees, everywhere. If neighborhood patrol saw me running down Sparrow Lane, they'd assume I was guilty of something and bruise me good, to get a false confession out of me.

Two blocks from being free of that moneyed neighborhood altogether, I felt a car roll up behind me and was like *crap*, figuring it for patrol.

Only two blocks.

They wouldn't harass me beyond the bird streets, I knew, and I was about to make a run for it, but the car sped up alongside me—an Escalade limo with Nuñez looking out the front passenger window. He motioned at the back door.

"Get in."

The way he said it, I didn't think it was negotiable. More like if I tried to run, things would get immediately violent.

I hadn't been lucky, after all. I should've known there were security cams inside the Tudor. Hesitating on the sidewalk, I almost voiced some nonsense about having needed a phone because my cell was dead, and also that I'd been looking for someone to tell about the fridge in the elf shed which didn't seem to be working right. But then I remembered what Wilt had said: I should speak as little as possible when in trouble, talking always made things worse. Funny that all his advice seemed to be about me talking less.

I kept quiet and got into the limo, as I was told. I expected some cushy, decked-out interior with platinum-and-diamond seatbelt buckles, a TV screen that unscrolled out of the roof at the press of a button, disco lights, a bar with vodka and gin and scotch in crystal bottles. Instead it was like a minivan without any cool entertainment stuff—two bench seats facing each other and a ton of empty space between. A vaguely familiar guy was there. His hand butterflied out, letting me know I should sit across from him.

"Drive," he said, and the limo started rolling.

He wasn't a scary-looking guy, not brick-muscled and square-headed like Nuñez. He didn't have any of that dead-eye quiet about him either, the kind psycho bosses in gangster movies have that's supposed to mean the quieter the boss-man is, the more probably he'll bludgeon a character's face if that character accidentally pisses him off by doing something he couldn't have known would piss boss-man off.

So but yeah, not scary. I mean, the guy's toupee? It was the same as the ones I'd seen on the mannequin heads in the Tudor—just laughably obvious. And now that I was seeing it on a live person, I thought the thing should've capped the head of some young government official-type. Except this guy wasn't young. He had a good amount of facial sag going on and seemed to've got his gray suit off a bargain basement rack without checking its fit. It bulged loose in some places and was too tight around the armpits and elsewhere. The exact opposite of how Nuñez's high-end suits fit—all snug and cash-money smooth. The guy could've been somebody's not-too-successful accountant uncle.

"Do you know who I am?"

I thought I did but waited for him to say.

"I'm Titus Yang. You work for me."

"Oh," I said. "Hey."

His tongue was too big for his mouth. It was like a fish flipping its tail out between his lips, flinging wet at me. Which is when I realized that TV and movies can screw you up. Not for the reasons some people think, but because they give you the wrong idea of how criminal boss-men look in real life.

Out my window, the bird streets were gone. Restoration Hardware and Saks Fifth Avenue bleared past. Starbucks, Dean Caruso Is One Tough Cop Wednesdays at 9pm, Pacific Sunwear—Clothes that Fit Your Head. I didn't ask where we were going.

"I was sorry to hear about your brother," Yang said.

"Yeah."

"What happened?"

As if he didn't know. Keeping it general, not mentioning St. Benny, I told him about Wilt's crash.

"Your mother handling it okay?"

I wasn't thrilled with him bringing up Mom, which must've shown on my face because next he said, "No, how could she?"

Liquors Beer & Wine, Lost Our Lease Everything Must Go!, If You've Been In An Accident You May Be Entitled To Monetary Compensation Call For A Free Consultation 1-800-LAWYERR. The neighborhoods out my window were getting crappier.

"I hope," Yang said, "that taking a week off from night shifts at UPS hasn't added to your mother's stress level—the loss of much-needed income coupled with the loss of a son."

I kept my face to the window, my heart crashing against my ribs like Manson trying to escape the dog run. *He's warning me*, I remember thinking. *He's telling me he can find out anything he wants to about my family, that he's a threat to me and Mom and anyone who matters. He can get to us any time.*

"Wilt and I used to talk," he said. "It might be corny to say, but I saw a lot of myself in him."

I was like, *Yeah? Well no way Wilt told you Mom had skipped a week's worth of work after he was killed.* I hate when people lie to me and think I'm too big an idiot to notice.

Yang had made my heart go epileptic, I wanted to do the same to his. "They said my brother was murdered," I told him.

His forehead wrinkled under his unmoving toupee. His lips turned nozzle-like. He didn't seem to be dealing with a flipfloppy heart.

"Do they? Why?"

"Why was he murdered?"

"Do you know the answer to that?"

"Uh uh."

"Then why do 'they' believe Wilt was murdered?"

"Don't ask me. Nobody tells me anything."

I should've stayed silent. Yang probably already knew what the cops suspected. He probably had cops on his payroll.

Boarded-up storefronts scrolled past my window. To make sure I had things clear in my head, I went over the reasons he might be talking to me:

To find out what I knew about Wilt's murder.

To let me know he was a threat to me and Mom and I'd best stay in line, no matter what sketchy stuff I saw, or thought I saw, while working for him. This probably explained why he was willing to have his victim's younger brother as an employee: he wanted me close, the better to keep tabs on me.

"What's up with Manson?" I asked.

"Who?"

"The dog whose ear is glued together?"

"Ah. Had a bit of a skirmish with his roommates. It happens."

All of a sudden I wondered if there was another reason for Yang's talkfest. "I'm not gay," I said.

"Thank you for telling me, Curtis."

"No, but I mean . . . if you are, it's okay. There's nothing wrong with it."

"I appreciate your support."

"It's just, I'm not."

Yang reached for the inside pocket of his jacket and I dove to the floor, shielding my head with my arms as if it might make a difference. I don't know how long I waited, but when I figured I should have already heard the gun click, I looked up. Yang was holding a fat wad of cash my way.

"A month's pay in advance," he said. "I'm expanding your job duties. Get Nuñez to show you the dogs at the other houses."

I wasn't about to count the money in front of him, but from the heft of it, I could tell it was a lot.

"I included some extra. Use it to get flowers for Wilt's grave and help your mom with bills."

The limo slowed to a stop and Yang and I spent a while looking at each other.

"This is where you pick yourself off the floor and get out," he said.

Maybe it's rude not to thank your brother's murderer when he gives you a promotion and a ton of cash, but I was on the street by the time I thought of it, the Escalade already driving off, leaving me at the corner of my cruddy block.

25

Florence Gantry was trying to fit a dish drainer into an old VW van stuffed with boxes, chairs, folding tables, lamps and other household junk: vacuum cleaner, coffeemaker, toaster, mini stereo, sewing machine, untied garbage bags filled with blankets and towels. Her husband Max butted open the door of the building and came out carrying a drawer filled with unfolded clothes, which took him three tries to get into the van. Florence shoved the dish drainer at him and with serious effort he loaded that in too.

The Gantrys moving out meant only four tenants to go, including me and Mom, before Pappas's building would be totally vacant. I nodded hello/goodbye to them and went on into the lobby, which was cluttered with the last of their stuff. Pappas's door was open, the bushy troll probably coming out to gloat every two minutes. I chugged quick to the stairwell to avoid seeing his belly button worm and started the long trudge home, wondering how much longer it'd actually be home.

Not that I cared about our dumpy place.

It was just, Mom had made it clear more than once that we didn't have a lot of choices in terms of places to live.

"Where've *you* been?"

She was in militant mode. I'd barely stepped into the apartment but Mom was already laying into me.

"Why did you leave the morgue without telling anyone? Why have you been ignoring my calls?"

She'd left at least fifteen messages.

"I haven't been ignoring them," I lied. Some kid I had never seen before was attacking the ceiling corners with a broom. "Who's he?"

Okafur put down his lemon-fresh Pledge and twisted a dust rag in his hands like it'd keep him from hassling me along with the parental. Broom-boy, though? He didn't seem to hear anything and just kept swiping at the corners of the room.

"How many times have I asked you to keep me informed of where you are?" Mom said. "A text or phone call that'd take no more than two minutes of your time. Is that so impossible? You have no idea what it's like not to know if your child is alive or dead because the hours pass and he doesn't come through the door and you've gotten no message from him."

I tried to convince myself that it was better to get lectured by a parent than to have one who never cared where I was. Except it didn't work. I wasn't in the mood.

"Look at it this way," I said, "at least you know I'll always let you down."

"That's not what I'm saying."

"Who is he?" I asked again, meaning broom-boy.

Her sigh was like the hydraulics on a bus, the *chssssssh* a bus makes when it lowers to give some geezer an easier time hobbling up its front steps.

"Curtis, meet Narith."

Hearing his name, the kid left the corner spiderwebs alone and turned to us.

"He's come from Cambodia to meet you," Mom said.

"No, he hasn't."

The parental had clearly moved beyond overcompensating for devastating loss into delusional territory. I didn't know if the side effects of too many nicotine patches/lozenges was partly to blame or what. I didn't care.

"You remember that a while back, you got your fallopian tubes knotted?" I said.

"What kind of question is that?"

"I'm just wondering if you remember telling me and Wilt why you were having the procedure done. You said it wasn't 'cause you thought too many people were being born, or that there were enough orphans in the world and wannabe parents should choose from them instead of birthing new kids. No, what you said was, being a working single mom of two boys, you couldn't risk getting pregnant again—"

"I couldn't!"

"—and you went about the whole thing in an extended huff, like having your tubes tied was revenge, like you were never gonna let yourself be tricked into bringing another guy into the world to wreck a family when he grew up, the way you thought Dad did. But here you are, bringing not one but two guys into *my* world, wrecking what little family *I* have left."

Her fingers worked at the front of her neck like she was trying to button a coat against the cold. "It's been a stressful day," she mumbled, as if that might explain something.

"No, really?"

I stalked to my room. There was a time I would've already

been punching walls, and I don't know if it was because my meds were working or that I just didn't have the energy any-more—or even if I didn't have the energy anymore because my meds were working—but I didn't feel like punching a wall. I was going to hurl Narith's beat-up suitcase out a window, though. The thing was on *my* bed waiting to be unpacked.

"Babe?" The parental had nudged open the door.

"I don't want to see you," I said. What could she possibly tongue-wag to me that I'd ever want to hear? "Get out," I said. "Leave me alone."

She lifted Narith's suitcase off my bed and sat in its place so that I had to turn to keep from looking at her. I knew she'd wait however long it took for me to give in and talk to her. I would've gone over to Mrs. Holt's apartment, except how was I supposed to get the keys without Mom following me? She was trying to force us into a Hallmark moment, but no sentimental mush could make up for her weirdness with the kids-from-other-countries deal. And because she didn't get it—that cheesy Hallmarkiness couldn't make up for anything—I started to feel more depressed than pissed.

"Mom," I said gently, "you don't have to tell me the truth about Okafur and Narith if you don't want to. If you think it's safe to have them here—fine. Except I'm going to believe that you're foster parenting them for the cash it brings in, even though I've checked and wannabe foster parents have to wait something like four months to get approved. But that's what I'm going to believe, okay? It's just easier."

I don't know if she heard me or not. She stayed mute. Maybe she didn't want to jinx it with words—that I wasn't going to make a bigger stink about Okafur and Narith.

"As for extra cash . . . "

I turned my back on her so she wouldn't see how much I had. She didn't quiz me about where I'd gotten the money, just pocketed the sixty bucks I handed her and asked if I'd talked to Wilt.

"He's not calling as regularly as he used to," I said, "but yeah."

"Do you think he'll keep calling?"

"I don't know."

I wondered what she told herself about *why* he was calling, since she didn't want to think it had to do with his murder.

"If I'm not nearby to talk to him the next time he calls," she said, "please tell him I miss him and love him very much."

She stood up and I let her hug me. I've never been a big hugger, but considering my mood a couple minutes earlier, it was all right. The hug, I'm talking about. It reminded me there were times, not frequent, when I sensed what things could be if Mom and I had a friendlier, more easygoing relationship.

"You could've clued me in about you and Dr. Murray," I said. "I'm telling you now, I'll never tolerate that guy as a stepdad."

"Babe, you're getting way ahead of things. We're just good friends."

"Uh huh."

She pulled away from me and smiled like she was about to drop an awkward secret. "It so happens I'm seeing someone else in half an hour."

"What? Who?"

"He's in law enforcement."

"You're going out with Detective Abrams?"

I didn't care if Abrams shouldn't have been dating a person connected to one of his cases. Anybody was better than Dr. M.

26

Lou was like, "What can I tell you? Everybody's a little off. Your mom's just more off than pretty much everybody."

"Dude, maybe it's a good thing," Jeremy said. "She won't be focusing all her craziness on you."

We were mid phone conference and I'd just told them about my pseudo-brothers, keeping my voice low since Mom was only a few feet away—in the bathroom, doing something with makeup.

"The sooner we figure out this Wilt thing . . . " I said, extra quiet. And Lou was all, "Returning to which subject, we're agreed, right? Tomorrow night we stakeout St. Benny for real. You're sure it was 'tomorrow at wholesale' you heard Yang say?" he asked.

"Yeah."

Okafur passed by me for the tenth time, waving shy at my phone's screen on his way to fold laundry or whatever. As always, he stopped and stared in awe when Jeremy waved back. At least Narith'd seen a smartphone before and was in the kitchen, wiping down cabinets, not being a pain.

"If those St. Benny warehouses are where dogfights usually happen—" Jeremy said.

"Not usually," I cut in. "According to the interwebs, organized fights don't happen at a single venue. They move around."

"Yeah," Jeremy said, "but why would this Yang dude still have fights there if he knows it's where Wilt died and the cops think it was murder?"

"You mean 'cause it'd be stupidly risky?"

"Yeah. And why'd Wilt have been called to the Tudor in the first place if they knew he was dead?"

Jeremy could surprise you sometimes.

"Keep talking back to your elders," Lou said, "see where that gets you."

"Dude, you're a week older than I am."

"So what if it's not Yang then?" I said.

"Exactly." Lou acted like he'd thought of it. "It could've been somebody else who bets on the fights or is otherwise involved in them. Maybe Wilt was supposed to have handicapped one of the dogs but didn't, and the bettor lost a lot of money because of it."

"People into that stuff are always into other bad stuff," Jeremy said.

Lou laughed. "'Always'? You have a lot of experience with these kinds of people?"

"Gotta go," I said, because I was getting another call.

I clicked off the conference and stepped out of the apartment, leaving the door ajar so I could scope for Mom.

"I found the Romans," my brother said first thing.

"Huh?"

He explained about how he'd picked a direction at random, his plan to keep walking till he found an exit. Turned out the Aftermart had more than one Entertainment department, but he initially seemed to be caught in a kind of loop. Like, even though he was walking a straight line, he kept passing the *same* Entertainment department over and over again, with all the same recently discontinued merch on the shelves—stuff recent enough that he'd known some of it in life. So then he walked in the opposite direction and noticed that the TVs in the Entertainment departments were getting progressively older and out-of-date, and then there weren't TVs anymore at all, just radios. Vintage radios. Old-timey radios.

"Imagine what it must have been like to live in a time when state-of-the-art family entertainment meant radio," he said.

"Like the Romans?"

"No one has ever missed a therapy session before. They—whoever 'they' are—have been calling my name over the intercom system, asking me to report to the manager's office. I don't have any idea where *that* is. They're doing it right now."

"Yeah, but what do Romans have to do with—?"

"I'm getting to it, feminine hygiene product. During my lengthy perambulation, I saw that the same way the dead crap in the Entertainment departments was getting progressively more historical the farther I went, so was the dead crap on all of the other shelves. I was eventually surrounded by crap I'd seen only in museums—steam-powered crap, frock coat crap, all kinds of crap. The shoppers had also changed. They'd become people out of history books. And when I came to where I am now—the shelves stocked with ancient clay pots and sandals and togas, and with gold ornaments for pimping out chariots—I knew I'd found them: the Romans."

"Wilt?"

"They don't call it Aftermart. To them it's just a less dusty bazaar than they were used to. And their Entertainment department is pretty lacking, although they're not above strolling into newer aisles. Their therapy when they first got here—I think they somehow wrote to living relatives, but they've been here so long none of them *has* living relatives anymore. What's it tell you about how boring this place is that they haven't gotten used to being here after centuries and are still in therapy? We all speak the same language now that we're without body. There are centurions around. You know what those are, doucheface?"

"I know that dogfights happen on St. Benny," I said.

He let the silence hang—didn't deny it, didn't tongue-wag squat.

"You still there? Hello?"

"I'm here."

Not that we'd ever had a pet or that Wilt had ever waxed misty-hearted about canines, but I knew dogs were his favorite animals. Back when our parents were still together he used to beg Mom to take us to this dog park, where he'd get shriek-happy with whatever beasties were panting around. So like, he must've seriously hated Yang's canine death matches, and I was really starting to think maybe he hadn't kept his mouth shut and his head down and just done his job the way he'd told me to do. Which I might have asked him, just to hear him deny it—to hear the quality of his denial, I mean—except

I didn't get the chance. The stairwell door screeched open and Abrams staggered out, about to cough up a lung but getting cop-squinty when he saw me on the phone.

"Yeah, naw, that's cool," I said to Wilt, pretending he was Lou or Jeremy, "I'll see you tomorrow."

I felt kind of guilty hanging up on him. Hang up on your dead brother, you don't know if it'll be the last time the two of you ever talk. You don't *think* it'll be the last time, but you could be wrong. Plus, I forgot to pass along Mom's message—the one about her missing and loving him. Which maybe I'd subconsciously forgot on purpose since Wilt and I'd never said the word "love" to each other before, not even to talk about somebody else's.

"What's up?" I said to Abrams.

He wheezed something I couldn't understand and showed me his index finger, like he wanted me to see a splinter he had. He was decked out in lumberjack shirt and pleated khaki pants. Instead of generic Lonely Old Guy, he'd become Lonely Old Guy Rejected from an L.L. Bean Catalog.

"He's here!" I yelled.

Abrams followed me into the apartment. His breathing settled into its normal clotty-rattle, but I pegged him as nervous because he seemed to be watching a hyperactive fly, never turning my way or noticing Okafur and Narith. And what wasn't to notice? Okafur and Narith were at the feeding table, polishing our stock of plastic cutlery from fast food places as if the stuff was legit silverware.

"Where you taking her?" I asked Abrams.

"Red Lobster."

"She has to be at UPS by ten."

He finally registered the new brothers. "Friends of yours?"

"Yeah, I often invite my friends over to help clean."

He ignored the snark and glanced at the bathroom, which Mom would be popping out of any second. He lowered his voice so only I could hear. "That kid you mentioned earlier, the one interested in your brother's girlfriend's pants? This him?"

He pulled a copy of a class photo from his pocket, with Rick Calvados's picture circled.

"Yeah," I said.

At first I liked the idea of Rick being hassled by cops, even if maybe he hadn't had anything to do with Wilt's murder. I liked it less after I realized the reason I'd told Abrams he should interrogate Calvados was the same as what Lou and Jeremy were accusing me of—wanting to get with Suzy. Except it's not like I was *trying* to get into Suzy's pants. I mean, if it happened, yeah, it'd be a game-changer, but I wasn't Rick-level trying.

"Sorry to keep you waiting!"

Mom gazelled out of the bathroom, painted over with eyeliner and lipstick and whatever else, the way she always was for a date. She stood about four inches taller than normal on account of strappy platforms that looked like outdoor lounge chairs for her feet, and I guess she wanted to prove she wasn't as thin as she used to be since she'd squeezed herself into the kind of dress reality stars wear to get attention.

"Curtis introduced you to everyone?"

It was the singsong voice she put on whenever she met new people. She was pretending that Abrams wasn't the detective investigating her son's murder, that he was just some guy she'd chatted with online, this their first face-to-face.

Unless she wasn't pretending but really believed it.

Which wouldn't have surprised me.

Anyway.

I've always kind of known Mom was okay-looking. I've seen guys check her out, and Lonely Old L.L. Bean Reject stood goggling her like he couldn't believe his luck. Thinking about the two of them bumping nethers was going to make me sick if I didn't act fast. I elbowed him.

"Wow, you look great," he said.

"Don't stay up too late!" Mom singsonged. "Homework should be done before you turn on the TV or play video games! Dinner's in the fridge!"

She was so taken up with the impression she was making on salivating Abrams, at first I thought she was telling *him* to finish his homework before zoning out with media.

I locked the door after them. Okafur and Narith laid off polishing plastic to watch me.

"Dinner's not in the fridge," I told them.

I was thinking about Yang and why he'd have dogfights at St. Benny if he knew it's where Wilt had been murdered. He wouldn't, I figured. Which meant, in solving my brother's case, I was probably nowhere.

27

The links Lou texted me about Titus Yang were all from legit business sites and tagged the guy as a serious mogul who'd made a billion dollars from five-hour energy gluggers, then invested in real estate and telecom and turned that first billion into a couple more. He'd allegedly spent something like eight million on his creepy doll collection, which Doll Experts with No Lives claimed had either doubled or tripled in value. Everything Yang put money into doubled or tripled in value. I saw pics of him from before he'd gone bald, back before he started wearing hair that looked like hair had taken a dump on his head.

While building up a database on Yang, I thought I'd do another smart thing. Because I'd seen it before on media: how cops trying to solve a murder explored a bunch of possible scenarios at once, not knowing which actually happened and which didn't. By clueing themselves in to what didn't happen, they sleuthed out what did. So to prove Mom *couldn't* have been the murderer's target instead of Wilt, I searched for evidence that'd somehow prove she *had* been the target. I didn't know what kind of evidence I was looking for, but I pawed through the living room closet, the TV-console-thing she used as a dresser, and the cabinet under the bathroom sink where she stowed tampons—basically, wherever she kept personal junk. Okafur thought it was all some elaborate cleaning ritual and imitated me, lifting clothes and whatnot out of drawers and putting everything back exactly as found. Meantime Narith reunited with his favorite broom and swept the ceiling, always trying to anticipate where I'd be and stay out of my way.

"You don't have to do that," I said to him, and mimed working the broom, but he just gave me this blank stare, so.

My snoop didn't turn up anything out of sync with what I knew of Mom's life, nothing that might've somehow clued me in to if/why she'd be targeted for murder. But under a stash of old sweaters in a plastic storage bin by the feeding table, in this manila envelope stuffed with drawings and homework from my and Wilt's elementary school years, I found what I wish had never existed: a couple shrink reports on me back from when I was six years old.

```
Children's Medical Center
Outpatient Department
        Diagnostic and Evaluation Center
          Medical Consultation

Name: Curtis Brooks          Parents:
Birthdate: 7/8/99            M/M David A. Brooks
Date of Consult: 11/09/05    7416 Clearlake, #412
Roman K. Peele, M.D.


Curtis is 6 years of age and was the product
of the mother's second pregnancy, which was
completely uncomplicated and 9 months in length.
```

He weighed 7 lbs. 4 oz. at birth. The mother
said he was born by natural childbirth and took
his first breath without any problem. There were
no problems in the nursery or in the neo-natal
period. Curtis sat alone at 6 months, walked
alone at 13 months, and his words and language
came along normally. At about 18 months of age
Curtis began to have trouble relating to other
children; he wanted to play with them, but he
didn't get along with them. Curtis is sometimes
hyperactive; other times, he is not. The mother
says that if he is interested in television he
can sit still and watch it without moving for 30
minutes. On the other hand, if she goes to the
store with him, he is constantly touching things
and running all over the place. Curtis sleeps
well at night, tends to have a lot of misbehavior
at home in that he does not mind, has outbursts,
temper tantrums, dawdles at getting dressed
for school in the mornings, argues frequently
with his mother, and does most things just to
aggravate her and manipulate her. He was placed
on Ritalin by Dr. Finkelman last July and he is
currently on 10 mg. three times per day. Recently
the mother feels that his misbehaviors at home
have increased and she is wondering if there is
anything wrong with his central nervous system.

PAST HISTORY: The child has had no serious
illnesses. He can see and hear well. He has never
been unconscious, fainted or had a head injury.
He does not wet the bed.

FAMILY HISTORY: The father and mother are
separated and are in the process of getting a
divorce. The mother says that there was never any
fighting or arguing before Curtis.

PHYSICAL EXAMINATION: Height: 122 cm. Weight: 22 kg. Head circumference: 52 cm. which is within the normal range. Blood pressure: 96/60. Neck normal; heart and lungs clear; abdomen normal; external genitalia normal; neurological evaluation completely normal. On the Peabody Picture Vocabulary Test, the child scored a Mental Age of 9 years, 6 months. The Conners behavior rating scale contains 39 items and on this the child's scores were significant for poor sociability, aggression, and anxiety.

IMPRESSION: Both the medical history and the behavior rating scale are equivocal for hyperactivity. I think the child has developed behavior problems that have "turned off" his parents, his peers, and probably his teachers as well, and sensing this he has therefore developed some secondary anxieties. Many willful behaviors are being reinforced by his family.

RECOMMENDATIONS:
1.   I think that the Ritalin dosage is adequate, since Curtis is having no adverse effect to it.
2.   I concur with Dr. Finkelman's assessment that the parents need to implement a program of behavior modification with Curtis's willful behaviors. Curtis is a very intelligent boy who may be bored by the routine first grade work and need more of a challenge than is ordinarily offered by the first grade. I think that there is going to have to be a consistent set of rules and expectations at home, with his father, and at school. I think that this has been the greatest problem. The adults are inconsistent in providing the punishments and rewards for inappropriate and appropriate behavior respectively. There is

no other medicine indicated here or surgery for curing Curtis's "condition." I think that he should continue the psychotherapy as long as Dr. Finkelman thinks it is warranted.

Roman K. Peele, M.D.

RKP/ch
cc: Dr. Greg Finkelman
     3613 Cedar Road

- - - - - - - -

INDIVIDUAL AND FAMILY TREATMENT CENTER
CLINICAL PSYCHOLOGY

Greg Finkelman, Ph.D.
3613 Cedar Road
October 17, 2005

Re: Curtis

Dear Mr. & Mrs. Brooks:

At your request I will try to summarize my impressions and recommendations regarding Curtis's special needs, etc.

First, I see him as an exceedingly bright six-year-old who is functioning reasonably well, but who occasionally demonstrates symptoms of a "hyperkinetic" child, including impulsivity, overactivity, low frustration tolerance and distractibility. These symptoms have in my view resulted in parental frustration and anxiety, as well as partial rejection of Curtis, which in turn aggravates his own anxiety and behavior problem.

Curtis needs a carefully structured and consistent environment that is clear cut in its ground rules and in the consequences of behavior, but that is

also flexible enough to accept a certain degree of
overactivity and impulsivity, which I think Curtis
cannot avoid. He needs the same expectations
from both of you and you need to communicate and
cooperate with each other in order to achieve this.

The transition from full-time parent to full-time
work is a very difficult one for most single
parents, or for that matter any married parent.
Doing this with an energetic and anxious child like
Curtis is even more demanding. I recommend periodic
professional counseling for whichever parent has
custody of Curtis, ranging from twice a month to
once every two to three months depending on the
needs.

I feel that for the time being Curtis continues to
benefit and to want individual psychotherapy for
himself.

> Sincerely,
> Greg Finkelman, Ph.D.
>
> GF/jk

A lot of times I've wished I wasn't trapped in my own head, that every now and then I could remove my brain and stop being so annoyed by doofuses like Dr. M. I also figure that, with a detachable brain, I'd get breaks from always feeling there's this big canyon separating me from everybody else— even the people who're supposed to know me best. Because in general it's like I have to get across this canyon if anyone's ever going to really understand me, except I can't, it's impossible.

Whatever *that* means—to be really understood by another person. How can you know if another person understands you if you can't even peg down the "you" you're talking about?

Anyway.

The shrink reports took me out of myself, but it wasn't good—the rest of the night one big WTF till Suzy texted me "Nite!" with a picture of her lying on her stomach. She was in bed, like I was. Her hair looked pillow-mussed, her eyes sleep-drunk—as if she'd woken up just to send me the photo. It was hard to tell if she was wearing pajamas or a sleepshirt, but I zoomed in, wanting to see as much as I could. I studied that pic of Suzy so hard, it got to where I could smell her—that soapy, sweet apple smell of hers with its under-whiff of cigarette smoke.

"Nite," I texted back.

Okafur was snoring in Wilt's bed. I didn't know if Narith, on the floor with his sheets and blankets, was awake or not, but I was all, *No way I'm going to get to sleep if I don't do it.* So I rolled over to face the wall and took care of myself to Suzy's picture, then like every night I drifted into Sandman territory, hoping maybe tomorrow would be different even though it never was, or never in the way that I hoped.

Because the parental worked graveyard, she tended not to sack out till after I was off to school. Most mornings she'd be pretty beat, which suited my a.m. shufflings just fine, but sometimes she'd be wired, cleaning like a fiend and nagging me about homework or how much time I wasted on the phone/computer/TV. The morning after her date with Abrams, though? That was different.

"Won't a Sunday picnic be wonderful!"

It was her singsong voice, so I thought maybe Abrams had met up with her after her shift at UPS and spent the night. It wouldn't have been the first time I'd woken up to find one of her dates in the place. I'd just never heard her be super happy about it—singsonging and all.

"Yes, we injoy sanwich an fruity salads," a voice that wasn't Abrams' said.

I pulled on my clothes from the day before and slogged out to the feeding table. Okafur and Narith were serving breakfast, refilling Mom's coffee and whatever, both holding sheets of paper in front of their faces. On the table next to Mom was another sheet of paper.

Seeing me, she palsied her head at the only other place setting and at the print-out lying by its plastic knives and forks. "Your lines are highlighted. I got it from a book called *How to Keep Your Family Together and Still Have Fun.*"

I must not've been fully awake because I actually sat down and let Okafur put a plate of scrambled eggs in front of me. The highlighted dialogue I was supposed to read was stuff like, "We should acknowledge more often how much we appreciate one another's company," and "This is a delightful excursion, mother. Let's take a stroll along the picturesque creek."

"Nice when fambily best friensame," Okafur said.

From the gloss of his eyes, I could tell he wasn't reading. Mom had probably gone over his lines earlier, but it was news to me that the kid didn't really speak English. I'd thought he was faking.

"How was your date with Abrams?" I asked.

"Let's stick to the script."

Narith brought me a cup of coffee. Okafur poured OJ into my glass. I was like, *For where we are, there is no script,* but didn't bother verballing again. I snatched Okafur's and Narith's print-outs, wadded them up and tossed them at the parental, slung on my backpack and was out the door.

∿∥∼

An opening had been cut in the fence around this vacant lot where a lavanderia used to be. I ducked through it, jammed Peele's and Finkelman's reports into the open top of a cinder block and set them on fire. Watching them burn, I thought I could take myself off meds without waiting for Dr. Polk to give the okay. It wasn't as if he or anybody else ever made sure I popped my dailies. I could just stop taking the pills while pretending otherwise. Except I'd been on meds so long, I couldn't remember what it felt like to be off them.

Like totally and completely, I mean.

The one time Dr. Polk had tried to wean me off, I punched a lot more walls and loudly exercised my vocal cords in adults' faces—whenever I wasn't ignoring adults altogether. But what I remembered of these things? They might as well've belonged to somebody else. They were just pictures in my head without any feeling to them.

So med-free? I didn't fully know what I'd be getting into and had to think about it. Which, considering I didn't have any idea what I was getting into when I decided to hunt down my brother's murderer—calling the phone number on the $50, showing up at the Tudor for the first time and taking over Wilt's job—was maybe an unusual place to get cautious.

My phone buzzed.

"If you ever hang up on me again . . . " Wilt threatened.

"What, you'll kill me?"

He laughed and I told him how Abrams had shown up in the middle of our last conversation.

"If he'd heard I was talking to you," I said, "he would've made me put him on the phone."

"And I'd have advised him to stop his useless investigation. You remember about the intercom system here? The voice asking me to report immediately to the manager's office?"

"Yeah."

"The voice sounds offended. As if I've hurt its feelings

by not doing what it asks. And it got that way *before* I started stealing."

"You're stealing?"

"If I skip therapy, I don't earn my quota of credits. If I don't earn my quota, how am I supposed to buy anything?"

"Um, you can't?"

"So now I take what I want. If we're going to break the rules to see what happens, doucheface, we might as well really break them."

We, he said. As in *me and him.*

I was like, "Yeah, I guess it makes sense, except how come the powers that be don't cut your phone privileges? Do you have a certain number of minutes you're allowed, or—"

"We don't have 'minutes' here. I told you."

"I remember. You don't experience Time as I understand it. But why don't the powers that be cancel your calling plan or something? Couldn't they do that?"

"How should I know? But turns out I'm not the only one who's bored. I've convinced some Romans to skip therapy and steal crap. I've been dumping my stolen crap in Claudius's donkey cart because my locker's far away at the moment. FYI, and at the risk of being redundant, I'm speaking metaphorically when I say things like 'far away' and 'I took a walk.' It's impossible to get a handle on the physics of this place."

The shrink reports in the cinder block were mostly ash. One page—curled black and glowing at the edges—drifted out onto some weeds. I stomped on it.

"People in high school think they're tons different from how they were in elementary school," I said, "always talking about how much they've changed."

"Are you attempting profundity?" Wilt snarked. "Should I sit down for this?"

"Some people do try to change, I guess. But from what I've seen, nobody does. Not really."

My brother let out one of his bodiless sighs, as if I'd tongue-wagged something he didn't need to be reminded of. "Take it from one who's no longer among you," he said, "human beings stay the same more than they can usually admit. An asshole at six years old is an asshole at sixty. A thoughtful, generous person at six is a thoughtful, generous person at sixty."

"Huh," I said, thinking, *How do you know?* The same way dying had given him a mature perspective on things, had it also given him knowledge about life in general, just not about specific lives? "Wilt? What do you remember?"

"I thought we've been through this."

"Not about the night of your accident. I'm asking about back when Mom and Dad were getting divorced."

"Not sure I understand the question." His voice had suspicion in it. "I remember having to sit through a movie starring talkative meerkats."

I explained about the shrink reports—how they were from the time of the parentals' split and one of them said my behavior had recently gotten worse.

"If you're asking what I think you're asking," he said, "I remember you being the same before the divorce as you were afterwards. I'm going to tell you something I've thought for a long time, brother, but never considered useful to say aloud: Mom and Dad putting you on meds had more to do with them than it did with you."

"Then maybe *they* should've taken the meds."

"Should, you mean. Present tense."

"Yeah."

Our voices had smiles in them. And that canyon separating me from everybody else? I don't know, but I thought maybe there'd be times it might not seem so wide and I could jump across it to feel understood. Then Wilt asked a question that made my heart beat double-time.

"What's the latest on the girlfriend front?"

"Huh?"

"Calvados getting anywhere in his play for Suze?"

My heart slowed but still felt loud enough for Wilt to hear. "It's hard to tell. But maybe. Yeah."

"Hold on." He said something I couldn't make out, like he'd turned away from the phone to talk to someone. "Anyone you're hoping to get more intimately acquainted with?" he asked when he came back online. "Anyone in particular causing you to mistake raging testosterone for love? Because let me tell you, love's when you make compromises to please someone, when you give way over and over to this 'loved one,' and she doesn't hear what you say even though you've said it a hundred times."

"Are you . . . you're not talking about you and Suzy?"

"I'm talking about the wisdom of experience. You going to answer my question?"

I thought about naming a girl—*any* girl—from my grade. Or making up a name. But my mouth had its own ideas. "You've never taken an interest in this kind of thing before."

"These chats of ours are full of firsts, in case you haven't noticed. But forget it, you don't have to answer. I already know. You've been with her enough times when I've called, and I can hear it in your voice every time her name comes up. You try to sound casual but wind up talking too fast and breathing heavily. You like Suze. It's all right. You *should* like her, if you're at all hetero."

"I'm *all* hetero."

" . . . "

" . . . "

" . . . "

"Okay," I said, "I'm not admitting you're right or anything, but if you *were* . . . I mean, wouldn't you think it kind of, I don't know, weird? Me wanting to—"

"Why? She's not my girlfriend anymore. There's no chance we'll be getting back together. And if I had to choose between you and Calvados? Suze can do better than Rick Calvados."

I had to play back that last bit in my head: my brother had said I was better than Rick.

"Calvados has always been competitive with me," he said. "His big thing's lacrosse. Mine was Suzy. He used to give me crap about how lacrosse was going to open up a lot of doors for him in life, and what was being with Suzy ever going to do for me? But I *know* he would've given up lacrosse for Suze any day of the week. And if he thinks he's going to be with her now just because I'm dead? If he thinks he's going to have lacrosse *and* her? Uh uh. I can't let that happen."

"So this is another time when that mature perspective you have on things doesn't mean you'll actually act mature?"

"If she ever asks you to go somewhere or do something— the slightest thing at all—don't answer *yes* like an eager beaver. Pretend to consider it, as if you'd really like to go with her but there's so much you have to do, before you say yes. You know that she likes M.C. Freak of Nature? And the poet Sylvia Plath?" He turned away from the phone again. "I'm coming!" To me, he said, "I have to call you back. Claudius and I are about to hold our first rally against quotas and therapy. We're trying to incite a rebellion."

He hung up before I could ask if it was smart to talk about rebellion when his counselor or any of the Aftermart's managers/assistant managers might be tapping into our conversations.

I probably shouldn't have called where I was a vacant lot, though. And not just because the place was littered with bricks, cinder blocks, rotten lumber, broken glass, car tires, smashed shopping carts, and lint-like tumbleweeds that might've been leftover from the lavanderia. More because life, or at least evidence of it, was everywhere: a steel garbage can someone had turned into a fire pit, wrappers from McDonald's and Taco Bell and wherever, paw tracks in the dirt, swarming ants, skittering lizards, birds dive-bombing abandoned window screens and using the metal wire for their nests. The lavanderia lot was a place of desperate, scavenging life—pretty much the opposite of vacant. Everything depended on how I looked at things. And probably I would've seen it sooner if I hadn't been preoccupied with Wilt's murder: that on account of my phone gabs with him, it was like I had a special power. He'd been through tenth grade already. He'd taken all of Mrs. Jensen's tests, done all her assignments. Over every other guy at school, he'd gotten Suzy Painter to be his girlfriend. I don't want to sound corny, but it was like my better self had gone through the basic-life stuff I was supposed to be dealing with and could tell me how best to get through it. I had access to info that could maybe tilt my

future toward an improved status quo. So my better self sometimes called me doucheface? I decided to think of it as a term
of endearment.

29

I spent an hour copying Sylvia Plath poems and sketching M.C. Freak of Nature graffiti onto notebook covers. Not wanting any of it to look too obvious, I crowded the spaces around these things with doodles and scratches. I got to school after the first period warning bell and found Suzy behind the humongoid HVAC, smoking cigarettes with Nisa and Janelle.

"Hey," I said.

The three of them goggled me like I'd stolen the conversation out of their mouths. I knew Nisa and Janelle only by sight and only because they were Suzy's friends. I wasn't used to being seriously goggled by three of the hottest girls in school and would've slunk off if I hadn't thought what a loser I'd be if I did.

"I'll see you guys in class," Suzy said.

Nisa and Janelle took their time grinding out their cigarettes. After they left, I shifted my notebooks around in front of me to give Suzy a clear view of the poetry and whatnot, but she didn't notice—actually seemed to forget about me for a while. So I gave it up and just stood in awe of the way her chest pushed out every time she sucked at her Marlboro Light. When she finally verballed, I almost didn't hear her because of the pulsing in my pants.

"Remember the other night, when you said what if you move away but wherever you go, everything's the same, just with different scenery?"

"Yeah."

"Well, haven't you ever thought that sometimes you need to change your environment to get out of bad mental habits? That to knock yourself out of looking at the world in your usual way, you sometimes have to leave what's familiar, put yourself into a new environment where old habits have no place because *you* have no place?"

"A person doesn't have to be in a new environment to feel he has no place," I said, failing to be interesting through silence. I looked out at what little I could see of the bike racks, trying to seem mysterious. "I took over Wilt's job of feeding rich people's dogs," I told her.

It came out like a sneeze, involuntary: "No," she said. Then, quieter, almost embarrassed: "Don't."

"I know all about the dogfight operation," I said. "No way Wilt didn't tell you about it, so don't bother pretending. You're still scared that what happened to Wilt could happen to you. I get it. But you wouldn't be scared if you didn't know something you'd be better off not knowing. Except, who exactly are you scared of? I'm starting to doubt it's Yang or Nuñez. I'll have a better idea about them after tonight, though."

She wanted to come off as nonchalant, but the hand holding her cigarette was trembling. "Why? What's tonight?"

"I'm staking out this old Wholesale Electric building on St. Benny. If there's a dogfight like I think there's supposed to be, that's pretty much a guarantee Yang and Nuñez didn't kill Wilt. It'll mean somebody else involved in the dogfight op did it."

I was hoping for some kind of clue in her reaction to all this—other than her general nervousness. I didn't see one.

"Can't you just leave things alone?" she asked. "Hasn't enough *bad* already happened?"

"*Yes* to the second question. *No* to the first."

I heard quick footsteps and then Nisa was with us, out of breath.

"What?" Suzy said.

"Rick's being interrogated by the police about Wilt," Nisa spewed, "Ann heard it from Judith who heard from Mark who was driving to school with Rick when the police picked him up."

Suzy jammed a fresh cigarette between her lips, her hands so jittery she had trouble lighting it. The final bell for first period rang and Nisa mumbled something about how she couldn't be late for class again. I figured Abrams wouldn't get anything from Calvados. There was nothing for him to get: Rick had nothing to do with anything.

Alone again with Suzy, I said, "Tell me what you'd be better off not knowing. I've got connections with the police. What happened to Wilt won't happen to you. I won't let it."

Cheesy! I thought, expecting her to be, *Oh, you won't let it, huh? Some sophomore thinks he can play hero and save the girl, and so I don't have to worry?*

"What makes you think your brother didn't already go to the police?" she asked.

I'd never thought of it—not really. I mean, yeah, I remembered Jeremy one time saying that Wilt could've gone to the cops and let them deal with gathering the evidence to bust Yang, but I'd kind of glossed over the idea. Because if Wilt hadn't kept his head down and done his job? I don't know, I guess I just figured he'd have been scheming against his employers on his own—without cop intervention, I'm talking—since he'd never been a confide-in-authority-figures kind of guy.

I'm not exactly a confide-in-authority-figures kind of guy either. If Wilt hadn't been murdered and detectives already thrust into my life, I probably wouldn't have ever suggested to Suzy that we go to the cops.

"Wilt and I were going to rescue the dogs he looked after for Yang," she said, in a voice like she was tired of having to keep a secret, like maybe it was a risk to clue me in, but right that second it was easier than not. "We knew that even if we success-fully got the dogs to no-kill shelters, Yang and his friends would just get more and nothing would really change. So Wilt made an anonymous call to the police. He gave them the addresses where he fed the dogs, and the venues he knew about where fights took place. But the police never followed up."

That's it? I was thinking. *That can't be it.* I expected more, a lot more.

"I bet he has cops on his payroll is why nothing happened," I said. "Yang, I'm talking about."

"Didn't you just tell me you don't think he's the killer?"

I had, yeah, but she thought I was wrong.

"Yang must've found out what Wilt was up to," she said, "and since he probably knows about me, I don't need you or anybody else doing things that get him concerned about my continuing existence. Oh, and if he has police on his payroll, your connections are worse than useless. They're dangerous."

She was right about that last part, but by then I was only half listening. Her story didn't make a lot of sense. Or—it made sense up to a point. She wasn't telling me everything. That original feeling came creeping back, the one I'd had about her being involved in Wilt's murder. Maybe she hadn't meant to be involved and felt bad about it, but so what? Feeling bad about something didn't change the fact that it'd happened. Also I was like, *Yang's not the killer but has cops on his payroll? He bribes them to protect the dogfight operation?* What really freaked me out was the possibility that Abrams might be on his payroll, dating Mom as part of Yang's plan to keep the Brooks family close, in case the billionaire mogul had to be concerned about *our* continuing existence. It brought me around again to Yang having ordered a hit on Wilt. But then, why'd the guy still be allowing dogfights on St. Benny?

"Isn't it all a lot of trouble to go through for whatever money Yang makes off frothing dog-beasties?" I asked. "Even if he makes a lot of money from it—a ton, even—it can't be near as much as what he makes from his legit businesses."

"I don't know what to tell you," Suzy said. "Some people do things just to do them, because to them it's entertainment."

It didn't help my confusion that while I wanted to go off alone somewhere and think stuff over, my nethers wanted to be with Suzy for as long as possible. Whichever was about to happen, though, I knew it wasn't going to involve sitting in class, so I poked my head around the HVAC to scope for teachers. I'd forgotten that, because of city budget problems, teachers weren't patrolling school grounds anymore. There were hardly enough teachers to teach, never mind play security guard wannabes. So no teachers. Just Rick Calvados steaming toward us from the student parking lot, lacrosse stick in hand, leaning slightly forward like he was stalking through a heavy wind with a turd in his pants.

"Crap," I said.

"In some Eastern religions they believe a person's soul can't be at rest unless the body's properly buried," Suzy said. "I thought Wilt . . . maybe that's why . . . but he's at Forest Lawn, isn't he? I was at the service. I *know* he's at Forest Lawn."

She didn't need to hear that Wilt's body had been dug up for tests and was in a morgue freezer.

Rick was past the bike racks. A few more seconds and Suzy and I'd have no chance of getting away without him seeing us.

"Crap crap crap," I said.

"How much do you miss him?" she asked.

The question caught me off guard and I stopped worrying about Rick. How was I supposed to answer? *A lot*, I wanted to say. *I miss my brother a lot.* But because Wilt and I were talking more than ever, it seemed more accurate to say a *little*.

"I miss him constantly," Suzy said.

"What'd I fucking tell you?" Rick stomped around to the HVAC's private side, slammed me against the brick of the school. "What'd! I! Fucking! Tell! You?"

"Quit it, we're just talking!" Suzy shouted, except she had to shout it ten times before Rick laid off.

"What do you need to talk to *him* for?" he wanted to know, the twisted front of my shirt in his fist.

The look Suzy gave him, it was like I could see the full-on adult she'd become if I didn't get her killed by Yang or his associates. She had morphed into a parent silently telling her kid, *You know better. Don't be an idiot.*

"You're right. I'm sorry," Rick said to her. He let go of my shirt, but it stayed twisted, looking like the inside of an ear. "If you *have* to talk to Wilt's baby brother—I don't get why you do, Suze, and I don't recommend it—but if you really think it's not a bad idea, how about you do it another time, because right now I have a lot of pent up emotion to share with you?"

"Ew," I said.

Rick turned me by the shoulders in the direction of anywhere else. "Get out of here."

"The police," Suzy said, and I was like, "Yeah, why'd the cops want to question you?"

Rick spun his lacrosse stick by the handle and glared at the little net going round and round. "A couple of homicide detectives wanted to know how long we've been friends," he said to Suzy. "They asked if we were as good friends before Wilt died as we are now. Like they thought our friendship had something to do with Wilt's murder. Hey," Rick turned my way, "how'd they come to this line of questioning, I wonder?"

"They're detectives," I shrugged. "They detect things."

"Yeah? Well, I do not need detectives all up in my shit right now. Recruiters from Duke will be at our game against Marshall and I have to stay focused."

The guy was focused enough on himself, he didn't notice the tears streaking down Suzy's face. Whatever was making her cry, she shouldn't have had to deal. That's how I wanted it.

"What'd you do?" Rick said when he finally got his head out of his self-absorbed ass. "What'd you fucking do to her?"

"*You* did it," I said.

"Stop fighting!" Suzy yelled, and ran off.

Rick stabbed me hard in the chest with his lacrosse stick

and chased after her. I was going to have more than a couple bruises thanks to him, but it could've been worse.

I took out the lists I always kept with me and updated them.

WHAT I KNOW I KNOW

Wilt says he died by accident but he was definitely murdered.

Wilt had a job feeding rich people's dogs. (NUÑEZ, YANG.)

Yang is definitely NUÑEZ'S Boss.

The $ Wilt had when he died he made feeding Yang's (mostly) scary dogs.

YANG runs a dogfight op.

Wilt and Suzy were scheming to try and shut down the dogfight op

Wilt reported the dogfight op to the cops: nothing happened.

The car Wilt died in had been rigged with some kind of device

Rick C. is (probably) not involved with YANG / NUÑEZ.

Rick C. is an asshole.

WHAT I KNOW I DON'T KNOW

If YANG knew about Wilt's anonymous call to the cops.

If cops on YANG's payroll = why nothing happened when Wilt called them.

If Abrams himself is on YANG's payroll.

If Suzy told me everything or is still hiding something about Wilt's death.

What exactly Suzy is hiding.

If Yang (NUÑEZ) killed Wilt or if somebody else in dogfight ring did.

How exactly the murderer knew Wilt would be driving Mom's car.

How Wilt first started working for Nuñez and Yang.

WHAT I DON'T KNOW I DON'T KNOW
???

WHAT I KNOW THAT I DIDN'T KNOW I KNEW

Wilt loved dogs. He would have hated YANG.

The extent of Rick's assholeness.
It's way more than I thought.

I read the lists over a bunch of times, and then, because I had nothing else to do, figured I might as well go to class.

I wasn't going to be able to ignore homework forever—sympathy for a kid with a murdered brother only lasts so long—but teachers were still letting me slide. If Mrs. Jensen asked whether or not I'd done some essay on American Reconstruction, I'd puppy-face her and shake my head and she'd shuffle off to breathe mothballs on somebody else. In science class, before the last round of teacher layoffs, I'd sit at my desk puppy-facing no one in particular while everyone passed their homework to the front and Mr. Hearns wouldn't even bother asking if I'd done the assignment. Except now his class had like twice as many kids in it than it used to, and with so many of us there, I didn't have to puppy-face *at all* to get the homework go-by from him. Mr. H probably didn't even know I was in the room half the time, since there weren't assigned seats. A lot of us sat on the floor, on file cabinets, wherever we could find an open spot. Which wasn't easy if you straggled in a good twenty minutes late, which I did after being with Suzy and Rick.

Mr. H was reading from the textbook, trying to put us to sleep, when Winkleman stepped into the room. Big-time eruption, everyone winging pens, pencils, rulers, and erasers at the kid. Mr. H kept reading as if he were alone instead of at the front of an overfull class. Only after an eraser landed on his book did he stop.

"And you're here because . . . ?" he said to Winkleman.

"I have a note from Dr. Murray."

I was moving to the door before Mr. H finished scanning the note.

"Curtis Brooks?"

"Yeah, yeah," I said, dodging school supplies and trailing Winkleman to the hall, where I was like, "Why are you always running Dr. Murray's errands for him? If the guy wants to talk to me, let him pull me out of class himself instead of acting self-important and getting you to play fetch."

"You talk to corpses!" weasel-boy said, and ran off toward the cafeteria.

He wouldn't have been worth chasing even if I hadn't had questions for Dr. M. Which questions I almost didn't ask. Because showing up outside the guidance counselor's office and seeing him Krazy-glue a laser-printed "Murray" onto some new Murphy's Law poster he was about to hang up? It was a reminder: I didn't want to prolong the nightmare of being with the loser any longer than I had to—by quizzing him about stuff, starting new topics of conversation, whatever.

"C. Park yourself."

I dropped into the hard plastic chair next to his desk. He swiveled to face me.

"How you maintaining?"

Even before Wilt died, adults used to constantly ask how I was, as if they'd already decided I couldn't be well, I was a kid with major problems, and if I'd only admit my problems to them, I might somehow get better—*try* to admit my problems, I mean, since I wasn't clever enough to know what they were without an adult's help.

How was I maintaining? I didn't know how, but I was. I hadn't gone nuts or had a nervous breakdown. Yet. No thanks to Dr. M or anyone else.

"How do you think?" I said.

"You want to hate on everyone and everything because of what's happened. I understand. There's no justice in Wilton being taken before his time. But hating on everything won't bring Wilton back. Know what I'm saying?" The doofus nodded encouragingly at me.

"How long've you been dating my mom?" I asked.

He blinked, opened and shut his mouth a couple times like some sea-beast. "I don't dish the 411 on my personal life."

"You guys supposed to be exclusive or what?"

"I do *not* dish the 411 on my personal life."

I took that as a *yes* and almost told him Mom had been on a date with Abrams. I decided against it, though. In the future, I could use the info to hurt him, if I ever needed to.

"It's just," I said, "I'm asking how long you've been seeing her 'cause . . . haven't you noticed her acting kind of, I don't know, odd? Odder than usual?"

He dropped all hint of wannabe-gangsta, embraced his old-white-guy self. "She's lost a loved one. It'd be strange if she wasn't."

Had Mom told this idiot about Okafur and Narith? Did I want to tell him? No, I didn't. But did that mean I shouldn't? What if he could help? I mean, sure, I had serious doubts that Dr. Doof-Face's input could ever benefit anyone, but just because I doubted and hated the guy, was I supposed to let pass even the slightest chance he could somehow help Mom?

"Okay, but doesn't it ever seem to you that she might be, I don't know, a tiny bit delusional?"

Dr. M stared at me like I was the deluded one. "Why do you ask?"

"Maybe she didn't tell you about my new pseudo-brothers, Okafur and Narith? You should ask her how they came to live with us. Narith allegedly came from Cambodia."

Dr. M stroked his nose, no doubt debating whether he should report me to the Department of Major BS.

"I only ask about the delusions 'cause, remember how I'm supposed to be on a first-name basis with my feelings? I've been spending a lot of time with worry. I'm worried about my mom, I'm saying."

I figured that if the parental hadn't told Dr. M about Okafur and Narith, he'd ask me to spell their names so he could write them down. That's what I would've done. But he didn't ask or write down squat. Instead, he crossed his legs and ran a stubby hand along his thigh, the rusty gears in his head wheeling.

"These new brothers of yours, do they act as if they're being held against their will?"

"No."

"Hmm." He said it like he'd made a point I was too dim to understand. "Well, I haven't noticed anything I'd consider notably unusual under the circumstances."

He turned to face his desk. The bell rang, and after a couple seconds he checked the glue-job on his moronic Murray's Law poster. "Don't you have English class?"

I avoided Calvados as best I could the rest of the day: tried to keep a buffer of people between us in the cafeteria or wherever, and asked Lou or Jeremy to stand watch outside the bathroom every time I had to go, because the last thing I needed was Rick ambushing me as I stepped from a toilet stall.

Senior captain jock-boy still got to me, though. The first time was between third and fourth periods. I'd relaxed vigilance for no more than a few seconds when Rick passed in the hall and hit me behind my knees with his lacrosse stick. The second time happened in the early afternoon. I was leaning against the school's trophy case, texting Suzy, and all of a sudden Rick's lacrosse stick slapped my head and shoulders. He never said a word, just grinned like, yeah, he had hit me all right and if I wanted to start something, he'd be happy to oblige.

I assumed Suzy was mad since she never texted me back. Also, that she'd skipped out of school after our HVAC scene. But I saw her just before final period.

"Naw, dude, cherry has its places," Jeremy was saying, the both of us at our lockers, "but give me a stripper with big boobs over berry-pickin' any day."

"Boo!"

Jeremy tumbled his locker-innards into the hall. Suzy had snuck up on us. I immediately scoped for any sign of Rick.

"Hey," I said.

Jeremy crouched down, making like he was too busy picking up his junk to notice Suzy.

"Are you going to tomorrow's game against Marshall?" she asked me.

My first thought was *I don't need to be reminded Calvados has talent,* and I repeated it over in my head twenty times to keep from saying it or anything that Wilt might've called "eager beaver." Then I tried to put on this look like I was considering everything I had to do around the time of the lacrosse game. But who was I kidding? I *was* an eager beaver, not just because of how cool and sexy Suzy was, but also because, however much she missed my brother, which I didn't doubt, she was definitely hiding something and I needed to find out what.

I heard Dr. Polk's voice in my head: *compartmentalize.* I had to hope Suzy wasn't guilty of something that'd make my being with her impossible. The last thing I wanted was to be cock-blocked by my investigation. Or no, that was the second-to-last thing I wanted, the last being not to let my feelings for Suzy get in the way of my investigation.

"Yeah, I'm going to the game," I said.

"Good. We can go together."

She reached past me for a notebook in my locker, the one with lines from a poem called "Contusion" written on it. *Colour floods to the spot, dull purple / The rest of the body is all washed out, / The colour of pearl.* I expected her to say something about how she didn't know I was into Sylvia Plath, at which point I'd tell her yeah, I'd copied out the lines because my life felt like a bruise, but instead she just shifted her books from one hand to the other, not looking at me or at anything really. She seemed to be studying the inside of her eyeballs, deciding whether or not to describe what she saw. Jeremy was meantime trying to hide inside his locker.

"'Kay, I'll see ya."

From the way she met up with Nisa and Janelle down the hall—all OMG gossipy—you would have thought nothing had ever been wrong in her life.

"I'd definitely hit that," Jeremy said, playing like no one had noticed him bungling his books.

My phone buzzed with a text from Suzy:

must b sumway I can get u not to do wht ur gonna do tonite ;-)

To make sure my hard-on wouldn't influence my decision-making, I said quick to Jeremy, "You and Lou meet me at the Carnova Way bus stop at six-thirty, to head out to St. Benny."

"Oh, joy."

30

New England Colonial. Greek Revival. Art Deco. Mid Century Modern. Nuñez had taught me which houses were what architecturally, hinting that more than a couple of them belonged to Yang. My entire route was in the bird streets, though it changed from week to week, depending on which beasties were being put through training exercises Nuñez didn't want me to see. Elsewhere, in other neighborhoods, I assumed, other psycho dog-beasties were being fed by kids pillowed into Michelin Man outfits, and I wanted to ask Nuñez if the whole op was like a league thing, with dog-beasties from specific neighborhoods fighting teams of beasties from other neighborhoods. But that would've given away I knew too much, so.

I went to the most exclusive bird streets, their names out of science-fiction—Trogon, Jabiru. But whatever style mansion I visited, the setup was the same as at the Tudor: steaks in the fridge of some guest/pool house or gardening shed, filtered water, bags of dry food, cans of wet, the usual collection of pooper scoopers, muzzles, noose-on-a-sticks, car tires, heavy-duty collars and chains. Locked drawers or cabinets somewhere. And hanging on the back of a door or in a closet, on extra-strength hooks: a Michelin Man outfit.

Nuñez didn't need to school me about the different dog-beasties as much as he had with the houses. Pit bulls. Dobermans. Rottweilers. Mastiffs. The only breed I didn't know was the presa canario—a hard-packed thing whose chest and front legs could've belonged to some hairy, midget, Olympian weightlifter. He had a pointy-eared head perfect for breaking things against, and a mouth wide enough to take in like an eight-inch frisbee. He lived behind a New England Colonial on Ibis Street, in this kind of super cage with support posts secured in concrete, chain link twice as thick as normal, and coils of barbed wire crossing every chain link panel in a big X. Nuñez had said there was a reason the beast lived alone and I didn't doubt it. I felt lucky every time I made it out of that SuperMax without having my padding jawed off.

If it was in my route, I started at the Tudor, feeding Manson and his cage-mates, refilling water bowls and scooping poop, then sitting someplace in the run I hadn't just cleared of dog turd. Manson's wounds were as healed as they'd ever get—the hashtag cuts on his legs gone, most of the fur on his right side grown back. The ear that'd been shredded looked like an artichoke leaf scraped clean by someone's teeth. I'd sit there, naked-handed, petting Manson while he rested his chin on my outstretched leg, and I'd maybe talk about Suzy or how I was going to rescue him and keep him in Mrs. Holt's apartment till I could figure something else out, except he couldn't have too many rabid episodes in Mrs. H's—not that I figured he would, since he'd no longer be locked up with other psycho beasties or forced to fight for his life anymore, but still. All this buddy-buddy between us didn't change how frothy he got every time I left the run, though. He'd flare up along with his aggro cage-mates, same as always.

"I have confidence in you," I'd tell him, which was the kind of thing Dr. Polk sometimes said to me.

Whenever my route included the presa canario, I left him for last, since who wants to deal with psycho dog-beasties after having squeezed the balls of the beastliest one of all?

Because yeah, I squeezed Presa's balls.

It was the only way I could get out of the run. He would attach himself to one of my limbs before I ever tried to leave. I'd maneuver over to the gate, and with as much of my body blocking the opening as I could manage, I'd unlatch the gate and toss the pooper scooper out to the yard, then reach quick for the beast's nuts and squeeze as best I could with my mitted hand. Unfanging whichever of my limbs he was trying to gnaw to a stump, he'd twist around to snap at his balls, and by the time he reared around to have at me again, I'd be outside the run, slamming the gate.

But the day of the St. Benny stakeout—when I didn't feed the beast, only cleaned his run, per instructions—it was like all our previous battles had been practice and this was the main event. I had to squeeze his balls over and over to get out to the yard, and when I finally did, I wasn't in one piece. Michelin Man's vinyl skin flapped loose along my arms and legs. Chunks of padding were still in the SuperMax. My left calf, my right thigh: another bite and Presa would've punctured actual flesh.

"It isn't right!" a girl yelled from I didn't know where. "He shouldn't be locked up all the time!"

She was on a next-door balcony, suspended above the fancy landscaping that bushed up between the two yards. She had to yell because Presa was barking insanely, repeatedly launching himself at his prison gate with a running start like a bull who gives himself room to really charge at some dickwad matador.

"He never gets taken for a walk!" balcony-girl yelled. "It's why he's so aggressive!"

"Yeah, he's not mine! I just feed him and stuff! Believe me, I wish he wasn't like this!"

I didn't have the best view of her, but balcony-girl seemed pretty hot. She had on these tight little black shorts with white trim, kind of retro shorts like you'd see high school track geeks sporting in some campy movie about the '80s. Her yellow tank top wasn't even close to baggy and she looked top-heavy in a good way. I guessed her to be about Suzy's age, a senior in some private school.

Presa decided to try and bite his way through the gate, unbothered by the barbed wire cutting into the flappy skin above his side fangs.

"I'm Meredith," balcony-girl said.

"Curtis."

"You look ridiculous, Curtis. But cute. Want to hang out?"

I figured that Wilt's advice might work on this girl as well as on Suzy, and I counted slowly to ten before answering. "Yeah," I shrugged, having no idea if it came across the way I was dressed.

"Come around to the front and I'll let you in."

"Okay, I just . . . can I get this thing off first?" I meant my chomped-on outerwear.

"Why?" she said, which probably should've been a warning

sign, but I didn't want to overthink the situation more than I already would, and so I just Franken-walked to her drawbridge of a front door—this massive thing with wood planks at least a foot wide and hand-hammered iron bands bolted across them. If Nuñez had quizzed me, I would've said it was the entrance to a Mediterranean castle, and I stood off to the side of it, not wanting to get flattened in case it really was a drawbridge. I thought Meredith might be eyeing me from inside and tried to act casual, which basically involved nodding and looking out across the front yard till a regular-size door inside the drawbridge opened.

"Hi."

I hadn't been wrong. Meredith's water-balloon breasts wanted out of her top. Her legs weren't knobbly thin like on some pretty girls whose knees are wider than their thighs. Her legs were shapely—I'm talking athlete-shapely, dancer-shapely. Her straight, crayon-black hair was short enough I could see most of her beautiful neck. The only reason she wasn't Suzy-league was because her cheeks and forehead had the tortilla texture of someone who used to have bad acne. Still, she was a girl I could've easily shown off to Lou and Jeremy, the kind who would've had Jeremy reaching for his crotch, all, "Dude, I've got topping to put on *that* spread."

"My room's upstairs," she said.

"Cool."

I scoped the front hall as if her bedroom didn't interest me more than any other room and I might ask for a tour of the entire place. I followed her up a carpeted staircase, her hypnotic butt swinging left-right-left-right, each swing ticking off some episode from my piddling sex life.

Tick. On the playground in fourth grade, June Thomas asked if she could show me something. I'd barely talked to her before. We went to her locker where she took her time dialing in her combination and giving me funny looks. She finally asked if I liked her. I was like *yeah I guess*, and she brought out this box from the bottom of her locker. The box was full of notes written with color markers: J.T.+C.B.=♥ Forever and other sappy nonsense. No one else was around so I let her kiss me, then said I had to go, and I avoided her ever afterwards, pretending the whole thing never happened.

Tick. A bunch of us at Lou's in seventh grade, pairing off to make out in closets and wherever. Ellen Clayman and I'd been in the hall bathroom when she said that she didn't want to change partners anymore, she wanted to be with only me the rest of the night, and I was like *okay* because she was a good kisser. Lou and everyone went silent with surprise when we told them, except back in the bathroom Ellen and I hardly had time to do anything before Lou knocked at the door saying Ellen's dad was there to pick her up. I hid in the shower stall while Ellen nervously checked herself in the mirror. She whispered that she'd see me at school, turned off the light as she left, and I waited five minutes before stepping out of the dark stall.

Tick. Eighth grade. Claudia Evans sent me photos of herself. Nothing too porno, just teasing poses in front of a bathroom mirror, but enough for me to use.

Tick. The photos I got in ninth grade were like actual sexts. Claudia topless. Mary Lopez in her underwear or completely naked. For a long time I didn't know how to respond to sexts. I couldn't just say thanks, could I? So I searched the web, trolled online chat rooms, eavesdropped on Wilt's calls with Suzy for ideas. Eventually, like I was some senator, I sent both Claudia and Mary pictures of my nethers, and I stole ideas from erotica blogs and texted what I'd do to them if we were naked together. That was the year Dad came the closest he ever would to a Birds & Bees speech: "I'm offering you the same thing I did your brother when he was your age. If you and a girl find your-selves in a certain kind of trouble, you can come to me." It was also the year Wilt told me that if I ever got caught whacking it by some prude, I should say I'd only been exfoliating and what was the big deal since exfoliating was good for your skin.

Tick. The summer before tenth grade, Wilt and I were spending the usual month at Dad's apartment. Wilt was out somewhere with Suzy, and Dad wasn't around either. To avoid being alone with stepmom Maria, I went to hang in Ann and Melissa's apartment on the fifth floor, the three of us watching TV when Melissa suddenly asked if a girl had ever told me I was the best sex she'd ever had. "Yeah," I lied. She wanted to know how many girls had said it to me. "Two," I lied. She asked me to kiss her cheek, which after I did, she smiled at her sister and asked me to kiss her again. I kissed her three times total, the TV did the talking for a while, and when Melissa left the room to answer the phone, Ann was all, "My turn." We tongue-wrestled, then she stood up like a stretching cat and led me out to her dad's old Cadillac in the parking lot where she gave me my first and only blowjob.

Anyway.

Piddling, like I said.

But Franken-thumping up those stairs behind Meredith's butt, the thing I noticed most about these sexpisodes: girls had always been the initiators. Which I figured probably wasn't the case with my brother. Wilt had never been shy that way. Or any way really. If I was going to be more like him, I had to make the first real move on Meredith. Except I didn't get the chance. Soon as we stepped into her room, she came at me like a heroine in some movie who'd been lusting after chewed-on marshmallow-me but tragedy had kept us apart till we were finally alone and so now she couldn't help but release her pent-up passion.

The girl knew how to use her tongue, though. She stepped back and asked if I had protection.

"What do you think this is for?" I said, meaning my Michelin Man get-up.

She laughed. "It's okay if you don't."

When she pulled a Trojan from her nightstand drawer, I got kind of worried, not knowing if I should tell her I was a virgin or if I should wait and say something only when it became obvious. And maybe it seems weird for me to have sweated over this next thing, since I had a hard-on more often than I didn't, but I also worried about not being able to get it up. I'd heard somewhere that it could happen to guys their first time: you've wanted to get laid so bad for so long that when it's finally happening, you're too busy thinking how you can't believe you're actually getting laid, and so actually you don't— psyching yourself out of boner-town.

I started to take off my Michelin Man mitts.

"Leave them," Meredith said, which was pretty odd, but I wasn't about to overthink *that* too, so.

"I just had to . . . you know, readjust," I said.

WWWD? I kept thinking. *What would Wilt do?*

I Franken-walked a lap around the room, pretending to be interested in her collection of snow globes. I was trying not to think of floppy noodles, of words like *limp, soft, mushy.* Then, as casually as I could, I lay back on her bed as Michelin Man.

"You want some of this or don't you?" I said.

I'm still not sure if the next thing was an accident or on purpose, but she threw herself on top of me, bouncing off my puff-mound stomach onto the floor. She laughed and was more careful the next time, easing herself onto me. I felt her start to move and lifted my arms to hold her but couldn't reach. I tried wiggling, like I was responding to what she was doing even though I couldn't really tell what *that* was. A picture developed in my head: I was a large turtle, helpless on my back, my arms and legs paddling nothing, while some naturalist girl did her thing on top of me, trying to be one with the creatures of the earth.

She wanted me to keep on as much of the Michelin Man suit as possible, which she knew how to manipulate better than I did. For a little while—with her on top of me and everything working the way it was supposed to—I didn't stress about the coming stakeout at St. Benny. I didn't stress about the parentals, Yang, Nuñez, Calvados, Okafur, Narith. I didn't even stress about Suzy or Wilt.

But only for a little while.

31

At the bus stop outside the bird streets, I stood rock-still and breathed, trying to feel the difference: I wouldn't ever be a virgin again. I'd expected some magic transformation, I guess, but I was starting to wonder if losing my virginity wasn't as major as everybody said—not one of those life milestones—because I felt pretty much the same as always.

Except, life milestones? I'll never again be the same as I am this second, right? Never again have the exact same experiences in my head, the same thoughts and feelings as I'm having at any given moment, in whatever surroundings. Every second I'm breathing, every heartbeat, is kind of a life milestone, so maybe, in a way, nothing is.

"Why do people always say 'losing virginity'?" I asked, meeting up with Lou and Jeremy on Carnova Way. "I get that virginity's supposed to be precious and nobody wants to lose something that's precious, but why doesn't anyone ever talk about what they gain when they lose their virginity?"

"Gain when they lose?" Jeremy said.

"Why don't they say, I don't know, that they've 'graduated' from virginity or something? Put it in positive terms instead of negative ones?"

"Some people probably do," Lou said.

"But maybe it isn't positive," Jeremy said, which was funny, coming from him.

"You lose training wheels: that's a positive," Lou said. "You lose baby teeth: that's a positive. 'Lose' doesn't always have to mean something negative. Where's all this coming from anyway?"

I didn't answer and sat through slow minutes of Lou eyeing me on the bus.

"Jer, you notice anything different about our friend?" he finally said.

"Has he lost weight, Lou?"

"No. It's something else. But there's definitely something."

I'd always figured getting laid would be brag-worthy. It might have been because there'd been a fat layer of padding between Meredith and most of me, but before I stepped off the bus at St. Benny, her smell, the taste of her mouth—it had all faded. As if my body had already forgotten it'd had sex, and so I was like, Maybe I hadn't lost my virginity, only misplaced it?

32

Living in the city, there are never a ton of stars overhead, but if I try hard enough I can usually see the brightest ones. In the sky above St. Benny, though? No matter how hard I looked: nothing but nothing, void. Which, wasn't it supposed to be the opposite? City lights kept me from seeing stars, so at St. Benny, where there weren't any city lights, I should've seen a sky full of them. Or at least a couple clouds. But instead the stars and clouds seemed to have floated off, as creeped out by St. Benny as I was, leaving the quarter-mile dead-end darker and creepier than ever.

The wind didn't help, stealing through abandoned buildings, making stuff creak and moan. It was the kind of wind that promised nothing good.

"Dudes, better get in on some of this."

Jeremy had come armed with nunchucks, slingshot, a set of steak knives in his backpack. The nunchucks he was keeping for himself. The slingshot was beyond stupid. The steak knives were the right amount of stupid. Lou and I each took one.

"It's only 7:50," Lou said, checking his phone.

The darkness made it seem later than it was, and I didn't feel like admitting the possibility that we'd be stewing in it for hours since I hadn't heard Yang mention a definite time. We had no idea when the dogfights were supposed to happen, or *if* they were even going to.

Our motive for being at St. Benny—my having overheard Yang say "wholesale" to Nuñez the day before—seemed pretty thin all of a sudden.

We kicked at the dirt outside Wholesale Electric awhile, not going inside in case Yang's crew showed up and trapped us. I spilled to Lou and Jeremy about how Suzy and Wilt had been scheming to rescue Yang's dogs, how Wilt had anonymously called the cops but nothing happened, how Suzy didn't think Yang was the killer but didn't want us hanging at St. Benny or anyplace where we might get seriously maimed.

"That's nice of her," Lou said. "But what makes her so sure it's not Yang? She know what happened?"

I'd been about to say that Suzy was probably hiding something, that her wanting us to stop nosing around Yang's business—to me, it suggested guilt as much as fear, and how could she know what to fear unless she was guilty of something that'd make her afraid? Or unless she knew about guilt-worthy doings by others? But something in Lou's voice . . . it was like he figured I'd grilled Suzy all wrong, like he needed to hear specifically *how* I'd grilled her to tell me what I should've done instead.

"You're trying to get me to suspect her again," I said. "You don't want us to hook up."

"You're the guy who said he wasn't trying to get into her pants." He watched me a second. "Unless you've been in them already? You have, haven't you?"

I expected to be bum-rushed by Jeremy's congrats, high-fives, pelvic thrusts and whatnot, but he just stood looking like he'd been asked to interpret a foreign language. The possibility that one of us might ever sleep with Suzy: it'd been the stuff of fantasy only weeks earlier.

"Jer, remember when I asked if you'd noticed anything new about our friend here?"

"Yeah, Lou. I think I do."

"I've figured it out. He has more confidence in his step, a way of carrying himself that's less boyish. I'm saying—"

"What *are* you saying, Lou?"

"I believe our friend Curtis has gotten laid."

"That why you smell like a wet soccer ball?" Jeremy asked me.

I told them about Meredith and the Michelin man outfit. I didn't brag, was just matter-of-fact, my voice so flat I could've been describing some video I'd watched ten times out of boredom, more than because I actually liked it. Jeremy started thrusting out his pelvis and trying to high-five me.

That canyon between me and everybody else? The one I said I had to get across to feel understood by another person, but which was basically impossible to cross? There was another. Between the guy most people thought me to be and the person I felt I was. Unless that was the same canyon described in a different way? I deflected Jeremy's air-fucks at St. Benny and was like, *The person my friends think I am. The person I feel I am. Who's right? Who's more right, if anyone?*

"I might become one of those guys who fixes up dead people to look good," Jeremy said after his air-fucks.

"A mortician?" Lou said. "Why would you want to do that?"

"Job security. Always gonna be funerals, dude. How many people want to sew dead people's eyes shut, empty them of their insides and whatever else? I heard there's good money in it. Six figures a year, easy."

"I think you have to go to school for that," I said.

"So?"

"One time I drank water too fast and threw up," Jeremy said an hour later. And half an hour after that: "Look, my hand's as big as my face."

We were kicking dirt under one of Wholesale's busted side windows when two vans rolled up. Nuñez and his crew—skinheads whose muscled bodies might've frequently exercised themselves in hate crimes—popcorned out of the vans, unloading electric generators, lights, sandbags, stacks of what were possibly doors. Lou, Jeremy, and I could see into Wholesale from between the iron bars of the busted window—the four stacks of thick boards being unfolded, the boards of each stack hinged together and Nuñez's guys inserting them edge-wise into grooved bases made of steel or something heavy like that. The finished setup was an octagon for midget wrestling. Nuñez's hate crimers dumped the sandbags on the bases for added support while he went outside and parked the vans with their open backsides perpendicular to the building's entrance. He set two cafeteria tables in front of the open-assed vans and then this junky old Crown Vic jalopied down St. Benny. And the guy who unfolded out of it? The backs of my knees got sweaty when I suspected who it was. He shook Nuñez's hand before positioning himself at Wholesale's front door like a bouncer. I used the binocular app on my phone to get a closer look and be sure.

"That guy seem familiar to you?" I whispered—a dumb question. Lou and Jeremy had never met Abrams' partner. "It's one of the detectives working Wilt's case."

"What you know you know," Lou said, "cops are on the take."

With Abrams and his partner on Yang's payroll, I was screwed. I didn't think it possible to skunk out Wilt's killer without busting up the dogfight op—which, if Abrams and his partner were benefiting from money-wise, they'd never let happen. They'd permanently silence me instead. Abrams' partner—or worse, Abrams himself—could've even killed my brother. It was never more real to me than it was right then: that in sleuthing out Wilt's murderer, I might only be hurrying myself after him.

I wanted to go off and be alone somewhere, but cars started rolling onto the street, headlights shining this way and that. No chance I wouldn't be goggled if I tried to skip out, so. Chrysler 300s, Dodge Challengers, Jags, Maseratis, Escalades, S-series Mercedes, pimped-out Lincolns and Beemers: the people stepping out of the cars whose paint jobs might as well've been actual cash? I don't know if they were hardened criminals or what, but they were obviously used to being in iffy places because they all had guns.

The cafeteria tables and vans outside Wholesale's entrance turned out to be a weapons check. No comer was allowed into Wholesale without surrendering his weapons, and even then Abrams' partner patted everyone down before letting them into the building. Nuñez walked around flexing his muscles, supervising everything, and in case I wasn't already seeing more than enough, landlord Pappas stepped out of a limo. It took me a second to recognize the guy because he wasn't his usual slobby self. He had on this jacket, a collared button-down, and actual pants instead of sweats. No ratty T-shirt two sizes too small for him, I'm saying, and so no chance of his belly button worm wiggling "Hello!" in the open air. He seemed to know how the weapons check worked, which he explained to the four investment-banker types he was with, guys whose fat wallets had no doubt given them bloated ideas about their personal value. The cockiness that comes from money: you could see it in the way they walked.

Leashed, harnessed, muzzled like they were canine Hannibal Lecters—beasties started showing up. I recognized about a third of them. I'd never seen any of the handlers before, but all of them had a hard time maintaining the Alpha role, the dog-beasties so aggro I figured they were amped on meds, though I knew from the web that some of them had also probably been given some passive mutt to use as a chew toy, getting jacked up on their own adrenaline.

I didn't risk speech, watching the prep. But when the beasties started going at each other? I felt like I might never speak again. On TV or in some movie, super fast edits would've made it hard to see what was happening. There'd have been blink-fast close-ups of bloodslobbery teeth, foaming mouths, wet tearing flesh, and sound effects with over-the-top snarling. I used to hate that kind of editing and would always be *just show the fight*, but that was before St. Benny. Because actually seeing two rabid beasties vying to rip each other's throats out? When no one's trying to make it look sick, it's even more sick. Like, even seeing lions chomp on a zebra on NatGeo doesn't come close to being at a beastie death-match. And boxing and the UFC? They're commercialized up the wazoo, yeah, but maybe they come close to the viciousness of a dogfight—a live boxing or UFC match, I'm talking, not one on TV. Not that I really have any idea, since I've never been to a live match. I'm just guessing.

I held my phone up to the busted window, recording video, aiming it around to take in as much of the scene as possible. Fights lasted anywhere from five minutes to an hour. Losers were dumped onto one of those big dollies people use at Home Depot to wheel around water heaters and sheets of plywood. A guy in a Michelin Man suit worked the octagon like a cross between a ref and rodeo clown, but mostly he sacrificed a padded limb or three after a fight so that handlers could get winning dog-beasties harnessed and muzzled again.

It went on for hours. Fight, winning beast taken away, loser beast tossed onto dolly whether dead or not, fight, winning beast taken away, loser beast tossed onto dolly, fight. Lou, Jeremy, and I had to keep stepping back from the window to stare up at the sky, it was so hard to watch. But what made the violence worse—eerier—was the silence. The relative silence, I mean, because besides what the beasties themselves made, there wasn't any sound at all. Yang had shown up by then, and he and everyone else just stood mute, eyeballing the fights, not egging on the dog-beasties with shouts, nothing. I never once saw money exchange hands, and because the dog-beasties Yang paid me to look after fought each other, I didn't fully understand what was happening. Or why. Maybe bettors didn't need to have their own dog-beasties? Or maybe Yang's op included a kennel's worth of fighters and he had stat sheets on each, which people scoped before placing their bets?

Like horse racing, except with dogs and no racing.

Anyway.

Just when I thought the whole brutality parade might finally be over, Nuñez dragged Manson into the building with one of those noose-on-a-sticks. The free end of the stick was wedged in his arm-pit and he had his right arm clamped down to hold it firm, his left hand gripping his right wrist at about the level of his belt buckle, and his muscles getting a good workout with Manson thrashing around like he was trying to choke himself to death. I'd never seen Manson that aggro before, and I felt this mixture of sadness and pride—sadness because he was basically a slave to his aggression, which he had too many chances to exercise, and pride because, as bad as I felt for him, the way he was bucking and snarling, I felt worse for the dog-beastie who had to fight him.

Until I saw which dog-beastie that was: the presa canario, brought in at the end of two-by-fours—five of them hooked to his anchor-chain collar in a star pattern, Presa at the star's center and five hate crimers from Nuñez's crew manning the free ends of the lumber.

With serious difficulty, Presa was maneuvered into the octagon, and all at once the two-by-fours unhooked from his collar like someone had pressed *release* on a remote control somewhere. Before the lumber was lifted clear, Presa and Manson were fanging each other.

I couldn't bring myself to film it and put my hands over my ears to keep from hearing the yelps and snarls. Jeremy lasted longer at the window than Lou, but pretty soon they'd both stepped away and were shaking their heads. I don't know if Yang overestimated Manson's psycho abilities or what. He must've had some idea what would happen to Manson, to *any* dog, against Presa. But maybe that was the point, what people paid for: they didn't bet on the outcome of fights, they just liked to watch dog-beasties get their intestines clawed out by other dog-beasties.

Even with my ears covered I heard it—the last bark that dropped into a long, fading whine—and I made the mistake of braving a look through the window. Presa was getting tasered, his handlers chaining him up to take him away, while Manson's body was tossed onto the pile of the night's losers.

I've no clue how much time passed before the Escalades and Maseratis cruised out of St. Benny. Yang had disappeared. Pappas and his banker-friends too, and then it was just Nuñez and his guys breaking down the octagon, the lights and the weapons check, loading everything back into the vans—everything except Manson and the rest of the loser beasts.

"Let's get out of here," Lou whispered.

"Not yet."

I skulked around to the front of Wholesale. Nuñez and his guys were wheeling the losers to the end of the block—the forest of six-foot tall weeds behind the collapsed fence, where escaped mental patients lived and mafia types and gang-bangers buried their kills. Some of the beasties were making low whimpering noises, and I watched Nuñez's guys carry them one by one over the fence into the dark, where I'd sworn I'd never go.

"How about now?" Lou whispered. "Now we leave?"

"Not yet."

I creeped toward the dead end. Lou and Jeremy followed. The stink hit us like a slap to the nostrils before we even lightfooted it over the fence. An irregular glow was coming from far back in the weeds and we moved toward it real slow, careful about each step, getting through the roughage without a machete all right, but not wanting to break twigs or anything else that might make a sound. In the middle of this small clearing: a pit too big to be fresh, which I figured had been dug on some earlier night and had been used loads of times. Flames danced above its edges, and Nuñez stood off to the side smoking a cigar while his guys threw the losers—dead and alive—into the fire.

Manson had been the uppermost beastie piled onto the dolly, because of which, he was the first carried into the clearing. He wound up at the bottom of the pile next to the pit and so was the last to get tossed in—just as Lou's phone rang.

"Shit! Shit shit shit shit shit!"

I took my eyes off the cremation pit for half a second tops, but it was too long: only Nuñez and one hate crimer were there the next time I looked. I thumbed my phone, sending the video I'd shot to Lou and Jeremy. Not that I knew what they were supposed to do with it. I'd have to puzzle that out later, if I ever got the chance. I would've given them my phone altogether, but no way Nuñez would believe a kid had been on St. Benny without one, so.

"Skip out," I said.

They didn't need to be told twice. "Thanks for an alarming evening," Lou said, and they were gone.

I stomped deeper into the weeds, making as much noise as I could, wanting Nuñez's hate crimers to come after me and let my friends get away, at the same time poking Trash on my phone, to delete the video, which I barely managed to do before being grabbed by the back of the neck like a puppy.

"I work for Yang!" I shouted.

They weren't gentle, lightening me of cash, phones, ID, steak knife. I don't know if they believed me about Yang, but I was still standing.

"You alone?" one of them wanted to know.

"Yeah. I work for Titus Yang. And Nuñez. I should probably talk to Nuñez."

"You shouldn't talk at all. Check for others."

One of the hate crimers gorilla'd off into the dark. The other pushed me through the brambles, not caring what sliced or thorned into my skin, till I tripped out into the clearing where he held me firm, way too close to the cremation pit with its flames throwing up a vomitous stench.

If Nuñez was surprised to see me, he didn't show it. Unless I did something to mess up one of his expensive suits, he had a single expression, which threatened violence but otherwise revealed nothing. His cigar made the overall stink worse and I breathed through my mouth.

"What the fuck are *you* doing here?" he said.

I didn't have an answer so I didn't give one.

Hate crimer #1 handed my two phones to Nuñez, who recognized the burner he'd given me right off. He started scrolling through my data, and if he ever saw *Wilt* in the log of incoming calls, he didn't say.

"I'm going to ask you one more time. What the fuck are you doing here?"

Staying mute wasn't going to work, was maybe going to get me the kind of beating where I ended up tossed into a fiery pit with a quarter of my skull busted.

"I come here sometimes," I said. "To St. Benny, I mean. It's where Wilt . . . " I let the sentence hang, nodded back toward my brother's crash site, the dead telephone pole. "I was over there just thinking about things when cars started pulling in. I don't know why I didn't make myself known, but I didn't. I wanted to see what the action was about, I guess."

"And what did you see?"

"A lot of expensive cars, people getting out of them and being patted down like they were going into a club."

Some pops and hisses came from the cremation pit. I tried to pretend there wasn't any cremation pit. The rest of the hater crew gorilla'd into the clearing, shaking their heads. So at least Lou and Jeremy had made it out.

I'd been wrong about Nuñez having only one expression, though. His rigid facial lines had softened somehow, as if he was dealing with a curious surprise.

"You say Wilt died here? He crashed *here?*"

It seemed like genuine news to him.

"Back there. Yeah."

"Show me."

I walked him to where the telephone pole lay alongside the blacktop, pointed out the splintery stump that was about the height of a car's bumper. There weren't as many glass crumbs around as there used to be, but he could see the skid marks, which I showed him using the little pen-sized flashlight he had. He spent a long time eyeing it all, then gave me back my stuff—my phones, ID, cash, even the steak knife—and told me to go home.

I had a pass to keep living. Maybe only a temporary one, but still.

33

Two-and-a-half hours later, Okafur opened the door before I got my key into the lock.

"Hey," I said.

He stood there—and Narith too, a little ways behind him, a rag in his hand like he'd been dusting.

"What?"

A note from Mom, safety-pinned to the front of Okafur's shirt, said the results of the DNA test on Wilt's body had confirmed what everybody but Dad already knew. Also, that Mr. Birch on the fourth floor was moving out.

Mr. B was supposed to be the kind of guy who'd never let a slumlord out of paying him cash to live elsewhere. As long as Mr. B was in the building, Mom had always said, the rest of us tenants still had hope of a dinky apartment, and unlike with most things, I'd never had a reason to disbelieve her. Mr. B hadn't shuffled out of his place in over a year, afraid Pappas would change the locks on him. His adult son Tom lived with him and did the grocery shopping and other errands. But the Birches moving out meant Mom had been wrong, which wasn't something she usually admitted in a note or otherwise, and maybe I would've killed more brain cells thinking about it if my phone hadn't buzzed. I'd been texting/calling Lou and Jeremy ever since Nuñez had let me live—my texts unanswered and their phones always just ringing till I got their recorded voices saying I should leave a message.

Which I'd done thirty times.

"Why haven't you answered any of my texts?" I said first thing, like I was a parent hassling them after they'd been out late.

Jeremy leaned into frame, phone in hand. "I'm answering them now."

"You're fine?" Lou asked me. "Everything's actually okay?"

"Depends what you mean by 'okay,' but yeah."

I held up my phone so they could see I was home.

"Dude," Jeremy said, "when we didn't hear from you, it started to feel like we weren't *gonna* hear from you."

I waited for more but it didn't come. Not really. My phone buzzed. To my first text of *I'm ok call me,* Jeremy'd sent *on it.*

"We showed your video to that detective," Lou practically whispered, no doubt wishing I wouldn't hear.

"What!" Narith and Okafur jumped in my peripheral vision, but I couldn't help yelling. "If cops are on the take, *why* would you do that?"

"We panicked."

"We didn't hear from you for over two-and-a-half hours," Jeremy said.

"But I texted you! I called!"

"No reception in the police station," Lou said. "We just got your messages."

I thought about that last bit. It'd been about twenty minutes between the time Lou and Jeremy left St. Benny and my

first text to them afterwards. Even if they'd immediately bee-
lined to the cops, they should've gotten a screenful of my texts
before stepping into any reception-lacking police station.

My phone buzzed. *Too late* Jeremy had sent in answer to
my *really I'm ok call me don't do anything stupid.*

"What'd Abrams say?" I asked.

"He mostly listened."

"What'd you tell him?"

A whole lot more than the basics of when and where the
dogfights had taken place, it turned out. More even than how
the three of us had wound up at St. Benny on that particular
night and had all personally scoped Titus Yang and Nuñez.
They told Abrams I'd taken over Wilt's job of feeding Yang's
dog-beasties, that my brother and Suzy had been scheming
to rescue the dog-beasties but never got the chance to actually
do it because someone had killed Wilt to shut him up, which
hadn't completely worked but *had* scared Suzy off the idea.

"What about his partner?" I asked. "You say anything
about seeing his partner?"

Jeremy said: "What happened was, before we talked to
Abrams, we panicked and kind of forgot about the cops being
involved. But after we told Abrams stuff, we remembered."

"We didn't mention his partner," Lou translated.

"The dude wasn't happy," Jeremy said.

"Did he seem surprised?"

"Not really."

"More tired than anything," Lou said.

"Where are you?"

"My house," Lou said.

"Were you followed? After spilling to Abrams, I mean?"

They looked at each other, didn't answer, and there was a knock at my front door, which Narith opened before I could stop him. Uninvited, unlit cigarette crotched between index and middle fingers of his right hand, Abrams walked in and locked the door behind him. He was there either because Yang wanted to know if I could be trusted to keep silent or else he was supposed to inflict harm. But why have Abrams do the violent work there and then, instead of letting Nuñez and his guys charcoal me earlier at St. Benny? As a means of controlling bent cops?

Without hanging up, I eased my phone into a pocket, microphone side facing out.

"It's late," Abrams said, which I took to mean he knew Mom was at work.

If he'd come to bleed me, Okafur and Narith must have been a problem. Like on date night, though, he didn't really register their existence.

"You've been busy," he said, and when I didn't say anything was all, "Should've left the investigating to professionals."

Should've? Past tense? A tense that couldn't be undone.

"You're going to tell me everything you think you know," he said. "Right now. And I mean everything."

Narith was swiping a rag across the window blinds in a way that had to be flinging dust everywhere. Okafur was messing with the vacuum, bumbling with its attachments, uncoiling and recoiling the power cord. I started by telling Abrams what he already knew—how I'd taken over Wilt's job of feeding rich people's dog-beasties, that all the beasties probably belonged to Titus Yang even though they were kept at different bird street mansions, and that there were more dogs elsewhere, but I didn't know anything about them except that they were brought to St. Benny and other places to fight for their lives. But the dog-beasties I fed? I'd only had to meet them once to see they weren't normal, which was partly why I'd guessed they were being trained as fighters in the first place, the other reasons being that the specifics of how they were cared for matched what I'd read online about dogfights, and also Wilt had kept his job secret. I hadn't found out about the job till after he'd died, and why would he have kept it secret unless there was a good reason to?

"Wilt still hasn't admitted anything to me about the dog-fighting," I said, which made Abrams wince like he had tweaked a muscle somewhere. "Right. You don't believe in an afterlife. Sorry. But he hasn't denied it either. He was a big fan of dogs. I heard about him wanting to sabotage the whole op from his girlfriend. Ex-girlfriend, I mean."

"Suzy Painter."

"Yeah."

Maybe I shouldn't have volunteered so much, but I didn't think it was necessarily a bad thing. It showed I was coming clean and that he and Yang could trust me, even if they couldn't.

Abrams put the unlit cigarette in his mouth and chewed so that it bobbed out between his lips. "Your brother worked for Yang?" He said it more to himself than to me, but I was like, *Uh, being on the guy's payroll, shouldn't you know Wilt worked for Yang?* Could I trust my impression that he didn't seem to know? Why was I still breathing? Just because Okafur and Narith were in the room?

"My brother says he wasn't murdered." Again, Abrams

winced. "He says we're wasting our time trying to prove that he was. But okay, since you want to know everything: I'm pretty sure Wilt's calling because, never mind what he says, I'm supposed to help bust his killer, and his afterlife counselor Sean knows all about it—maybe not who the killer is, but that Wilt can't rest in peace till the killer's found. Wilt's supposed to think he's calling me only as a way to get used to being dead, which is apparently a thing, the dead not always being thrilled at finding themselves dead, being pretty neurotic about it actually."

If Abrams had come to kill me, he was sure taking his time.

"You really want me to believe this afterlife nonsense, don't you?" he said.

"I don't care if you do or not. For me, the hardest part is believing that any higher powers would concern themselves with me and my family. It's not like they've ever done it before. Or if they have, they did too lame a job for me to notice anything positive from the interference."

Okafur tapped me on the shoulder and bowed good-night. "Tomorrow laundry," Narith said, and the pseudo-brothers chugged off to the bedroom without coming out again to wash up or use the toilet.

Abrams stared after them, chewing on his cigarette. "I'll give you points for imagination, but here's what I think. I think you've always known who's responsible for your brother's murder and that for some moronic reason you think you can play the hero. Unfortunately, what's going to happen is, you're going to get yourself hurt, and your mother's going to get hurt by virtue of you being hurt. But that might be your goal, huh? To drive your mom crazy with more unnecessary suffering."

She was already well on her way to crazy without my help, I didn't say.

"I also think this story about receiving calls from your brother is bullshit."

"Ask Mom, if you don't believe me. She's talked to him too."

"Your mother is grieving."

"I am too, asshole!"

"You have a funny way of showing it."

I stewed, trembling all over, like I always used to get before I started swinging my fists.

"For all I know, you put your mother on the phone with someone who pretended to be Wilt," Abrams said. "You have an on-again/off-again relationship with what most people call 'reasonable' behavior, don't you? Isn't that why you're on medication?"

"You want to date my mom, you should stop pissing off her only surviving son."

We stood in silence, me trying to breathe through the adrenaline tremors, him putting his lip-soggy cigarette back in its pack.

"Arresting men of Yang's stature and importance is not something to be done lightly," he said.

"Yeah?" By then, I'd pretty much decided he wasn't there to off me, but I still had more reasons to think he worked for Yang than that he didn't, and I wanted to find out how weak my position was. "I guess that's why nothing happened when an anonymous tip about the dogfight op was reported to the police. You guys never followed up. Yang's too important, I guess."

"What's that supposed to mean?"

"What I said: Yang's too important."

"No. The anonymous tip part."

I reminded him about what Lou and Jeremy had already spilled: that Wilt had hoped to somehow rescue the dog-beasties. Then I said that Wilt had also anonymously reported the dogfight op to the cops but nothing ever came of it.

"I can't speak for how police in other departments do or don't do their jobs," he said when he regained verbal. "By the way, I got the report about the device we found on the car."

"And?"

"Not the most sophisticated device my people have ever seen. An odometer seems to have been the trigger, instead of a timer. The device caused a sudden increase in acceleration, which may or may not have been irrevocable. A pretty imperfect method, in my opinion."

Imperfect as a way to murder someone, I figured he meant. So maybe the killer's goal had been only to scare Wilt? Maybe Abrams didn't work for Yang, but he'd still have to know about his partner, right?

"What're you going to do about Yang?" I asked. Though I felt horrible about the beasties, I needed the op to keep running a while longer. If it was shut down, the killer would get spooked and disappear before I could bust him. And as long as I was alive, I was going to work toward busting him. "'Cause like you said, it's not something to be done lightly—hassling Titus Yang."

"Uh huh."

I was losing him. "Your partner was at St. Benny tonight," I blurted. "He worked the door."

Abrams didn't say a word, as mannequin-faced as I had ever seen Nuñez be.

"I'll put in a good word for you with Mom if you leave the dogfight op alone for another couple weeks," I offered. How I'd find my brother's killer in two weeks, I had no idea.

"Tell you what," Abrams said after a long think, "I might hold off on Yang, to investigate further, but only if you don't mention my partner's alleged moonlighting to anyone."

"Deal."

He took out his Zippo lighter. *Chk chk. Chk chk chk.* "Those things on your head just ornamental?"

"What?"

"Your ears. Because I'm going to give you some advice, in case they're capable of taking anything in. Two weeks or not, I don't recommend you engage in any further doings related to this case, although I have a feeling you'll do what you want despite recommendations from me or anybody else. So you'd better at least keep me informed." He unlocked the front door, said the next thing out to the empty hall: "When you've done this job as long as I have, it's impossible to believe in heaven or hell. Where's your brother allegedly calling from?"

"He says it's kind of like a Walmart."

"Uh huh. And who's in charge?"

"He doesn't know. Maybe you can trace a call one time?"

"Maybe." Abrams pulled a crushed red rose from somewhere in his coat. The thing looked like it had been squished for days. "Please give this to your mom. Say it's from me."

Soon as he'd gone, I took hold of my phone.

"You catch all that?"

But Lou and Jeremy had hung up. Later, I found out it was because they hadn't been able to hear a word. I'd pocketed my phone with the microphone side facing out, yeah—except *upside down*, with the mic at the bottom of the pocket.

After Abrams left, with the front door bolted and Okafur and Narith asleep, I wound up at the feeding table, studying the first picture Suzy had ever texted me—the one of her lying on her stomach in bed, eyes sleep-drunk, hair pillow-mussed, the soles of her feet upturned and blurry in the background. I've thought Suzy Painter the most beautiful girl in the world ever since I first started noticing that kind of thing. By seventh grade, *most beautiful* also meant *most do-alicious*, but lots of girls have boobs, so I sometimes wondered what about her, specifically, had always made me think she was the *most* beautiful. It couldn't be just her eyes, the lay of her mouth, or her nibble-worthy nose. Couldn't even be the shape of her butt and thighs in a pair of tights. Divvy out those things to other people—put her eyes on another girl, I mean, and her nose on someone else—and they wouldn't have been as nice.

But pictures of her on a phone? No matter how good they might be, 2-D still-lifes or GIFS couldn't do her justice. Because there was something else. I don't know how to explain it. She could've been gossiping with Janelle behind the school's HVAC unit or just staring thoughtfully across the playground during lunch, but that's when I'd swear she was beautiful beyond belief and there'd never be a girl I'd love as much.

She'd been texting me all night, at first asking how things were going and if I was okay, then every five minutes messaging me with *still there?* and I'd text back *yeah.*

She answered the phone on the first ring.

"I was afraid you'd be asleep," I said.

"What happened?"

I meant to tell her about the dogfights, about Manson and everyone and everything I'd seen, but that's not what came out. "I was wrong," I said. "No dogfights while we were there."

She exhaled like she'd been holding her breath. "Good. That's really good. You're not going to try again, are you?"

I wasn't sure. I thought I'd probably have to, even if I wished otherwise. "No," I said.

"I'm glad you're safe."

I heard rustling on her end, which I thought might be shifting bedcovers. My words came out needy, not confident and flirty the way Wilt would've wanted me to sound. "Really? How glad?"

"What do you mean?"

Her voice had this teasing little upswing that told me she knew exactly what I meant. I sprung a third leg, but I was mad at myself for having sounded weak, and besides, it was bugging me that I still didn't know why Wilt had been on St. Benny the night he died. He obviously hadn't crashed while Yang's people were around, which meant either he'd gone there on a night when he knew no fights were scheduled, or after they'd happened.

"Why do you think he's in denial?" I asked.

The flirt drained from Suzy's voice. "Who?"

"You know who. Why won't he admit that your plan to sabotage Yang's dogfight op probably got him killed?"

"I think he knows better than you do what happened."

"Do *you* know what happened? Why was he on St. Benny the night he died? To set up surveillance equipment and get proof of mass canine graves too solid for the cops to ignore even if they were given it anonymously?"

The questions had vomited out of me, but I'd messed up. If nothing had happened on St. Benny, like I'd told her, how would I have known about the mass graves? Except she didn't ask how I knew—if Wilt had maybe mentioned them. She seemed to take the existence of mass graves as a given, and I lightbulbed: she'd always known about them.

"All my friends are either depressed or angry and most can't tell me why," she said. "Everything I see on TV and the web about how happy my life could be? It's depressing."

I was schizo between not wanting to let her change the subject and always giving her whatever she wanted. "We must not be using the same internet," I said. "Whenever I check out the news, all I read about are down-in-the-dumps assholes."

"I'm sleepy," she said, her voice so whispery, for a second I felt like I was in bed with her, tucked between soft sheets that made what I usually slept on as rough as canvas. "Maybe I'll dream a nice dream of you tonight."

She left me with a hard-on seriously testing the thread-count of my jeans. My phone buzzed.

"I know what happens in the field at St. Benny, after the fights," I said, answering it. "Why didn't you admit you tried to get Yang busted?"

"Suze tell you that?" Wilt said.

"Not about the field, no. I *saw.*"

From his silence, I knew he'd seen it all too. Maybe he'd even helped Nuñez at the fights. I doubted he'd have let himself be a dog-beastie handler, but I had no clue, really—the extent of what my brother might've done for money.

"Any people who bet on the fights your enemies?" I asked.

"Those people barely knew I existed."

"So no one ever asked you to handicap a beastie somehow—which, 'cause you didn't, they lost a lot of money?"

"Get a life while you still have a chance, doucheface. You've been wrong about most things from the start. Ask me how long I'll be able to call you?"

"How long will you be able to call?"

"Uncertain. But shoppers here aren't all victims of unsolved crimes, which rules out your theory that we're supposed to help living relatives solve our own murders in order to get out of here."

"Wait. They remember? How they died, I mean? I thought—"

"Some of them do, if they died peacefully in their sleep. Some remember a greeter welcoming them when they first arrived, although they no longer know where that greeter and entrance are. I myself don't remember a greeter. But here's something you might not have considered in your 'philosophizing'—that the idea of *getting out of here* implies there's somewhere to get out *to*, which I have no reason to believe even if I hope it's the case. Remember what my counselor Sean used to say, that this Aftermart 'is what there is'? There are other

ERIC LASTER

theories, by the way. A lot of the Romans—medieval ages guys too—don't think it's a crime we're supposed to solve in order to leave this place. They assume it's a deep-buried personal or emotional issue, which explains the therapy."

"But I thought you were supposed to have achieved perfect maturity?"

"Listen when someone is talking to you. I didn't say I subscribed to the theory. To me, it's just another flavor of shitty. But there are legions who, in case this emotional theory is true, have stopped trying to understand what their problem is, never mind fix it, because they can't fathom what might happen if they *do* fix it."

"The Aftermart you know being better than the afterlife you don't," I said.

"Exactly. But screw it. Sean could be bluffing and I *really* can't take it here much longer. I tell you our rebellion's gaining momentum? Claudius and I have recruited shoppers from every epoch. We've got Mongols, Ottoman Turks, Renaissance guys, seventeenth- and eighteenth-century people, you name it—thousands of us, skipping therapy, ignoring quotas. The voice on the intercom's been going nuts. Claudius and I have already been questioned by assistant assistant managers."

"But you're . . . this rebellion? You were only supposed to ignore quotas to lure Sean out, get him to tell you what he knows about your death. And anyway, what if they're listening to this?"

"I'm betting they are."

I didn't understand. Was he hoping to bring about change without having to launch a full-on war?

216

"Not yet sure how big of a problem it is," he said, "that unlike a terrestrial superstore, this place doesn't sell legit weapons, not even bows and arrows. Baseball bats and things that could be used as weapons are practically useless. Swing a bat at Claudius, it passes through him. I've tried it. Security doesn't seem to be armed either, but it'll make most of us feel better—to outfit ourselves with makeshift weapons when the time comes. There are bulletproof shower pans in aisle 109 x 10E7, which we'll use as shields. The whole thing's going to start like a flash mob when I give the signal. If I'm being held in a back office for some reason, not around to give the signal, then Claudius will give it. If he's being held in a back office, somebody else will."

"What if Sean's not bluffing? What if there really is nothing else?"

"Too bad for us, I guess."

"Okay, but maybe you could at least demand a sit-down with the general manager? Ask about clues you don't seem to know you've been giving me, and also for some kind of improvement in store policy?"

"I don't think a mere change in policy's going to cut it. Death induces one hell of an identity crisis. I feel like the residue of the person I used to be. See what I mean?"

"How can you *feel* anything," I said. "*You.*"

"You impress me more and more as a reasoning creature, brother."

There was snark in his voice, but still. "Thanks for noticing."

"We're going to demand release, dispersion as pure energy with no recollection of the humans we used to be. Because the way things are, I'm worried I'll forget what Suzy looks like—what you, Mom, and Dad look like, and I don't want to eternally remember that I've forgotten the people who meant the most to me. As pure energy, there shouldn't be anyone for me to have forgotten since there won't be any particle of 'me' left. Although really, I'm mostly worried about Suzy and people forgetting what *I* looked like."

I thought of Suzy's chin, apple-bottom dimpled, and the slide of her eyes under those long lashes when she looked at a person sideways, as if in that glance she was passing them a secret. I thought of the pulsing hollow at the base of her neck, like a tiny bird's visible heartbeat, and the way she held her pinky straight out when she picked at the cubes of fried tofu she ate for lunch. I thought of her small white teeth and her provoking lips and the way she brushed her hair sometimes, bending completely forward with it hanging straight down parallel to her legs.

"Wow," Wilt said, which was when I realized I'd said all this out loud. Then we got disconnected.

34

I had too many thoughts ricocheting around in my skull to get any sleep that night. Okafur was in Wilt's bed, murmuring dreamily, Narith on the floor between us spewing Cambodian every once in a while, which he sometimes did like a frightened little kid, other times like he was furious and about to pummel someone.

I'd been told more than once that entire populations had it worse than I did. Usually by some self-important know-it-all who thought he was teaching me a life-lesson. And sure, Okafur and Narith were probably examples of people who'd had it really bad, but so what? So there were people struggling through situations suckier than anything I'd had to deal with? How did that help me—to hear that their allotment of daily crap was bigger than mine? Like it was supposed to put my allotment of daily crap in perspective, which'd somehow give me strength to cope? Like I shouldn't have felt bad about my life because it could've been worse? Whenever I hung out at Forest Lawn, it wasn't that the Dobbs, Lindhursts or Millers might've suffered more than me that calmed me down. It was that their *having lived* reminded me how everything bad, good, and otherwise passes. The nonstop, impersonal shove of time—not the particulars of anybody's life I imagined to be worse than my own—gave me a kind of peace. Anyway, what about all the people who had it better than I did? Whose older brothers didn't die on them in high school and who kicked back in large, cushy apartments without having to sweat about a Mom surprising them with a new sibling? Was I supposed to feel worse about my life because those people had won the birth-lottery?

For the record: I didn't think my life would have turned out better if Mom and Dad had stayed together. I doubted being stuck with them both under one roof would've been an overall improvement. I used to think it might be, especially those first few years after they split, but no. For some parentals, the best thing to do is divorce.

Mom came home after her shift at UPS and I listened to her bang around the apartment, apparently not too worried about waking anyone up. I rolled out of bed and shook yesterday's stink from my clothes. When I made it to the living room, she was sitting on the couch, staring at nothing.

"What's this?"

I had tried to make Abram's rose look fresh—picked off dead petals and fluffed up the rest. But the thing still seemed exhausted, leaning in a glass of water I'd set on the coffee table.

"It's from Detective Abrams."

Mom's got ten gigabytes' worth of sighs in her repertoire. The one she let out then was part resignation, part defeat.

"He means well," she said, as if it didn't matter how well-meaning Abrams was, things between them just weren't going to work out. And even though I feel that way myself most hours—that the big stuff won't pan out no matter how hard I try or how well-meaning I am—it pissed me off to hear her. She'd already decided that no matter how much she and Abrams liked each other, they'd wind up on the junkheap of relationships, except she couldn't possibly know.

"He's a thousand times better than Dr. Murray," I said.

"Is there any news from Wilt?"

I was like, *Depends what you mean by "news,"* but she didn't need to hear about afterlife therapy, quotas, rebellions, any of that. Which would've boggled her more than she already was, so. "What kind of news?" I asked.

"I don't know."

"If you want to hold on to this for a while, in case he calls . . . ?" I offered her my phone, but she didn't reach for it.

"Are we sure this isn't a nightmare?"

Yes and no. "Pretty sure, yeah."

"Part of me wants to hear his voice as much as possible because it gives me hope he might somehow come back," she said. "But another part doesn't want to hear it, not if he's never coming back. Because then, hearing his voice just makes everything harder."

For no reason, I remembered how, about a year after her split from Dad, she and her friends used to tongue-wag as they guzzled white wine before heading out for a night of man-hunting, how she used to say my grandparents had raised her old-fashioned and she'd grown up expecting to be a stay-at-home mom, so she'd married young, pushed out my brother and me, and never imagined she'd have to sweat being a breadwinner. "Fuck him," I'd hear her say, *him* being Dad.

"He made his choice and I have to move forward with my life, to live the way *I* would like."

Except what I hadn't known then was that she couldn't live the way she would've liked: not as a single mom with two kids to raise, with no training or education to help her earn the cash necessary to feed and clothe them.

The problem was in having expectations, I decided, in ever expecting anything specific—just as Mom, on the couch, did something I'd never seen her do: closing her eyes and lowering her head, her lips moving but her words too soft to hear, she prayed.

We might've talked about so much.

35

Landlord Pappas was hosing down the front sidewalk, showing it more care than he'd ever shown his actual building. It wasn't light out yet and I was surprised to see him on the troll so early.

"Hear about Birch?"

He wanted to gloat. The Birches abandoning us meant only three tenants would be left in the building.

"Yeah."

He turned his hose in my direction, water splashing closer and closer to my duct-taped Converse while he acted like it had nothing to do with him, his belly button worm peeping out from his shirt, all, *What're you gonna do about it?*

"I heard about this motorcyclist one time," he said. "He was part of a pile-up on I-10. Didn't appear hurt and helped people from their wrecked cars. His head started to ache. He had kept his helmet on while helping people from their cars, but now he took it off. Big mistake. His skull had fractured in the crash. His helmet was holding it together. Soon as he took off his helmet, his skull fell apart and he died." Water splattered my jeans and Converse. "It's what he gets for not wearing a helmet. Especially in this city."

"Uh, you just said he was."

"Not *him*. Tom Birch."

Turned out, Mr. Birch's son had died in a moped accident. Tooling back from the 99¢ Store with groceries strapped to the back of his seat, he hadn't seen stalled traffic up in front of him until it was too late. With no time to swerve, he laid the moped down, purposely losing his balance and crashing into the asphalt instead of the cars, but his momentum slammed him into the back of some Toyota so hard his body got lodged under one of its rear tires. Old Mr. Birch, the homebound recluse now with nobody to look after him, was being forced to move in with a younger sister somewhere in Georgia.

"Sad as hell," Pappas said, smiling, "but what can you do?"

36

It was as if nothing at the Tudor had ever been different—the landscaped yard, the pool with its phony hot spring, the way the dog-beasties in the run strained against their chains when they got their first whiff of me, the moneyed air of the bird streets in general. All of it was the same as on every other day. Except different.

Rinsing off Michelin Man after my work, I was about to skip out when Nuñez came up behind me and said, "Inside."

He followed me to the kitchen door, blocking me from going anywhere but into the house. In the kitchen, I pretended to be at a loss, as if I had no idea which garage door-sized opening led to the front entry, or where the back rooms filled with dolls and head-carpets were. He motioned me out to the atrium, then to one of the white living rooms where Yang was waiting in a suit that looked like it'd recently been balled up in a bag—all rumpled and askew, totally at odds with the sharp, ultra-clean surround. The guy's "hair" was as rigid as a Lego character's.

"Why didn't you tell me Wilt died on St. Benny?"

I thought about admitting the truth: that at first I didn't say anything because I figured, being the murderer, he already knew, and then when I had started to think he wasn't the murderer, I couldn't say anything because I wasn't supposed to know he was involved in an operation that held nasty dogfights on St. Benny.

"I didn't think it mattered," I said.

"Do you know what your brother was doing there?"

"He hasn't told me."

"Excuse me?"

"No."

"Did you see anything last night that upset you?"

"I don't think so."

"Really? Nothing you're curious about because you're unsure of exactly what you saw?"

That's when I lightbulbed: I had to admit a little of the truth or else he'd know I was full of shit. "I guess I could lie," I said, "but you'll know, so what's the point? You're hooked into some kind of dogfight operation. The beasties I feed in the bird streets are part of it. But how you make money from the whole deal, assuming you do, I have no idea."

"Do you think you need to?"

"No."

That might've been the moment to say that someone betting on the fights or otherwise involved in them had probably killed my brother, except I thought it'd lead to questions I couldn't answer. I had to let Yang figure things out for himself as much as possible.

Nuñez was somewhere behind me. I didn't try to scope where exactly, in case I wouldn't like what I saw—him with fishing wire pulled taut between two fists, waiting for a nod from his boss.

"Most people are greatly offended by dogfighting," Yang said. "They can't comprehend how one might find pleasure in exploiting the violent instincts of animals that, I'm told, can occasionally be cute. But whoever claimed that pleasure was the motive? Or monetary profit? For me, the fighting serves as a reminder that we are all of us creatures of instinct, largely at the mercy of biology. Natural tendencies can be developed. Manipulated. But only so far. Keeping this fact top of mind, both as it refers to myself and those with whom I negotiate, helps me as a businessman."

Biology? Was the guy talking about electrochemical happenings in the brain? Because being at the mercy of *those* wasn't exactly news to me.

His toupee seemed different than most of his others. Almost canine. Maybe Nuñez had standing orders to skin any loser-beast with a specific fur color/texture before throwing it into the cremation pit? It wouldn't have surprised me if some of Yang's head-carpets were made of dog.

I had to focus. If I let my mind drift to the fact of Nuñez at my back, waiting for a nod, I would've freaked.

"Your father," Yang said.

"What about him?"

"He's presently in town, isn't he? He goes out of town fairly often, for extended periods. But right now, he's here."

He was doing it again, telling me he could get to anyone in my family whenever he wanted. I could've asked him what my dad did for a living, but that would've given away that he knew more about Dad than I did, so.

"Not being upset with what you saw last night, I don't imagine you can enlighten me about this?" he said.

He gave the nod. I spun around—arms up and elbows out to defend myself even though things would go faster and be a lot less painful for me if I just let Nuñez do what he had to do. But the guy only aimed a remote at a closed cabinet. A screen flashed on the wall above the fireplace—a computer desktop screen, with web browsers open to different sites. Nuñez clicked on the different browsers. One showed an anonymous post on a PETA blog ranting about how business tycoon extraordinaire Titus Yang was a kind of serial killer of dog-beasties. Nuñez said that whoever posted it had used an elaborate encryption scheme to route his data through different servers, some of which didn't store IP addresses or use tracking cookies, and so he hadn't yet found the source. Other browsers were open to the comment sections of articles on websites like *USA Today*, Fox, CNN, *NY Times*—all the major news outlets. Anonymous commenters had written about Yang being kingpin of a dog-fight operation and urged authorities/investigative journalists to probe into the matter. On Wilt's tribute blog, there were similar comments, but with links to pictures of a wasted, deserted afternoon at St. Benny.

"People at school set up the tribute page," I said. "But the other stuff? Couldn't the person or people posting it be anyone who's been to one of your dogfights?"

"It started after you came to work for me."

"I know nothing about it," I said, worried about someone who might. "I swear."

37

"Has to be Suzy. Think about it."

Jeremy put a hand to his chin and pursed his lips—his imitation of a thoughtful look, which he'd probably seen in an ad somewhere. Lou and I waited for him to reveal some insight, but he was just, "You know that girl with the head who sits at the front of Mrs. Jensen's class? What's her name?"

Lou turned to me. "You're saying it has to be Suzy because everyone else who knows of the op are participants, and why would they suddenly have a problem with it?"

"And the murderer is definitely out of the running," I said. "He wouldn't do anything that might bring attention his way."

We were in Mr. Hearns' overpopulated class, taking a test, kids scribbling away around us, some of them two to a desk, others on file cabinets or on the floor in the aisles and at the back of the room. Mr. H had either stopped caring that people talked during tests or he'd accepted that he couldn't keep it from happening. Most tongue-waggers were discussing possible test answers, trying for a consensus on which were the right ones. Not me. Seeing all those questions about eukaryotes and cytokinesis, having no idea how to answer them, and not trusting the brainiacs around me, I texted Wilt. He'd taken Mr. H's class and his grades had been okay. I knew I wouldn't get him if I tried calling the contact *Wilt* on my phone, but maybe if I texted?

"He answered!" I said. To my text of *viruses r living - tru? false?* Wilt had come back with *F*. "Number three is false," I said.

Lou put pen to paper, but Jeremy didn't bother filling out his test, probably lusting after the girl with the head in Mrs. Jensen's class, who might've been either Karen Hudson or Juanita Cruz.

"I thought Suzy didn't want you snooping around because she was afraid you'd implicate her in whatever got Wilt killed," Lou said.

I thumbed Wilt a question about which structure synthesized proteins in cells: Golgi apparatus, lysosomes, vacuoles, or ribosomes. "Yeah," I said.

"So you're saying she didn't want you to implicate her because she wanted to implicate herself?"

"Makes sense to me," Jeremy said.

Ribosomes, Wilt texted. I was going to ace Mr. H's test. "I'll get more out of her later," I said, "at the game against Marshall."

To me, lacrosse looks like a bunch of guys in baseball umpire masks hacking at one another with long fruit-pickers, but I would've had to be blind not to see that Calvados was the best fruit-picking guy on the field—storming around beating on Marshall's players, spinning, catching and passing the ball, scoring. His every move screamed he was MVP-material, born to dominate.

"I know Rick gets jealous easily," Suzy was saying to me, "but it's no biggie. I don't belong to him. And what's there to be jealous of anyway? It's not like you and I are doing anything."

That last sentence hurt. It might have hurt worse, though, because even she didn't pretend it'd be okay for Rick to see us sitting together, else why would we have been *underneath* the bleachers? But if she'd wanted to sit up in the front row, out in the open for Calvados to see, I'd have done it. I would've risked a pummeling for Suzy.

On the field, Rick scored a goal/point/whatever, and I figured if he didn't get a scholarship to Duke, he'd get one to some other school where he'd hook up with rich girls till he found one whose dad owned a law firm or hedge fund for him to take over.

"You believe in psychics?" Suzy asked.

"What?"

"Fortune-telling and stuff. Do you think there are people with a heightened intuition who can see things we can't?"

"Why, you read palms or something?"

"No. I just mean would you want to know when and how you'll die, if you'll be rich or not, if you'll have a family?"

"I sort of have a family," I said.

"Yeah, but wouldn't you want to know if you'll be married, have kids, that kind of thing?"

"I haven't really thought about it."

Besides, I didn't say, *nowadays when I brood about the future, I think about how you'll soon be going far away to college, but how far away exactly, and what schools did you apply to because maybe I'll apply to the same ones, or at least, after high school, live and work wherever you end up.*

"I've got plans," I said.

"Yeah?"

"I know what I don't want. It doesn't mean I can tell you what I want, other than I plan on not dealing with what I don't want. I've been dealing with what I don't want long enough."

She put her hand on my knee. Her touch was a major privilege and I wanted my body to remember it always. Sitting there with my hard-on, my pulse thumping, my breath so shallow I couldn't get enough oxygen, I was all, *What would Wilt do? What would Wilt do?* knowing that if the thought-loop kept up, I was going to psych myself out.

I'd been doing a lot of brave stuff around then—some people would've called it stupidly brave—but out of everything, what I did next felt like it took the most courage. I leaned forward and kissed school-famous Suzy Painter. She didn't say a word. I thought I'd screwed up and nearly apologized. But then she gave me one of her coy, fake-shy smiles and kissed me back.

"You have something on your . . . chest," I said.

I covered her right breast with my hand—didn't squeeze or caress or anything, just held it there. I was supposed to be asking about the anonymous online postings I had seen at Yang's, but instead I had my hand on her boob and we were both staring down at it, as if what was happening below the neckline was happening to other people and we could go along with it or not. It was a sweet feeling, though, even over her clothes—to be cupping that hefty, warm part of Suzy.

Out of everything two bodies can do, I think French kissing is the most awesome because it teases of *more* while being super pleasurable itself. Suzy and I were going at it pretty heavily when my phone buzzed. She got immediately uncomfortable.

"It's not Wilt," I told her, in case that's what was bothering her. I held up my phone for her to see: Mom was calling. "I don't have to answer it."

"I think you should," she said, so into the phone I was like, "Yeah?" After listening to idiocy squawk at me through the other end of the line, I hung up.

"I shouldn't have answered," I said, looking out to where Rick was clobbering guys with his fruit-picker. "I gotta go."

"Everything okay?"

"I don't think so. Actually—no, everything is *not* okay."

"You want me to come with you?"

"Do I want you to come with me? Yeah, I want you to come with me. Do I think you *should* come with me? Uh uh."

We kissed. She petted my cheek with her fingers and tickled my ear with a whisper: "I'll come over tonight."

I tried to convince myself it was a good thing I was leaving, that Wilt would say it proved I wasn't an eager beaver, which would make Suzy want me more. Also, it meant Calvados couldn't happen to glance at the bleachers and see me and Suzy stepping out from underneath them as a couple. Just because I'd risk a pummeling from the guy didn't mean I wanted one.

39

The manager of the 99¢ Store was frowning like a cartoon character, the corners of his lips practically below his jaw. On a table made out of an old door and two saw horses: vacuum bags, toilet brushes, latex-free gloves, dustpans, glass cleaners, bleach powders, sponges, Pledge and 409 knockoffs in spray bottles, a bunch of other crap.

"The only reason I haven't called the police is because you're regular customers," he said. "That's over $100 worth of merchandise."

We were in the back office—me, Mom, Okafur, Narith, some Indian girl I'd never seen before.

And by Indian, I don't mean Native-American. I'm talking a girl from India.

Anyway.

Over $100 worth of merch, but there weren't 100 things on the table. At the 99¢ Store. Go figure.

Frowny Mr. Manager played a minute's worth of closed-circuit surveillance footage for my embarrassment. It showed Mom, Okafur, Narith, and the Indian girl pretending to browse the cleaning supplies. They were sucky actors—the parental clearly scoping for anyone who might be watching them, her head swiveling back and forth before she arm-swept glass cleaner into her tote, Okafur then stuffing packs of vacuum bags under his shirt, Narith loading up on latex gloves and toilet brushes and sponges, the Indian girl on dustpans. Next I saw the parental and her gang of found children on their way out of the store, clothes bulging with their hoardings, being stopped by the manager and a security guard.

The manager paused the footage, and I don't know how else to describe it except—all I heard, all I felt, was anger pooling into my fists. What'd the parental need so many cleaning supplies for? Our own apartment had been dusted and vacuumed to the point of sterility. Was she hoping to use her found children as a way to make extra cash, pimping them out as housekeepers?

"I've explained that your siblings are new to this country," she started, but I gave her a look that shut her up.

"I was kind of expecting your father," the manager said.

We'd been shopping in the 99¢ Store for as long as we'd lived in Pappas's building, but that didn't mean Mr. Frowny knew jack about our family. I unpocketed a wad of cash, making sure he saw how big it was. I lightened it of $200, which I put on the table. I waited.

"I can agree to let this incident pass," he said, "but only if your mother promises never to set foot in here again. You yourself are okay. But your mother, these kids here—I don't want to see them again. And they have to promise."

Why he'd trust the word of people who'd just been caught stealing from him, I didn't get. But whatever. I turned to the parental.

"All right," she said, like a pouty kid being forced to apologize. "I promise."

"Me too," Narith said.

Okafur nodded.

"Arundhati?" the parental said to the Indian girl.

"I too promise."

By the time we were outside the store, I needed to swing and kick out at something.

"Please don't tell Detective Abrams about any of this," the parental said, ripping open a fresh nicotine patch. "Or Dr. Murray."

I shoved a ball of twenties at her. "Next time you want a new dustpan, *buy* it."

Her lips quivered, a sign that she was about to cry, and I was like, *At least she feels bad for making Okafur and Narith and this Arundhati girl play at thieves.*

"You're turning into quite the young man," she said. "I must be doing something right."

That was it for me. I kicked over the garbage can on the street corner, punched the air, ripped flyers off the streetlamp, punched the air. As if they were glad for something to do, Okafur and Narith set about righting the garbage can and cleaning up the tumbled bottles, greasy wads of paper, and scummy plastic and Styro bits. Arundhati stood button-eyed, unmoving, probably doubting that her new situation was going to be an improvement over where she'd been before.

"Whatever I am or will be," I said to the parental, "assuming it's any 'good' at all, is *despite* you."

Huffing away, I saw Nuñez standing across the street. He was out in the open like he wanted me to see him, not trying for stealth. I assumed Yang had ordered him to tail me, but when the parental and her found children moved off in the opposite direction, he followed *them*.

40

The one time I'd officially tried to go off meds—completely, I'm talking—I didn't get far. Dr. Polk said it was best to take things slow, so he'd lower my daily dosage from 300 mg of Effexor to 225 and we'd see how that went. I didn't figure the change would be any big deal, but after a week I was sparking into rages at everything—being given detention, having to wait in line at 7-11, it didn't matter. Also, there was no difference in how angry I got, whether what set me off was large or small, like Dad not showing up for a court-approved visit or Wilt eating the last of the chocolate chip ice cream in the apartment. After a couple-few weeks on 225 mg, I stopped getting angry so often, but only because I had this soundtrack of constant negativity in my head.

Everything I said and did was wrong or stupid.

Everything I *thought* was stupid—except the thought that everything I thought was stupid.

I was ugly.

I only caused problems—for others, for myself.

I was in this deep wide long crater that I couldn't get out of. Worse: I knew that the negativity in my head had no basis in fact—that like, I was mentally beating myself up for no real reason but couldn't keep from doing it—because of which, I fell deeper into depression and self-hatred.

Dr. P had me scribble all this down on a piece of paper from his yellow legal pad, which he put in my file, saying he'd show it to me again if I ever doubted my meds were working. I figured it just wasn't the right time to go off meds and went back to swallowing 300 mg of Effexor a day. My mental state returned to the less imperfect balance I was used to, where the craters weren't so wide and deep that I couldn't climb out of them. By that point I wasn't sure if I was popping meds because I was supposed to be hyper, depressed, some combo of the two, or what.

"Depressed," Dr. P said when I asked him.

The Effexor eventually stopped working. It felt like I'd stepped down in dosage when I hadn't. Dr. P switched me to Fluoxetine, gradually ramping up my dose while simultaneously, gradually, lowering my intake of Effexor, as a way to keep the electrochemical happenings in my brain from making me a truly messed up bummerwad.

Except after the 99¢ Store? I thought I should maybe increase my daily dosage. I needed *something* to help me cope better with family. In the short term, though, kicking garbage cans and punching air wasn't going to clear my head, so I took out my lists and added to them, in case *that* might.

WHAT I KNOW, I KNOW

Wilt says he died by accident but he was definitely murdered.

Wilt had a job feeding rich people's dogs. (NUÑEZ. YANG.)

Yang is definitely NUÑEZ'S Boss.

The $ Wilt had when he died he made feeding Yang's (~~mostly~~) scary dogs.

YANG runs a dogfight op.

Wilt and Suzy were scheming to try and shut down the dogfight op

Wilt reported the dogfight op to the cops: nothing happened.

The car Wilt died in had been rigged with some kind of device

Rick C. is (probably) not involved with YANG / NUÑEZ.

Rick C. is an asshole.

I have to talk to Dr. P about Mom. She needs professional help.

I shouldn't take my anger out on Okafur, Navitu, Arundhati.

YANG / NUÑEZ don't themselves seem to have killed Wilt.

Detective Abrams probably isn't on YANG's payroll.

I hooked up with Suzy Painter!

WHAT I KNOW I DON'T KNOW

IF YANG knew about Wilt's anonymous call to the cops. (Probably not)

If cops on YANG's payroll = why nothing happened when Wilt called them.

~~If Abrams himself is on YANG's payroll.~~

If Suzy told me everything or is still hiding something about Wilt's death.

What exactly Suzy is hiding.

~~If Yang (Nuñez) killed Wilt or if~~ somebody else in the dogfight ring ~~did~~ killed Wilt. Who? Why

How exactly the murderer knew Wilt would be driving Mom's car.

How Wilt first started working for Nuñez and Yang.

How I'll survive not just losing Wilt, but Mom's off-the-wall craziness.

If Suzy is posting damaging stuff about Yang online.

WHAT I DON'T KNOW I DON'T KNOW

???

WHAT I KNOW THAT I DIDN'T KNOW I KNEW

Wilt loved dogs. He would have hated YANG.

The extent of Rick's assholeness.
Is way more than I thought.

It might never be the right time to get off meds.

41

"We're going to have to move soon, and how's that supposed to work?" I was at Forest Lawn cemetery, on the phone with Wilt. I'd been hanging with the Dobbs, Lindhursts, and Millers when he called. "All the kids Mom's filling the apartment with? We'll need a bigger place, but that's not doable on her salary. And mine might be ending."

I explained about Tom Birch's moped accident and how Pappas's building seemed to be emptying of tenants by the week. I told him I'd been busted by Nuñez at St. Benny and interrogated by Yang at the Tudor.

"Damnit, what'd I tell you? Keep your head down, do what little was asked of you, and earn enough money to get out of living in slummy buildings forever, maybe even enough for college."

"I know," I said.

"And if you couldn't do that, what were you supposed to do?"

"Quit without complaining or making a stink about anything I saw. Swear on my life that I hadn't *seen* anything. But was that—what I was supposed to do—because *you* couldn't do it, and look what happened? You didn't just keep your head down and pretend not to see anything?"

"No. I didn't."

In the oldest part of Forest Lawn, where the headstones weren't flat plaques in the grass but ancient slabs of pocked cement leaning at woozy angles, a groundskeeper turned on the sprinklers.

"Out of newfound respect for your opinions," Wilt said, "I've been trying to entertain the possibility that I was murdered. But I haven't come up with a single reason why anyone would want to hurt me. Not Nuñez. Not Yang. Not anybody else. And do you know why? Because I never got far enough in my plan to torpedo Yang's dogfight syndicate that anyone could've known."

"So then you *did* have more of a plan? When the cops didn't follow up on your anonymous tips, you weren't done, right? Did you know the cops are on Yang's payroll?"

"Would I have made an anonymous call to them if I'd known they were on the take?"

"Okay, probably not. But did your plan involve spreading rumors about Yang, like creating a public awareness campaign tying Yang to the killing of dog-beasties, with untraceable links posted on blogs and sent to news sites? Because if it did, if that was your plan, I think Suzy might be carrying it out. It's apparently not okay for me to risk her life, but it's okay for her to risk mine. And her own."

"Suzy's good people. If I thought she was guilty of anything except being shockingly humble for someone so beautiful, do you think I'd help you hook up with her?"

"No, I know. It's just, if she's—"

"How're you guys doing anyway?"

It seemed like people were always wanting to change the subject with me, whatever it might be, and no way I would've let *him* change it if I hadn't needed his advice for what I hoped might happen with Suzy a few hours later.

"We made out a little," I told him. "At one of Calvados's games."

"Excellent."

"She's coming over later and I'm not sure how to handle it."

Excited, like he was the one who might get laid by the loveliest girl he'd ever seen, he said if Mom's apartment was as crowded with pseudo-siblings as I claimed, and I wanted anything more than kissing or copping a feel to happen, I should deck out Mrs. Holt's place ne xt door—candles, flowers, incense, music—and hang with Suzy there.

"I don't remember her being so shy back when I used to hear you guys going at it."

"That wasn't our first time," Wilt said. "The first time needs to have some romance to it."

"You don't think candles and flowers'll be, I don't know, too eager beaver?"

"Accept my wisdom without question, doucheface. I've been clueing you in on a need-to-know basis. There's a difference between off-putting over-enthusiasm and showing a girl you genuinely like her. With Suzy: in the beginning, yes, the more aloof you are, the less eager beaver you are, the more quiet and mysterious you'll seem, and that's good. But once she's interested in you, you surprise her with a blatant, tender show of affection, which she'll consider more special than she would have, because it's never happened before."

"Seems kind of manipulative."

"Do you like her like her or do you just want into her pants?"

"I like her like her." *Love*, I didn't say.

"Then you do everything you can to prove it. It's not as if you'll be lying. Just show her how you feel. You won't scare her off now."

After we hung up, I went back to the 99¢ Store and filled a shopping basket with candles, paper plates and napkins, plasticware and cups, a couple tablecloths, a gallon of bottled water, a two-litre bottle of root beer, and a 12-pack of condoms made in China. I bought a box of incense sticks from a street vendor—Nag Champa, the guy said, a favorite of ladies everywhere—and a bouquet of unidentifiable flowers. Then I went to Hugo's taqueria and ordered enough food to feed me and the pseudo-siblings for a week. In Pappas's slum, I left all this stuff in the hall outside Mrs. Holt's apartment, except for three chicken burritos, which I brought into my own hovel and gave to the pseudo-siblings. I interrupted their vacuuming and dusting and pantomimed for them to eat, even though I thought Arundhati might understand English as well as I do and Narith's probably wasn't as bad as he pretended. With them at the feeding table, gobbling dinner, I took sheets and a blanket from the front closet, two pillows off the living room couch, and Mrs. Holt's keys from the drawer in the kitchen.

"I won't be back for a while," I said on my way out. "Don't wait up."

I arranged Mrs. H's bedroom first—laid the blanket out on the floor where a bed might have been, flapped sheets open on top of it, and threw down the pillows so they would look casual. I put candles on both sides, as if they were on night-stands, and more candles in the corners of the room. I lit an incense stick, letting it burn in this little boat-thing I made out of aluminum foil that'd been wrapped around a taco. At first the Nag Champa smelled like wet dog, then like burnt paper, and then I stopped noticing it. I texted Suzy to tell her where I was and spent the impossibly long wait till she showed up checking the lay of sheets and blankets and rearranging the bedroom candles so many times I wound up with them back in their original positions.

"Oh," Suzy said, after her knock finally came and I let her into the living room, which I'd turned into a picnic scene, with plates and plasticware and neatly folded napkins on a checked tablecloth. She glanced toward the open bedroom, biting her lower lip and smiling, her eyes shifting up as if to read a thought bubble over her head. I was feeling pretty self-conscious and spit out what I said next:

"You hungry because I've got every taco known to man shrimp veggie beef pork mushroom cheese and burritos pork beef veggie shrimp three different kinds of salsa chicken quesadillas bean and cheese quesadillas guac and chips?" Suzy's bag beeped. "Tortas nachos rice?"

Suzy scavenged her phone out of her bag, looked at it like she might answer it, but didn't.

I poured root beer into cups for both of us and tried not to eat like a spazzy pig. My phone was in a corner, pumping out M.C. Freak of Nature, and we listened to him do his grunty thing for a while. *Aw. Unh. Aw. Unh.*

"Everything better with your mom?" Suzy asked.

"As better as it's ever going to get probably."

"That sounds sad."

"I don't mean it to. It's just a fact. Or feels like a fact anyway."

Suzy's bag beeped again. She pulled out her phone, glanced at it. "You know the surplus store on Shannon Road?"

"Yeah?" I said.

"I went there the other day. They were out of everything."

"That's a joke?"

"It's a joke."

She ate a shrimp taco with spicy salsa, half a veggie taco, some guac and chips. She lit a Marlboro Light and inhaled lungfuls of carcinogens while telling me something about Janelle. I tried to pay attention, but the way her under-jaw sloped down to her neck was distracting.

"If you're just an acquaintance and you're only 75% correct, that's okay," she said at one point. "But if I know you, it's got to be more like 90%, and I *know* Janelle."

Her phone beeped. She shut it off, stubbed out her cigarette. The M.C. Freak of Nature playlist had looped around to its opening track.

"So do I get a tour now that you've redecorated?"

The way she said it, with that teasing little upswing in her voice, I thought I was going to spooge my pants. I walked her around the living room, showing her where a couch would go, a coffee table, lamps, a desk. I moved toward the bathroom, figuring I'd explain about shower curtains and bath mats, but she stopped me.

"What about in there?"

She meant the bedroom. She was biting her lower lip again. I should've been the one easing us into the bedroom, but it was amazing to realize, even if already kind of obvious by her being there, that she was willing to fool around with me.

"Here's where I'd put a dresser," I said in the bedroom. "And against that wall, I don't know, a couple chairs with a little table between them."

"Wouldn't it be great if this really was your own place?" she asked.

"Except for the building it's in."

We stood against each other, so close our thighs touched. Her arms were around my neck. I had my hands at her waist, my thumbs pressing lightly on her belly. We let our mouths communicate by touch. When I eased my hand under her shirt, she shivered.

"Cold."

Yeah, because most of my blood's elsewhere, I didn't say, figuring she could feel that much through our clothes.

The worry I'd had with Meredith about things not working as they should? I didn't have it with Suzy. No matter where my head was, in stressville or wherever, Suzy's nearness always perked my body up. My boxers were stickywet from just making out. But with my nethers tingling intense like they wanted to get it all done with, for relief as much as anything, Suzy and I took it slow. Without acknowledging any kind of plan, we each stripped off one piece of clothing at a time—shirt, sock, another sock, pants—and spent the twenty minutes in between exploring the newly naked parts of each other's body.

I'd never been to third base, having kind of skipped over it with Meredith. I'd seen stuff online, sure, but not a how-to video, so.

Suzy and I were both down to our underwear, lying under the sheets. Maybe forty minutes had gone by and it was past time for me to get her naked. If I waited any longer, she'd think something was wrong. But before I could do more than touch her panties, she started working them down past thighs and knees and pedicured feet. And God, there's no bigger turn-on than seeing a girl like Suzy wiggle off panties. I shimmied out of my boxers, and we let our hands trace around on each other, toying, avoiding our money spots. My hard-on kept poking her leg, which was delicious enough, but when she stroked me a couple times? I'm not trying to be sappy, it's just—I didn't know till then that I was physically capable of feeling so much. Wonderfulness oozed out of every pore. The universe had become a boner of pleasure. I was tempted to just lie there and *feel*, but I finally went for it, reached down and petted her pubes like they were the fur of some gerbil.

"What would I, Suzy, do?" she said, guiding my fingers, teaching them what to feel for, what she wanted.

We used up a quarter of the condoms before falling asleep, and if I could've forgotten Wilt's death, which was pretty much what had brought me to that exact place in time, it would've been the best night of my life.

"It's not fair. Why me? *Me?*"

Dr. M's voice whined through the air vent into Mrs. Holt's bedroom. Suzy was still asleep, lying on her side with her back to me, and looking at that knobby ridge of spine, I thought I might not be as caged in as it seemed, that options were open to me I wasn't aware of. Because with or without Wilt's death, I wouldn't ever have imagined I had the chance of being with Suzy. But there she was, naked, close enough for me to run a finger down the length of her spine. I saw possibility in that spine.

"What did *I* do?"

Dr. M sounded like a bullied, helpless kid. And considering the way he always power-tripped at school, trying to come off as an authority figure, it was pretty funny. As in funny-lame.

"I'm sure it was just a misunderstanding," I heard Mom say.

"But what'd I do to be misunderstood by homicide detectives?"

Murray whined as if it was his new favorite hobby, and I caught enough to understand: Abrams and his partner had yanked Dr. M from school in front of Principal Chu and a student horde. They'd hauled him to the police station and asked him where he was the night of Wilt's death, could anyone verify his whereabouts, that kind of thing. No way Abrams considered Dr. M a suspect. He must've just wanted to screw with the guy, his competition for Mom. Still, it was good to know that lame-o Dr. M had squirmed through a Q&A with authority figures the way he was always making me do.

"Did I hear Dr. Murray?" Suzy had rolled over to face me.

"Yeah. He and my mom. Sometimes."

"Ew."

"Tell me about it."

I should've just lain there facing her. I should've kissed her, cuddled, let my body do the talking. But I guess I was too used to not having a good thing, so instead was all, "Those posts on PETA blogs about Titus Yang? The anonymous comments about Yang and dogfights? Those are you."

Suzy sat up and hugged her knees. The candles and incense had burned out. Her panties were on the carpet beside the bed, with the leftover condoms. She reached for them, started gathering up her clothes.

"I'm doing it as a tribute to Wilt," she said. "If enough people get angry and speak out against the cruelty, the police will *have* to look into it and Yang might be shut down for all time."

"Yeah, but he thinks it's me."

"I didn't know you were working for him until after I had already started."

"So, what? You didn't want me snooping around 'cause you knew how it'd look for me?"

"And I didn't think I should tell you either. Because then, if you were ever asked, you wouldn't have to lie: you really wouldn't know anything."

Fully dressed, she was at the bathroom mirror, hand-brushing her hair.

"One of the detectives working Wilt's case, the one who's probably not on Yang's payroll?" I said. "I told him about the dog-fighting. He's supposed to be looking into things."

"And you think if he has to choose between arresting a mega-mogul or toeing the line with the rest of his cop friends, he's going to arrest the mega-mogul?"

It was a good question. I didn't have an answer, or any idea what Suzy would've done if I'd asked her to lay off the public awareness campaign against Yang, to forget every bad thing as much as possible and just go back to anticipating whatever distant college she'd soon be at. But since Yang had already pegged me as the troublemaker, since I knew the overall situation couldn't hold much longer . . . if Suzy was helping bring it to a head with her online posts, why should I get in the way? So even though she hadn't come close to hinting she'd ever quit—

"Keep doing what you're doing," I said. "Don't stop."

Alone, I cleaned up Mrs. Holt's place. I felt warm and easy all over, and maybe because Suzy and I'd spent so many hours skin to skin and the whole of what we'd done hadn't involved just our nether regions, I didn't have to try to hold on to the feeling.

The total opposite of how it'd been with Meredith, when my body seemed to forget it'd had sex fifteen minutes afterwards.

The warm easy feeling made facing Mom easier—left me as relaxed as I could've possibly been after I'd stayed out the entire night, strutting into the apartment and seeing her for the first time since the 99¢ Store. I expected her to act like the 99¢ Store had never happened, to lay into me because a mother worries and why hadn't I texted or called to let her know she wouldn't find me in the apartment when she came home from her UPS shift but I was safe, and all that kind of crap.

Except she surprised me.

The pseudo-siblings weren't hustling about yet. She asked me to sit down with her at the feeding table.

"Curtis," she said, her voice gentle and cautious, like it was feeling its way through dark, unknown territory, "are you dealing drugs?"

"What?"

She put the cash-wad I'd given her on the table. "All the money you have these days. I'm concerned."

"But I'm not."

She thumbed through the cash, to remind me how much was there. "I'm going to ask you again and I want the truth. Are. You. Dealing. Drugs?"

"No."

"Because I don't know how I'd survive if anything happened to you. I can't have you involved in the same dangerous behavior that got Wilt killed."

She said that last sentence fast, as if she hoped not to take in the meaning of her own words.

"That's the first I've heard you admit Wilt's dying probably wasn't an accident."

"It's not only violence I'm worried about, hon. What if Detective Abrams catches you? Please, for all of us," she nodded toward the bedroom, where Okafur, Narith, and Arundhati were making wake-up noises, "get out of dealing whatever it is you're dealing. Completely and forever out of it. Please."

"Okay. But I'm not dealing."

"We don't have to talk more about it. You know how I feel."

I debated whether to tell her that my not being a dealer in no way lessened the threat of violence. That the dangerous behavior I was engaged in wouldn't get just me killed, but that if things went as bad as they seemed about to, I didn't think she and Dad would be around to mourn me—the pseudo-siblings either. Not that I expected *them* to mourn, but still.

"Dr. Murray believes you could be a great student if you made a little effort," Mom said. "He says there are kids who can't be good students no matter what, they don't have it in them, but that isn't you."

"To recognize brains, it helps to have some in your own head. Which Murray doesn't, so."

The pseudo-siblings were up and about, Okafur doing his breakfast-chef thing in the kitchen, Arundhati setting place-mats on the table in front of me and Mom, Narith laying out cups and plasticware and folded paper towels.

"You know what?" I said. "You need me to stop dealing? Here's what I need: for all *this* to stop." I flapped a hand at Narith, who was pouring OJ into our cups, and at Arundhati carrying out butter and jelly and a plate of toast. "I get that you're seri-ously upset and angry and disappointed and you've been that way even before Wilt died. We all have. But using Wilt's death as an excuse for recruiting kids to be your servants? Not cool."

The kitchen had gone quiet. Narith and Arundhati had stopped playing wait staff. The pseudo-siblings were standing close together, watching us—so close they would've looked like they were posing for some cultural diversity PSA if they'd been smiling.

Mom ripped open a nicotine patch.

"All they do is vacuum, dust, wash dishes, and clean the toilet," I said. "Whenever they're not serving breakfast or ser-ving you in some other kind of way, I mean."

She was genuinely surprised: did the same little chicken-bob with her head that she'd done the first time I answered Wilt's phone calls. "But they asked to do those things. It was *their* idea."

"Yeah. Like three of them independently asked to do chores all day long."

"Not exactly, no."

She explained how the first time Okafur saw her break out the vacuum, he stepped to her, shaking his head. She didn't understand what he wanted, unwound the vacuum's AC cord and plugged it into the wall socket. Okafur gripped the vacuum and pointed to himself. She was like *oh* and backed off to let him use it. Except he didn't know how to turn the thing on. He got mighty startled when he heard the noise it made, but Mom pushed it around on the carpet to show him there was nothing to be afraid of, so he went ahead and moved the vacuum up and back, real tentative, and because he seemed to want, almost need, encouragement, she'd given it to him.

I remembered the night I'd met Okafur, how I'd passed through the living room and seen him handling the vacuum like it was a possibly dangerous beast, Mom shouting at him over the noise, "That's it! Perfect!"

"It was the same with the dishes and everything else," Mom said. "Whenever he saw me start a household chore, he insisted on doing it himself. And when Narith came to live with us, he saw everything Okafur was doing and volunteered to sweep the ceiling."

"*I* thought it was a competition," Arundhati said.

"And what about the 99¢ Store?" I asked. "Was that their idea too? And the whole waiter/busboy thing?"

Mom folded the nicotine patch in on itself, took a second before answering.

"It wouldn't hurt them to learn a marketable skill, would it?"

"Stealing or cleaning?"

"Cleaning."

Maybe I don't make good decisions most of the time, but that doesn't stop me from being boggled by the stupid decisions others make. Especially a parent.

Mom blinked awhile at the plate of cold toast, then pocketed the unused nicotine patch and got up from the table. She led Okafur to her chair and coaxed him to sit. When she took a pile of mail and old magazines off another chair, motioning for Narith to pop a squat, I understood what was happening and pushed back from the table.

"Have a seat," I said to Arundhati.

Mom and I laid out fresh place settings, poured OJ and water into cups. In the kitchen, she scrambled eggs while I made toast and coffee. A few minutes later we were serving Okafur and Narith and Arundhati breakfast like we were waiters at Chili's, but they only eyed their food till Mom said, "Please, eat. It'll go to waste if you don't."

I ran into Abrams on the sixth floor landing, couldn't keep the smirk from my face. "You brought Dr. Murray in for questioning?"

"Yeah. That guy."

"He's a loser."

"I'd call him worse, but yeah." Abrams' breathing was creaky as an old rocker in the wind. "I've noticed chatter in the blogosphere. About Titus Yang."

"Huh. How's your partner?"

"Getting it sorted. Tell me you've been smart. Have nothing to do with the internet chatter about Yang."

"I have nothing to do with it."

"I don't believe you."

"You're not alone."

He jammed an unlit cigarette between his lips, which somehow calmed his lungs and gave him breath to say, "You asked for two weeks before I moved to shutdown the dogfight operation. That was because you had a scheme you wanted time to work. I'm not necessarily giving you the time you asked for—I'm just being thorough, an absolute necessity with a man of Yang's stature. But why do you assume those online postings won't make Yang uneasy enough to stop his illegal activities any less than if I was noticeably poking around?"

"I don't. I'm not happy about them. But you didn't make it obvious you had the balls to ever bust Yang."

Out came his Zippo. *Chk chk.* He lit his cigarette and inhaled once, deeply, before pinching it out between saliva-wet finger and thumb. "Just because you think something, that doesn't mean you have to say it aloud, you know." The cigarette slid back into its pack. "I foresee a day when you'll spend some time at the station, for your own safety. We'll call it Visit-Your-Mother's-Boyfriend-at-Work Day."

He'd elevated himself to boyfriend status, but I didn't give him a hard time about it—a reward for what he'd done to Dr. M. "You here 'cause you've got something new on my brother's case?" I asked.

It was weird the way Abrams could be the universe-weary cop one second, a guy with this shambling resignation to the fucked-upness of things, and the next second, whenever his thoughts turned to Mom, a self-conscious stutterer.

There was nothing new on my brother's case, he said.

I left him to his climb and his hope of rescuing Mom from her life in a dinky ten-floor walkup, as if she were some kind of Rapunzel. Did he know that he couldn't rescue her because she was her own prison tower? Probably. He wasn't stupid. Which meant he wanted her, prison tower and all.

One of the ground-floor apartments was open, Pappas showing a bunch of paunchy geezers around inside. I hid in the stairwell and watched them through the steel door's mesh. The geezers were moneymen, I guessed: the investor/developers buying the building. Some of them might've been the same guys I'd scoped Pappas with at St. Benny. It was hard to tell. Except for one guy whose ill-fitting suit wasn't of a piece with the others' and whose head-carpet I could've picked from a line-up in any wigshop window.

One guy I couldn't help but recognize: Titus Yang.

Pappas always kept the basement chained and locked. It had to be a fire hazard: access to any back door nil, the only exit from the building being through the front lobby. I waited until the troll and his moneymen waddled deeper into the apartment and out of view, then sprang from the stairwell, and almost before I could think *belly button worm*, I was through the lobby and outside. The street looked like St. Benny on fight night, with limos and Beemers and Mercedes parked in a line at the curb. Except no Nuñez. And none of Yang's goons that I recognized.

One Mercedes was a classic from the 1960s or whenever. Its hood was up, the chauffeurs gathered around inspecting its engine. Because I wasn't anyone's boss, they barely registered my existence. I went down the block and crouched in the tall weeds of the lavanderia lot and scoped them with the binocular app on my phone. When Pappas and his investors came out onto the street, the chauffeurs hustled to their respective fancy-mobiles—all except the driver whose Mercedes had its hood up, and who seemed to explain the problem to his boss and Pappas. Mr. Money lowered himself into the Mercedes and went to work with his phone. Pappas lay on his back, half underneath the car. Minutes passed. The chauffeur tried the ignition and the engine started up. Pappas got to his feet and shut the Mercedes' hood.

Not till later did I realize what I'd just seen.

42

I'd asked Abrams for two weeks. Why not three or one? I was still so clueless about how to skunk out Wilt's murderer, I was afraid I'd never be anything else, no matter how many weeks the detective let me have. But I figured the best way to show Yang that I wasn't responsible for the online postings was to go about my job as normally as I could.

Not that I expected to convince him.

It was just, Nuñez hadn't fired me and I thought it would look more suspicious if I stopped showing up. Besides, if I didn't try to run or hide, maybe Yang wouldn't hurt Mom or Dad or anyone else. Maybe he'd focus his payback on me alone.

So I kept to my bird street routines—before and after school visited the Tudor and other mansions, scooping poop, feeding organic steaks to frothing dog-beasties, filling bowls with filtered water, a mix of dry and wet foods, all while dressed as the mascot of a tire manufacturer. Then came the day Presa at the New England Colonial didn't go psycho at the first whiff of me—not as psycho as he usually did. His water and food bowls were full. No crap was piled anywhere in the run. I found the guesthouse unlocked and open, and on the back of the door where Michelin Man should've been hanging, the new Michelin Man that'd replaced the one Presa had fanged to shreds with me inside it? Nothing but an empty hook. Which I didn't look at for more than a few seconds before I heard laughter and stepped back out to the yard.

Splashing. More laughter. Coming from Meredith's place.

I went over, peeped between vertical slats of the fence that separated the two yards, and got an eyeful of Michelin Man standing by a lounger, Meredith rising up out of the pool, topless.

"Don't take it personally."

I jumped. For a cinder block of a guy, Nuñez had stealth.

"She's done it with everyone who's worn that suit," he said. "Your brother before you. Calvados before your brother."

Thoughts churned. My brother? Had Wilt cheated on Suzy? One thought foamed up above the others, though. "*Rick* Calvados?"

"He said he had to quit to focus on lacrosse."

Calvados had recommended my brother for the job? Did that mean anything? Like Lou had said, Calvados lived bird street adjacent. Maybe Calvados's dad knew Yang through business? Except why would Wilt be hush-hush about who'd recommended him for the job? Why not tell Suzy? So much info was coming at me all the time, it felt impossible to separate what mattered from what didn't.

Next door, Meredith and her new guy went horizontal on the lounger. What'd I care about Meredith when I had Suzy?

"That's Phil with her," Nuñez said. "He's your replacement, and *that* you can take personally."

"I didn't do anything wrong."

"Maybe you didn't, but this is the last you get."

He handed me a small fold of cash. Yang was firing me as a kind of protective measure, I knew, as a way of keeping me out of the loop. He was being careful, which explained why none of the beasties on my route had any fresh wounds: there'd been no fights since boss-man found out about the online postings. And there wouldn't be any fights until the chatter faded and was forgotten, which'd make skunking out Wilt's killer impossible.

Yang's precautions meant one good thing, though: rich as he was, he didn't suppose he was untouchable. I seriously hoped Abrams had the balls to bust him. Or wanted to impress Mom enough that he'd do whatever was necessary to catch Wilt's murderer, even if that meant arresting a mega-mogul instead of staying true to his on-the-take cop buddies.

Nuñez asked for the burner he'd given me my first day of work.

"It's not on me," I said, which was true. I always dropped it in bushes a block from whichever mansion I visited and picked it up again afterwards, wanting Abrams to eventually have it as evidence.

Nuñez frisked me and checked my backpack, shook his head like my being without the burner was another example of why I was being fired. He didn't have to tell me I'd be seeing him again. He followed me around to the front of the house and stood in the driveway to make sure I left the property.

Forget catching a killer or sabotaging Yang's op. I hadn't rescued a single dog-beastie. I'd risked myself and nearly everyone I cared about, and for what? A pocketful of cash? I'd blown it big-time.

43

I told Wilt that Yang had given me the boot and he said I was lucky, it showed that the mogul wasn't concerned about me, despite everything. He said at least I'd made some money before butting my way into real trouble, and as much as dogfighting sucked, I should forget Yang and leave things to the authorities.

"What about Suzy?" I asked.

"She should leave things to the authorities too, but you can't control her, can you?"

He never brought any of it up again—not dogfighting, St. Benny, Nuñez, nothing. Which made my failure to catch his murderer or rescue abused beasties seem worse. He also stopped calling so often, telling me not to read anything into it, he was just busy with the "logistics of impending rebellion."

Whatever.

I didn't like admitting it, not even to myself, but his not calling so much was sort of all right. Whenever I heard his voice, it only reminded me how much I'd failed him. Besides, I didn't want him to worry: Yang wasn't as free and easy about me as he thought, and the less Wilt called, the less tempted

I'd be to confess that I was seeing Nuñez's hate crimers every-where. They stepped unexpectedly from around street corners, appeared behind me in line at a 7-11, drove past as I was mak-ing my way to or from school. Something might flash in the corner of my eye and I'd think, *This is it!* It got so that before I left school or Dr. Polk's office, before I left anywhere at any-time, I'd peek at the wide world outside. If Nuñez's goons were in sight, I'd try for an alternate exit and lose them, but when they caught up with me again, and they always did, they'd make themselves more than ordinarily visible, as if to say there was no point trying to hide.

I had zero idea if the hate crimers were going to abduct me or what. Maybe they'd press me hard to confess everything I knew—which, even if I did, might not satisfy Yang. Or maybe I'd come home at some point and find the apartment ransacked, Mom and the pseudo-siblings lacking certain vital organs. It wouldn't have been all that consistent for the hate crimers to get violent on me or mine. If Yang was taking precautions to protect himself by easing off the dogfights, it made no sense for his underlings to bloody the extended Brooks clan, which could attract attention from honest cops. But since when are people consistent? Eventually, I almost convinced myself I was dealing with a best-case scenario, that Nuñez's goons were just keeping tabs on me till Yang was sure the smear campaign had ended and he could again crank the dogfight op into action.

Problem: the smear campaign wasn't going to end.

In Mrs. Holt's apartment, Suzy would show me her latest posts about Yang, complete with pictures of brutalized dogs she'd found online. Sometimes she would talk about the col-leges she was getting acceptances/rejections from, or about little things, like how Mr. Hearns droned on to his overstuffed classes or kids in school bullshitted about this or that. But her main subject was always Yang and how she wouldn't lay off him until dog-beasties were safe from his abuse forever. I'd bought another twelve-pack of condoms, and Suzy and I used most of them, but it was always while we were gabbing about trivial subjects that I felt, I don't know, like we were delving into the profound. Like in the brief minutes when we managed to (mostly) ignore Yang and everything he represented, being in each other's company made all looming danger seem trivial. The complaints we had about daily living became laughable. Unfair teachers, the tyranny of adults in general, the tests that were supposed to be evidence of whether we were stupid or smart, whether we had potential as maturing citizens or not: Who cared? For me, yeah, there was always in the background the idea that all of these things were ridiculous compared to the threat of Yang, which probably wouldn't end up being trivial. But when Suzy complained about her "ear-loogeys," the way I used to hear her do with Wilt, I could believe that nothing outside ourselves should be taken seriously.

Too bad the feeling never lasted. Not for me anyway. And especially not after we left Mrs. Holt's. I didn't know if Suzy and I were boyfriend/girlfriend and I wasn't dweeb enough to ask. At school, if Rick wasn't around, I'd hang with her between classes and during free periods—nothing more or less than I'd been doing since Wilt's death. Calvados would smack me with his fruit-picker every time we passed in the hall, and if he happened to catch me with Suzy, I knew I was going to get an extra smack or two the next time he found me alone and he'd be, "Hey, Suze, I need your advice about something important. Right now." She'd give me this glance that was supposed to imply Rick was a difficult character who needed humoring, that his jealousy was harmless and even kind of pitiable, and what else could she do but go with him? I didn't buy it. Why'd she want to hang out with that athletic ape instead of with me?

We fooled around behind the HVAC unit once, Suzy and I, but only because we knew Calvados was with recruiters from Duke, and even then we didn't go at it long. She was more worried that Nisa or Janelle might come looking for her than about Nuñez's hate crimers, who were staked out at the edge of the playground and had seen us duck behind the HVAC.

"Why're we being sneaky?" I finally asked.

"You know why."

"Rick Calvados can eat me."

I never stopped scoping her with the guy—in the cafeteria or wherever—and every time I did was one time too many.

Lou and Jeremy meanwhile kept at me with the usual sarcasm:

"There she goes, Jer."

"Who's that, Lou?"

"The girl whose pants our friend Curtis absolutely *shuns*."

Everything was a letdown. I'd imagined that being with Suzy would change my life. I'd thought asking Rick about his job for Yang and why he'd recommended Wilt to take his place would prove something. All he said was, "You have a problem with work?" Plus, I was seeing too much of weasel-boy Winkleman from seventh grade, who daily came into my classes with a note that Dr. M wanted me in his office.

Doofus-face, lame-ass, loser-man Dr. M.

Rumor had it that on account of his interview with Abrams at the precinct, he was undergoing evaluations. Principal Chu had to determine whether or not the guy was a liability to kids. Chu should've asked me. I'd have said the doof was a liability by nature, not because of anything he'd done to be singled out by the cops.

In Dr. M's pathetic office, I'd get an earful of how of course it was okay for me to mourn Wilt, it was the most natural thing in the world to grieve the loss of a loved one, but it wasn't okay for grief to turn me into a nutbag. Dr. M seemed to have given up on the wannabe-gangsta speak altogether, always tongue-wagging formal instead, with a lot of *one* should do this and *one* should do that.

"After a tragedy one has to re-engage with the world in a rational way," he said.

He babbled on about how it was past time for me to be done with my delusions and admit that Wilt's calls were imaginary. He spewed about "crisis apparitions" and "auditory hallucina-tions"—the same jargon I'd found online by typing "dead rel-ative phone calls" into Google. Every day he hunkered toward me in his chair, his under-eyes sweaty and desperation in his voice, like if he could convince me to give up my so-called delusions, it might somehow allow him to keep hugging his own. And yeah, more than often, I wanted to tell the loser to fuck off and leave me be. Probably I could've asked him how his relationship with Mom was going, snarked, "Tell her I say hello next time you see her," and he'd have pushed me out of his office quick enough, not wanting to dish on his personal life. But instead I'd just sit there, watching his mouth move, wondering what kind of kid he'd been at my age, what traumas he'd been subjected to by parentals and people at school.

I never lied, though. Never said that I'd made up the phone calls. Wilt was actually, literally calling me, I insisted, and no amount of pleading on Dr. M's part ever got me to say otherwise.

Except the suckiest thing? Or maybe I should say *another* suckiest thing? Dr. M seemed to be the only one who still remembered, let alone cared, that Wilt was (allegedly) calling me. Not that I needed the kind of popularity the calls had brought. Popularity's overrated, even if you have to be popular at least once in your life to find that out. It was just, people had moved on to other gossip—Rochelle Newton's pregnancy, Dennis Watley being busted for selling meth, who knows what. It didn't matter if the gossip-hounds had believed I was getting calls from Wilt or not. It didn't matter if they'd thought the calls made me a religious freak or a sort of Oprah Winfrey to the dead. It didn't matter if they'd thought I was inventing the calls to beg off homework or to attract attention from girls—everyone had gotten bored and moved on. They acted as if Wilt's calls had been entertainment, something to occupy them when there was nothing else to talk about, a story gone viral, passed around like the weirdest/creepiest thing ever but which the next week was replaced by another weirdest/creepiest story ever.

Anyway.

So much was happening/not-happening that I forgot to show up for a visit with Dad. He called the next afternoon and asked where I'd been.

"I don't ask where you are every day," I told him, which didn't make total sense as a response, but he seemed to recognize it as the non-answer he used to give whenever Wilt asked about his job.

We rescheduled, and a couple nights later, before leaving Pappas's building, I did my new usual—checked for any sign of hate crimers. I liked to know exactly where they were when I ventured out into the open. Not that the knowledge gave me any advantage. I spotted them easily enough, parked across the street in their Escalade, in front of the derelict auto body place. I stepped from the building. The city air stunk like an unwashed armpit. With a three-block hike to the bus stop and buses that showed up as erratically as Mom's sanity, I knew I'd be late to dinner with Dad. Nuñez's goons were eyeing me, and I don't know, but I felt exhausted all of a sudden and wanted to get whatever was ultimately going to happen to me over with, so I walked toward them. They both shifted, the better to access their weapons probably, and I remember thinking that if I lunged or made a quick move, they might overreact and put a bullet in me. No doubt I should've been scared, but like I said, I was more tired than anything else.

"You guys give me a ride to the Chili's on Larrimore?" I asked. "I'll save bus fare, and you're going to end up there anyway, so."

The driver turned to his partner. If any signal of agreement passed between them, I didn't see it. I got the nod to climb into the back seat, which was covered in this black leather soft enough that it practically swallowed me. I wouldn't have minded if it had. I didn't figure the goons would admit what Yang's plan for me was, so I didn't ask.

Larry's Taco and Pizza, Bargain Warehouse All Items Under $1, Politically Correct By Day, Bacardi By Night scrolled past outside my window. Junk! Up to 10% Off!, Disney Collector's Cup with Every Purchase of Happy Meal®—While Supplies Last.

"You know where we'll be," the driver said when we rolled to a stop in the Chili's parking lot.

The REVILED EW banner on the restaurant had been turned around to read WE DELIVER. I gave up the plush of my enemies' SUV for sooty concrete and an imminent reunion with Dad. It was pretty much a crapshoot, whether he'd bring his wife Maria to our meetups, another significant other like the gopher-lodge-hairdo geezer, or some lady he'd just met. He rarely showed up alone. This was the first time we'd be seeing each other since DNA analysis had confirmed the body buried at Forest Lawn was Wilt's, and I didn't figure he'd surprise me by showing up solo.

"Hey, kiddo!"

"Hey."

He squeezed me like I was fruit he was checking for ripeness. Before Maria could attempt a hug, I dropped into a chair.

"What's the latest? How're things?"

He was too upbeat, which meant he had something to tell me he'd rather have avoided. But the *latest*? I was like, *Do I tell him?*

"There are a couple hate crimers waiting for me in the parking lot," I said. "Soon as they're given the okay from their boss, they'll be responsible for my demise. Except they're only out there 'cause I screwed up trying to find Wilt's killer, and I'm not about to give up anyone's name even if it might clear mine, so I guess I'm really responsible for my own demise and the hate crimers are just the weapons I'll be using."

All around us: the clink and scrape of cutlery, the talk of diners. But at our table: silence, Dad and Maria losing verbal for what seemed a long time, Dad not even taking refuge in a margarita but looking through me so hard I turned around to see if anything interesting was at my back. At least he didn't come out and blame my meds for what must've sounded like BS. *That* would've been typical—using my meds as an excuse for anything I did or said that he didn't understand.

"You can go out and see the hate crimers yourself, if you want," I said. "They follow me everywhere. Sometimes they follow Mom. Have you noticed anyone following you?"

Slowly, Dad shook his head.

"He hasn't," Maria said, as if we needed a translator.

"You might want to take self-protective measures," I told Dad.

"I do. Every day."

The waiter came to the table and I ordered a bacon cheeseburger, fries, root beer. Maria asked for a Caesar salad. Dad said he'd have a margarita for appetizer, then surprised me by ordering bona fide food—a plate of ribs. He was trying hard, wanting us to have a regular family dinner the way most of the people around us seemed to be doing.

"I don't think there needs to be a second funeral, do you?" he said after the waiter had gone.

So *that's* what he hadn't wanted to talk about. "No," I said.

"Good. I told them just to re-bury the body."

Like the exhumation never happened.

Why hadn't he ever been as determined to find Wilt's murderer as he was to make sure the funeral people hadn't buried the wrong person? Why hadn't he railed at Abrams and the cop higher-ups to find the asshole responsible for my brother's death? Or *had* he, but out of my sight? Was my thinking I should've seen Dad rage to find the killer—that like, obvious rage on his part would've been an appropriate response to a murdered son—any different from Abrams being suspicious of me because I hadn't cried at the morgue the night of Wilt's crash?

"Why is it called a funeral 'home'?" I asked. "Is it supposed to sound cozy, comforting, what?"

"It's probably historical," Maria said. "Let me look it up." She got busy with her phone. "'Before the mid-nineteenth century,'" she read, "'deceased persons were often displayed in the parlor of the family home. Hence the term *funeral parlor* that is still in use today.'"

"Do you know," Dad asked me, "is it good that Wilt's at that store? Has he said if there's somewhere better he could've ended up? Or worse?"

"He's not sure. But if he calls, you can ask him."

I set my phone on the table. Now that science had confirmed the death of Wilt's body, I thought Dad might be doubting whatever afterlife beliefs he had, mentally scrolling back over his life, questioning if the things he'd done were on the whole "good" or "bad," because depending on which, he'd up where Wilt was. Or not.

"'As embalming became standard practice in the late nineteenth century,'" Maria read, "'private viewing in the family parlor disappeared in favor of funeral homes, where a preserved body could be presented in a neutral setting and families could receive guests and hold a formal service.'"

"Why'd you leave?"

The question had just kind of burped out of me. Maria turned statue.

"When?" Dad asked.

"Me and Wilt. Mom. Why'd you leave us?"

His answer was immediate, kneejerk. "You can't blame me. You have to take responsibility for your own actions."

I laughed, since he wasn't great at taking responsibility for his own actions. I told him I'd never blame him or anybody else for who I was, no matter how much I wanted to. The electrochemical happenings in my brain were partly inherited from him, sure, but it's not like he chose which ones to pass on. Still: "I'm only sixteen," I reminded him.

"What's past is past," Maria said.

"Not really."

Why did stepmothers never understand, their sleeping with Dad didn't give them a voice in his personal conversations with me?

"The thing is," I said to Dad, "I'm curious. I just want to know."

"I don't think now is the best time to talk about this. Maybe when you're older."

I didn't say anything, kept looking at him. He sucked on a mouthful of margarita ice.

"My reason won't sound good," he said.

I stayed quiet. He sucked on a second mouthful of ice so long I thought it'd never melt. Then he came out with something that floored me.

"I was uninspired."

If he'd said that he'd felt claustrophobic, being in his twenties and stuck with a wife and two kids, afraid he saw the rest of his life as husband and father stretched boringly out in front of him, if he'd said that he never loved Mom, that he'd been stupid, irresponsible, and had let his nether regions lead him into marriage: either would've been better. But *uninspired?* What kind of reason was that? Wilt and I didn't do it for him as sons? I mean, who doesn't want to have inspiring friends and relatives? Who doesn't want to be an inspiration to others? Am I supposed to go through life feeling constantly inspired by the people around me? Is it like an inalienable right or whatever? The idea seems more fantastic than getting calls from a dead brother.

I forced down a few bites of my burger, which someone at some point had put in front of me. Maria blabbed on about an architect from a previous century, and the longer she went on, the more I tried to insulate myself from Dad and his sense of entitlement re: inspiration. I picked at my fries. Dead architect this, dead architect that, Maria blabbed. Then we were stepping out to the parking lot, the three of us, and I nodded toward the hate crimers in the Escalade.

"There they are."

Dad walked toward them, scaring me as much as Maria, who fluttered along at his side. "What are you doing? Please, let's just go! Please!"

"Have a nice dinner?" driver goon asked.

Dad thumbed the Escalade's license plate number into his phone, went up to the driver's side window.

"I'd like to report an incident," I heard Maria's voice say— no doubt into her phone. I was watching Dad.

"You're obviously not a side-effect of Curtis's medication," he told the hate crimers, "so understand something. I don't care who you are or why you're following my son. But if anything untoward happens to him—and I'll blame you if anything does—I *will* come after you. Hard. You'll wish I was a good citizen who called the police in times of trouble. Your guns and your muscles will mean nothing. I've already lost one son and I *won't* lose another. Tell your boss."

He legged it to his jeep without saying goodbye, Maria at him about how he never needed to act macho to prove himself to anybody and why had he been so reckless.

"Old man has a few issues, I guess," driver goon said to me. "You want a ride?"

I didn't. The Escalade rolled along behind me while I tramped through less-than-safe neighborhoods, trying not to think of anything, to just focus on the motion of my arms and legs and lose myself in my physical doings. Almost home, my phone buzzed, and I'd barely breathed "hey" before I was telling Wilt that Dad had just floored me by threatening two of Yang's hate crimers but still he was clueless when it came to acting like a father, not that I wanted to care as much as I did, it was just kind of sad and I was tired of things being sad. And Maria? Forget her. Maybe if she hadn't been my stepmom always trying to get into my business I could've tolerated her as much as I might've tolerated any inoffensive geezer, but I'd never had a stepmom like that, so I couldn't know for sure.

A bunch of inexplicable stuff came gushing out of me. Not just about Dad and Maria. Not just about Mom's nicotine-patch habit or her way of always being needy while dismissing others' needs—by which I meant mine. Out of my mouth gushed little-seeming things, disconnected things, relevant to I didn't know what.

Like when I was five years old and Mom and Dad were still together and I was slick with sweat after a T-ball game one Saturday, sitting on a bleacher with a can of Orange Crush in my hand, listening to the coach say how impressed he was with my play.

Like the week-long road trip in a Winnebago—the family foursome trucking out to the Grand Canyon, Wilt and I taking turns sleeping on the foam bed above the driver's and front passenger's seats. I had these little plastic army men that I'd goof with, I remembered, and I'd stand each of them up in the foam's pits and divots, pretending not to hear the whispered angry voices that alternated with creaks and heavy breathing behind the curtain where the parentals "slept."

Like the games of Red Rover Wilt and I used to play with kids outside our old building on Parkland, when we'd form two human chains facing each other maybe fifteen feet apart, and every time my group called *red rover red rover let Wilt come over*, my brother would sprint toward where I held the hand of the person next to me, always knowing he could break the link.

Like when Wilt and I visited Dad at his first apartment after the split from Mom, when Dad had been out somewhere and Wilt decided we should throw a whole carton's worth of eggs off the balcony into the pool area.

Like how after the divorce there had been so many day-care centers and babysitters—strangers looking out for my and Wilt's welfare because we were supposedly too young to look out for ourselves, but I'd only ever wanted them to go away and leave us alone.

No doubt my complaining and weird skulk down memory alley weren't things Wilt wanted to hear, but I couldn't stop.

We'd never talked about it before—what it felt like to be Mom and Dad's sons. Maybe I figured that if anyone might understand the forces pushing and pulling on me, it wasn't going to be Dr. Polk or anybody, it'd be Wilt. Because he'd had the same forces pushing and pulling on him. Or if not the same exactly—the forces being different for him since we *were* different people—still more alike than what I'd find with anybody else. So out of my mouth came everything and whatever, in case a scrap of it might prod him to say, "I know what you mean." Instead, he shut me up with—

"There are a bunch of reasons to feel sorry for you, Curtis, but in a way, I envy you."

"Huh?" Besides what I had with Suzy, I couldn't fathom a reason why anybody would envy me. "Have you heard what I've been saying *at all*?"

"Sure. But as lacking as your relationship with Dad might be, it still has the potential to improve. Not mine. I assume I'm supposed to stuff a lifetime's worth of experience into these calls. But I don't even know what a full lifetime's worth of experience *is*. I got ripped."

"We all kind of did."

I was standing in the middle of a buckled sidewalk, the hate crimers' Escalade idling curbside behind me.

"I don't care what other people think of me or what I might've accomplished if I'd lived," Wilt said. "I don't care if friends and acquaintances think less of me because I didn't 'do much with my life.' But I have regrets. I regret the absences in my relationships with people like Dad, Mom, you, Suzy. Do *you* hear what *I'm* saying? These relationships were lacking and I didn't have the years to try and improve them. With you, maybe we've improved them a little, as much as possible in these short calls anyway. I hope so."

His voice was shaky with emotion, and even though the hate crimers were a reminder that I probably wouldn't have years to better my dealings with most people, I welled up. I wanted my brother to know that yeah, we'd improved our relationship. Absolutely. Maybe none of us ever changed as much as we might try to—maybe an asshole at six is an asshole at sixty, etc.—but that didn't necessarily mean people couldn't change how they treated one another, did it? And so yeah, it was hard to put things into words, but his referring to me by my actual name? His willingness to listen to my ideas, like the one about begging off afterlife therapy? And his help with Suzy, which I interpreted as more than him just teaching me how to finesse my way into her pants, which I took as him saying, *I want the best for you, little brother. I want you to have awesome experiences and, in a way that no one else can, I'll help you get them?* I would've told him it was all a major improvement, except I had no chance to stutter out a syllable. In my ear, he said, "I'm glad I admitted this to you before I lost the opportunity. I never know when will be the last we talk."

I'd once thought the same thing, that our last call might come anytime, and considering the circumstances, it might not have been all that unique. Maybe a lot of people would've thought it. But it was still unexpected to hear. A while back, Suzy'd said that I sounded a lot like my brother. I hadn't believed it. To my own ear, I didn't sound anything like him.

"I'm giving the signal for rebellion the next time *All in the Family* airs," Wilt said. "Claudius and I found a way to the management offices, we think: a door labeled Employees Only near one of the pet departments. We assume there are more of these doors and we just haven't located them yet."

"Pet departments?"

"Yeah. Depending where you are in the store, you can get a pretty good sense of what animals were popular during different historical periods. Parrots, snakes, goats, monkeys, sheep, horses, Komodo dragons. Dogs and cats are pretty constant, but not always top pet."

Manson. "Have you seen—he would've only gotten there recently—a mastiff with beige on his nose, hashtag scars on his legs, and an ear that looks like it was torn in half at one point?" I had no idea if Manson's fatal injuries would mar his afterlife "appearance" or if he'd look as he did before his lost battle with Presa. "He's a beast that seems like he'll bite your face off," I said, "but if you give him a chance, he'll just hang and be mellow with you."

"I've looked for dogs I'd recognize, but you might as well ask me if I've seen our grandparents or any of our ancestors. Odds are against it. Forever expanding as this place might be, it's still overpopulated. But listen, I've been mulling over some things and I need to hurry, in case *All in the Family* airs. What if I've been sure that I wasn't murdered and considered the idea absurd—even with Yang and Nuñez in the picture—because I wasn't supposed to be?"

"You're saying the wrong person got killed?" I asked softly, not wanting the hate crimers at my back to hear. They'd probably heard too much already. I started walking again, trying to put more distance between us.

"The car was rigged with a device, right?" Wilt said. "It was triggered by an odometer? The night I went to St. Benny, not even Suze knew. I drove there after a bunch of fights, when evidence in the cremation pit would be fresh. I wanted to thoroughly document the scene—time-stamped video, pictures, tire-tread patterns of everyone who'd driven to the fights. If I was lucky, I'd be able to collect bone fragments. I already had pictures of Yang and Nuñez at previous fights, but I wanted more. A smear campaign might only temporarily stop Yang, you know? I needed enough to shut him down for good. It wasn't possible to have too much evidence, only too little. Suze was already more involved than she should've been, so I didn't tell her what I was up to, and while Mom was in the middle of her shift, I borrowed her car, planning to bring it back before she was done. She was never supposed to know that I used it. But see what I'm getting at? If I hadn't taken the car that night, Mom would've been driving. She *should've* been driving— either on her way home from UPS after her shift or on her way to UPS the next night."

"Yeah, but who . . . I mean, *Mom?*""

I didn't like hearing it. Maybe it was further proof that my brother and I thought alike, but I'd already rejected the Mom-target possibility as ludicrous. Plus, if true, it meant that I had been wrong about everything.

"Why Mom?" I said. Then I remembered Pappas out front of his building, on his back under the money-man's classic Mercedes. "Pappas owns that slum auto body shop across the street, doesn't he?" I asked.

"It used to belong to his uncle or cousin."

"It seems a little too convenient, I think."

"What does?"

I glanced behind me. The Escalade was still rolling along, keeping pace at its usual distance. Drum & bass pumped out its open windows. "Tom Birch's accident," I said. "I told you, Mr. Birch was forced by his sister to move after his son died in that moped accident. What if there was a gadget on the moped like the one on Mom's car?"

I'd put it out there, yeah, but still. *Pappas a murderer?* A scumbag—definitely. Host of a parasitic belly button worm—not really, it was just fun to think so. But to fulfill his dream of selling a crumbling old building to developers for a ton of cash, would the guy murder his tenants? The more I considered it, and the more Wilt entertained the idea, the more I doubted it.

"Okay, so Pappas has never seemed like a genius or anything," I said, "but taking out stubborn renters one by one? Isn't it more idiotic than risky? His motive too obvious?"

"How many tenants are left in the building?"

"Three, including us."

"And you said the Gantrys moved out?"

I told him again how I'd come home one night and seen the Gantrys loading up their van.

"Once enough tenants were gone, the rest of you, faced with the inevitable, might have also left on your own," he said. "Then Pappas's killings would look more random, as they do now, with the Gantrys having moved out like they did. And if that doesn't cut it for you as far as 'obvious' goes, assume he didn't care. Greed encourages people to take stupid risks. Find out everything you can about Birch's moped accident."

"How, without involving Detective Abrams? Or do I ask

him to investigate it? Which'll get him on my case for acting the sleuth."

"No, never mind about Birch. I have a better idea."

We started forming a plan. We knew circumstantial evidence wouldn't be enough to really bust Pappas. If the guy was guilty, we didn't want him walking free thanks to some lawyer. I'd have to provoke him into compromising action with as solid evidence as I could get.

"Maybe I'll find it under a tenant's car?" I said.

"Or at our old clubhouse," he said.

An unexpected wave of sadness crashed over me. "I didn't know you remembered."

"Yeah. Sorry I left you hanging."

We schemed a way for Abrams and even Nuñez's hate crimers to be part of the plan, without their knowing.

"You'll have to use yourself as bait," Wilt warned. "Can't avoid it, I don't think."

"I know."

"It's going to be risky, easily the riskiest thing either of us has ever done."

"I know."

What option did I have *except* to go through with it? Let the hate crimers follow me around till they made their play? And meantime I'd keep a vigilant eye open for Pappas's murderous ways and try to convince Mom that we had to move out of the building asap, at which point she'd ask, since when did I feel such urgency about anything and who was going to fund this move?

I did have one option, I guessed. "Why don't I tell Abrams we suspect Pappas and let *him* sort out the situation, the way you told me to do with Yang and the dog-beasties?" I asked Wilt.

"Because until he does sort it out, you'll have to constantly check Mom's rental for the kind of device they found on her own car."

"Unless Abrams assigns cops to keep tabs on her and her rental," I said.

"Then Mom'll want to know what the protective surveillance is all about, and if she's been as mental as you claim . . . "

He didn't have to say more. Telling Abrams would be the same as telling Mom. I had no confidence that she'd be able to handle the probable truth—that someone had been trying to kill her when they'd done away with her oldest son. What her not-handling-it looked like, I didn't want to find out.

By the end of my call with Wilt, before *All in the Family* aired in his local Entertainment section and he yelled "It's on!" and hung up, our plan was fixed. Within twenty-four hours, I'd know if Pappas was the killer.

I was afraid to round the corner onto my block. What if I ran into Pappas? The guy would take one look at me and guess everything. From the way I folded my arms, he'd see that I assumed he was my brother's murderer. From the set of my shoulders, he'd know I was going to flush him out for the cops. The line of my mouth would tell him *how* I was going to flush him out. He'd see it all and stop me before I started.

The hate crimers' Escalade pulled up next to me. The drum & bass from its stereo went silent.

"Forget something?" the driver asked.

I peeped around the corner—no Pappas, so I legged it faster than usual down the block and through the building lobby, past apartment 1A to the stairwell. I listened but heard nothing. Still, I didn't trust the situation. Like I've said, usually when I don't want something to happen, that's what happens. I stopped on the second-floor landing, listened. No approaching footsteps. I creeped up to the third floor, stopped and listened, creeped up to the fourth floor, etc. When I made it safely to the tenth floor, I felt as if I'd gotten the better of the troll-landlord and was so self-congratulatory that I didn't register the oddity of the apartment door being off the latch. But then I pushed open the door and all self-congrats left me, along with most of my ability to remain upright.

Okafur, Narith, and Arundhati stood in a line, facing Pappas like they'd been called to attention by a drill sergeant. Pappas was sporting his usual troll-wear: skanky T-shirt at least two sizes too small, sweatpants that gave him shapeless duffel bags for legs, flipflops to show off his disgustingly hairy feet. He looked unwashed, murderous.

My voice came out like a gust of fear: "What are you doing here?"

"I own the place," he said.

I held my arms stiff at my sides so that he couldn't read anything into the way I folded them across my chest. I threw back my shoulders, not wanting them to hint that I planned to flush him out for the cops. And I kept my mouth open so that the squiggle of my lips couldn't possibly reveal how I was going to flush him out.

"You and your mom weren't here and I heard noises," he said.

How had he known that both me and Mom weren't home? Was he watching us? How long had he been watching us?

"Who are these people?" He meant the pseudo-siblings.

I almost answered. But I had to maintain my normal attitude toward him, to pretend that nothing had changed between us. "Get out," I said. "You're not supposed to be in here."

He moved toward me, flipflops slapping at his heels. "Neither are you," he hissed, and bumped me as he slouched out to the hall.

I shut the door, double locked it, and put on the chain. I scoped him through the peephole, pressed my ear to the door and listened till I was sure he was gone from the tenth floor. Then I swung round on the pseudo-siblings.

"What'd he say? Did he say anything to you? Did you tell him anything? Did he *touch* anything?"

"He only touched the doorknob." Narith's English had magically improved since the morning Mom and I made breakfast for him. "He said he wanted to make a list of what needed fixing."

"But you came in before he could go around and check anything," Arundhati finished.

Okafur nodded, shook his head, nodded.

Pappas was going to fix a leaky faucet or whatever? Obvious BS. So despite what Arundhati had said, I searched the apartment: the kitchen, bath and bedroom, the living room and closets. Nothing seemed in any way contaminated by Pappas.

"Always leave the chain on the door when Mom and I aren't around," I told the pseudo-siblings. "Never open the door even a few inches for anybody but us."

I had to try to calm down, to empty my head of everything except what I had to do the next day. But I didn't want to stress the details of the plan either, and with little to do but wait for morning—

"I'm going to sleep," I said.

I wasn't in bed ten minutes before I'd texted Suzy six times. By the twenty-minute mark, I'd texted her nine times and called her twice. Not that I knew what I wanted to say to her. Would I tell her about Pappas? Wasn't she already more involved than she should've been, as Wilt had said? Whatever I might've told her didn't matter: she never texted back and I only ever got her voicemail.

I didn't figure I'd get any sleep and planned to conduct periodic safety sweeps of the apartment throughout the night, triple- and quadruple-checking that Pappas hadn't somehow compromised the place. But it's weird how you can be both wired *and* completely beat, and at some point, in some way I didn't understand, Suzy and I wound up in a mattress section of the Aftermart. "Hey!" I said, but then she was gone and I was looking down at the never-ending aisles of dead merch like I was a security camera. A rumbling came up behind me, louder and louder, and then the aisles were overrun with Romans and Mongols and people from every century since civilization began—or so I guessed, because of the different wigs and hats and foofy-poofy outfits everyone wore. Wilt was at the front of the horde, leading the charge with Claudius the centurion, who'd decked himself out in armored skirt and breastplate. Some of the rebels carried bulletproof shower pans, but most were armed with baseball bats, golf clubs, canes, mops and brooms, and they advanced up the aisles, smashing and trampling merch. More than a few started looting.

Which I didn't get.

If the rebellion was successful and shoppers were dispersed as pure energy, it wasn't like pure energy needed a Pet Rock or Nintendo 64, right? And if the rebellion failed, wouldn't the Aftermart powers that be raid all lockers/donkey carts and take back the looted goods? I was about to shout out and ask somebody, not sure I'd be heard over the noise, when I woke up.

It was morning—Okafur snoring in his bed, Narith twisted in his sheets and blankets on the floor with a pillow over his head. I slipped on my clothes and out to the living room. Mom was at one end of the couch, sleeping with her mouth open, fully dressed like she had collapsed after her shift at UPS. Arundhati lay balled up asleep at the couch's other end.

Being the only one awake the morning of the Big Day, you'd think I would've taken a minute to eye Mom and even the pseudo-siblings. You'd think I would've stood there, assessing/regretting/appreciating our shared history, mentally logging all that had come before—good and bad—as a kind of acknowledgment that I might not see any of these people again. But I didn't. From the kitchen I took the yellow rubber gloves that Okafur wore when washing dishes, slung on my backpack and left, careful not to wake anyone.

I stepped lightly into the stairwell, stopped to listen for Pappas at every landing, and because I hoped to confuse the whole what-I-don't-want-to-happen-is-exactly-what-happens deal, I kept telling myself that I really wanted to run into the guy. I reached the ground floor without seeing him and huffed through the lobby as quickly and as quietly as I could. Outside, the hate crimers were asleep in their Escalade. The auto body place, fortress of junk that it was, mocked me from across the street: Auto Parts & Mufflers, Shocks Brakes Welding & Repairs. In its fenced-off concrete yard, where tall weeds had pushed up through the cracks, I could see a burned-out Dodge minivan on blocks, mounds of tires, rotted sheets of plywood, oil drums, stray car doors, bucket seats covered in gray, weather-pruned leather, scattered collections of what looked like exhaust pipes, and a moldy old love seat. The fence that kept all this crap from spilling to the street was no flimsy thing: seven-foot iron spikes bolted to the top of a three-foot cement barrier. I didn't want to struggle over it in front of whoever, and I knew the south side of the garage, where the water damage was, didn't have any windows. It didn't face the street either, so.

I let the hate crimers sleep, down the block ducked into the lot where the lavanderia used to be. I upended a battered grocery cart, stood on top of it, and climbed over the iron spikes into Pappas's property. I shouldered the dumpster aside, and for the first time in years, crawled through the rotted hole in the garage wall. I was unpocketing my phone, to use as a flashlight, when it vibrated.

"Uh, hello?"

"Wanted to check in, find out how's it going,"

Last thing I expected was Wilt to hit me up in the middle of his rebellion. "Aren't you busy?"

"Experiencing a lull in the proceedings at present. We're amassed at the edge of the pet department closest to the door that Claudius and I think leads to the management offices. An army of blurry-faced guys in dark blue shirts—they've got the word 'security' printed in bright yellow capital letters on their backs—have advanced toward us from a distant aisle. We're in the middle of a stand-off, each side waiting for the other to make a move."

Wilt had once said that he and the other shoppers couldn't physically interact, that when he'd tried to kiss some girl, his face had gone through hers, and that when he'd swung a bat at Claudius as a weapons-test, the bat had whiffed through the guy. But did that mean Security couldn't somehow physically stop Wilt and his peeps from rebelling?

"So tell me how it's going," he said.

"I'm in the auto shop. Just starting my search."

"Describe what you see and be specific."

I held the phone perpendicular to my face, so that I could use it as a flashlight and talk into its microphone at the same time. The shop looked like the workplace of some messy, greaseball hoarder. I described the unlabeled jugs half-filled with dark liquids tossed about among sooty fans and big spools of chain and electrical wire and rubber hoses. I described the spilled buckets of car handles, the metal flat file cabinets with open drawers full of bolts and screws, the milk crates cluttered with plastic funnels, wrenches, pliers.

"Holy . . . " I said.

"What?"

I described in detail what I'd found. On a bench between a vise and a pipe-cutter, in a space that seemed cleared for recent tinkerings because it was cleaner than its surround and had a single lamp aimed at it: two death-gadgets. I was sure they were death-gadgets. They looked like half-finished electronics projects wired to old-school odometers.

"And Wilt?" I said. "Whatever significance the number fifty had in all this, I figured either it'd already played itself out or there hadn't ever been much significance, mostly coincidence—you calling me every fifty minutes and Nuñez's phone number being on the $50 I found in your cash."

"I have always hated it when people ascribe meaning to coincidences, especially of the numerical variety."

"I know, yeah, but—"

"An airplane with a flight number of 370 disappears with hundreds of passengers onboard, some person says the plane vanished in the third month of year, on the seventh day, or a nut mumbles a bunch of so-called Law of Fives garbage, which is a bullcrap theory about how everything that happens in the world is related, directly or indirectly, to the number five. Flight 370. Three plus seven is ten. Divide ten by two and you get five. Or take 9/11. Nine plus eleven equals twenty, right? And the tragedy happened in 2001, which is two plus one, which equals three. Twenty plus three equals twenty-three, which can be broken down to two plus three equals five."

"And that proves what?"

"Exactly."

"Okay, but so, I stopped thinking the number fifty had any relevance to your murder. I mean, in the beginning, did you really call every fifty minutes, or was it sometimes more, sometimes less, and I just rounded off? But the death-gadgets on the workbench here? Their odometers are set to fifty."

"A target car has to be driven that number of miles before sudden acceleration."

"That's what I'm thinking."

It was like confirmation of what I'd believed about Wilt's counselor Sean—or if not him, then maybe the Aftermart's general manager: that he/she/it had arranged for Wilt's calls to lead to this, to me being in the auto body slum, staring at the kind of death-gadget that'd been wired to Mom's car and had done in my brother, and which I could use to catch the killer. For Wilt, the repetition of fifty probably *had* been coincidence, but the Aftermart powers that be had somehow used him, arranging it so that enough times in the beginning to get my attention, he'd unknowingly called me in intervals of approximately fifty Earth minutes. This possibility did open up some twisted lanes of thinking. If the powers that be could plant "fifty" in Wilt's doings, knowing I'd react in a way that'd kick-start a certain series of events, didn't it imply that they were all-controlling? And if they could control things, why were they letting Wilt and his fellow shoppers rebel?

"You know what to do next," my brother said. "Watch your back. I don't want you ending up in my place, wherever that might be, not for a long while."

I opened my mouth to say I'd have followed him anywhere, *except* to where he was, but then the roar of a massive waterfall or a stadium crowd came through the phone, and I thought I heard him yell, "Forces on the move!" before our connection cut out.

Wearing Okafur's yellow rubber gloves, in case Pappas was stupid enough to have left fingerprints, I put the death-gadgets into my bookbag. The troll-landlord would soon know someone was on to him. I had to hurry.

No part of hurrying included school, but I didn't want Suzy thinking all of my unanswered texts and calls the night before meant I was needy for her. Even if, yeah, I kind of was. But I knew I couldn't go up to her and be like, *Hey, Suze, it probably seems I've been desperately trying to get in touch with you for sixteen hours, except if you think I was even a little bit desperate—don't, okay? I wasn't.* I knew I couldn't say that because— duh—it would come off as totally desperate, so I figured to use Wilt as my excuse, pretending he was supposed to call and wanted to talk to her. Though really, I planned on being as non-verbal as I could get away with, especially since I'd decided not to enlighten Suzy about Pappas. I thought I'd benefit from a few minutes of her silent company was all. Being near her would give me strength and confidence to do what I had to do that day. She was the most incredible girl around and I'd been with her. Me. The sight of Suzy Painter would remind me what I was capable of.

Weaving past cars in the school parking lot, I passed a silver Lexus IS350 with two people kissing in the front seats. The girl had a hand on the guy's shoulder and I recognized it first: the long fingers, the black glitter nail polish. Then I saw the lacrosse gear in the back seat.

My insides went into freefall. A prickly sensation rode up the back of my head and my brain struggled to compute the nightmare scene. I guess I'd convinced myself—without realizing it, if that makes any sense—that Suzy still spent time with Rick Calvados out of habit and because it was easier than getting him to leave her alone. But I'd been a first-class idiot, a Grade A moron, the dumbest person who'd ever existed. I was too devastated even to kick Calvados's stupid Lexus, which no doubt would've earned me a beating if I'd done it. Not that I cared. Not right then. I would have welcomed a punch to the face. Or several.

I don't remember walking out of the parking lot and only became aware of the world again when I was slumped on the curb outside 7-11, where I stayed for who knows how long— first period at school might've come and gone, second period, I had no clue. I was numb, a vacancy wrapped in human skin. How was I supposed to trap a killer feeling like *that*?

I needed to talk to Wilt. With everything he had going in the Aftermart, I wouldn't whine about Suzy, but I could say that I'd lost my nerve to carry out the plan against Pappas. I'd let him convince me—better than I could convince myself— how there was no possibility of backing out. I couldn't even put off the plan till the next day, he'd say, since that'd mean sneaking a second time into the auto body shop and returning the death-gadgets to where I'd found them. Which, even if I managed, how could I know Pappas hadn't already noticed they were gone? No, he'd say, I had zero choice. I had to carry out the plan no matter how I felt. But he didn't call, didn't respond to my texts, and Suzy came walking toward me with a kind of bop in her step.

"Hey," she said.

"Hey."

It was all I could do to look at her knees, those lovely, dimpled knees that had me like, *Why, lovely knees? Why'd you do this to me?* She started humming no song I'd ever heard.

"Could you stop?"

"What?"

I imitated her. "Mmm mmm mmmm mm."

"I'm in a good mood."

A *good mood?* Because of Rick Calvados? The world was a toilet, flushing me down.

"Do you have to let it bleed over everything?" I said.

I braved a look at her face, scoping for evidence of jock-boy on her lips, her cheeks. It pissed me off that she wasn't going to ask about my onslaught of texts and calls, but she'd probably been too busy enjoying her good mood with Calvados to notice them.

"Why're you so cranky?" she wanted to know. "And what're you doing here?" She meant at the curb.

"I saw you," I said, but she didn't get it. "WITH THAT FRUIT-PICKING, FUTURE SCHOLARSHIP-WINNING, BIG-MAN-ON-CAMPUS-HEDGE-FUND-MANAGING JOCK RICK CALVADOS!"

She jerked with surprise and I experienced something I hadn't felt since my first months on meds. Not that I knew if I associated the sensation with meds because they'd made it go away or had produced it as a side-effect—either would've made a lasting impression on the thinkwad in my skull. But my back and forth with Suzy, the cars pulling in and out of the 7-11 parking lot, the birds flapping in the sky, the trees heaving like giant pompoms, it was all moving quickly and slowly at the same time—rushed but still in slow-mo—and laced with this menacing urgency.

Suzy sat on the curb and stared at the ground. "I thought we had an understanding," she said softly. "I guess I'll tell you what I told him."

I nearly crapped myself. "Wait, what? You told . . . about us? *Why? When?*"

"Last night. He seemed to know already, but he wanted to hear me say it aloud. Besides, weren't you tired of sneaking around? He had to find out sometime."

"No, he didn't."

I didn't know which was worse, that she'd spent the night with Calvados or had spilled to him about us.

"I never claimed we were exclusive," she said. "I really thought you understood the situation. What I do with other people doesn't change the way I feel about you."

"And how is that? How *do* you feel about me?"

I sounded pathetic, but whatever. If it was pathetic to show hurt when screwed over by someone I loved, fuck it, I'd be pathetic.

Suzy put a hand on my thigh, her touch the same electric jolt it'd always been, except I didn't want a boner. On principle I didn't want a boner—I *was* pissed, right? Too bad it wasn't up to me.

"I really, really like you, Curtis."

"But you've been fooling around with Rick this whole time?"

She answered by saying that until his death Wilt was the only person she'd ever been with. "I loved him. But after everything that's happened, I thought . . . well, that it couldn't hurt to have more experience before I go away to school, you know?"

"Depends who you ask."

She didn't appreciate that and huffed off into 7-11. A minute later she came out, cracking open a pack of Marlboro Lights. She stood over me without verballing awhile.

"I *am* sorry, Curtis," she said. "I didn't mean to hurt you."

I felt like crying. Like punching something. Like crying and punching something.

"We'll talk later, okay?" she said. "I have to get to class."

I watched her leave, watched what I thought was my only chance at happiness speed-walk away from me and out of sight, doubting I'd ever have the strength to get to my feet again, never mind do anything else, and then—

"Dude," Jeremy said when I answered my phone, "I wouldn't come to school until after Calvados graduates. He's in a rage to beat on you and seems willing to risk a scholarship to do it."

46

For a plan to work, you need luck. Particular events have to happen in the right order, one giving way to the next in a kind of chain reaction, and every minute there's a chance for something to go wrong. Change the original plan on the fly because those particular events didn't happen when you needed them to? Even then a successful plan relies on luck. Because a whole new set of events needs to happen, one event giving way to the next in a new right order, and there's a fresh bunch of variables to deal with, any of which could mess up any single event, which would botch the entire plan. And the biggest variable of all, in every plan?

People.

You can never be sure how people will behave, no matter how well you think you know them. People are predictable right up until they aren't.

I'd sneaked out of Pappas's auto body place with the death-gadgets, figuring to wake up the hate crimers because I needed them to be within view when I confronted the troll-landlord. I was supposed to play it like Yang and I'd made a deal against him. Wilt had said we didn't have to sweat what the deal might be. It didn't even have to make that much sense, my making *any* kind of deal with Yang—the idea just had to spook Pappas a little and excite his paranoia. But when I got back to the street after the auto body shop, the Escalade wasn't there. And if the hate crimers had thought I'd skipped out while they were asleep and they'd gone looking for me, they should've found me by the time I was on the curb outside 7-11. I'd made it easy for them, stopping off at school. Except they were nowhere.

So already events weren't happening the way they needed to, but because I didn't know if the whole plan was blown, I went ahead and did what I should've done soon as I'd found the death-gadgets: I called Abrams.

"I know who killed my brother," I told him.

"Is this a confession?"

"Not funny." I had to compartmentalize, to suck up the pain of Suzy and get on with things. "I have evidence."

There was a lot of noise coming through the phone. Stuff like maybe a helicopter, dogs barking.

"What kind of evidence?"

"The device you found on Mom's car," I said, "the one you said caused sudden acceleration that probably wasn't reversible? Did it have an old-school odometer? Not digital numbers, but the kind that spin around on a dial? And did it have this perforated circuit board about the size of an index card and little red pillow things wired to the board?"

"Sounds about right."

"Mom had been the killer's target, not Wilt."

Abrams let out one of his geezery lung rattles. In all the background noise, I definitely heard dogs and was like,

That's why the hate crimers stopped tailing me. Abrams and his cop-buddies had raided Yang's Tudor and other mansions. The hate crimers had probably been ordered to the bird streets to try and get rid of as much evidence as they could.

"Where are you? Are you at school?" Abrams asked, getting downright parental on me when I said I wasn't. "Shouldn't you be at school?"

"Meet me at the auto body place across from my building. Bring reinforcements. Eleven-thirty," I said, and hung up.

47

Two gadgets. Three remaining tenants, including the extended Brooks clan. I had to check under Mom's rental to see if it'd been rigged for death—the Lopez's Camry and Weiss's Buick too, if I could find where they were parked.

A couple blocks from 7-11, my phone vibrated. Wilt must've dialed me by accident because all I heard was noise-wash. The stuff in the background of my call with Abrams had been nothing compared to it, and I stood struggling to make out my brother's voice or at least sounds of a rebel horde in that afterlife static when tires screamed behind me and I turned and saw Calvados come stalking out of his Lexus.

"Prepare for pain, dipshit."

Phone jammed into my pocket, I backpedaled fast. "But wait, aren't we—"

"I was more than clear, but you just had to get your dick wet."

"Wait! Hold on! Let's commiserate!"

"Commiserate with this."

Next thing, I was on the ground, tasting the metal of my own blood. Lucky for me Calvados played lacrosse and not soccer. His kicks didn't hurt as much as they might have, though he did get in a good several before I was able to snag hold of his right leg. He kicked at me with his left and I snagged it also, and I hugged both his legs, trying to bring him down, but instead of falling outright, the annoyingly coordinated athlete dropped into a crouch on top of me, pinning me with his weight on his knees, and started punching. Too bad for me he played lacrosse. His upper body strength was scary. His fists hurt, knew just where to inflict the most pain. I could only pray he'd get bored with beating on me before he put me in the hospital, but it didn't seem like that was going to happen.

"What're you kids doing?"

Calvados held off rearranging my face. Abrams was out of his car, the siren light on his dash revolving.

"We're only goofing around, officer," Calvados said.

"That so?"

My left eye was going into hiding. Knots of swelling already bulged under my lip, at my jaw. I nodded at Abrams and a nostril's worth of blood spilled onto the front of my shirt.

"You. Leave," he said to Calvados.

At first jock-tyrant didn't move, but then he loped past his car to the bus stop, saying no problem, he'd be happy to leave, except state of affairs as they were, he had to rely on public transit to carry him out of the vicinity and everyone knew how prompt public transit *wasn't*, but hey, it didn't make him a criminal, waiting at a public bus stop, so if anybody needed him, that's where he'd be, keeping an ear tuned to us in case we *did* need him.

The snarkiness more than the fists brought it home: Rick Calvados wanted to kill me. Because for all his bullying, he was always respectful to authority figures, never mouthing off to anyone who even remotely had the power to mess with his upward trajectory through life. The rare times one of us lesser beings complained to authority figures about him picking on us, we were never believed.

"You should play a different game with your friend," Abrams said. "This one seems unhealthy for you."

I would have asked how he'd found me if I hadn't been sure about his answer: he was a detective, it was his job to detect things.

"I'm taking you to the station, Curtis."

"Don't worry, I'll bail you out!" Calvados called from across the street.

"And you will stay there," Abrams went on, "protected from yourself and others, unable to engage in any further idiotic behavior."

"Good luck with that!" Calvados called.

"Your mother's already at the station," Abrams said, "unaware of the precise form your foolishness is taking today. She thinks she'll be getting her car back once the proper paperwork is filled out. But she somehow knows that you're not at school—I didn't tell her—and she's worried."

Going with Abrams would have saved me from Calvados, but still, I couldn't be trapped in the police station all day. "Thanks for the offer," I said, "but no can do."

"You don't have a choice."

He grabbed my arm and held me in one of his special cop grips, and what with me trying to squirm free and my face bruised and bloody, I guess it looked like he was really letting me have it, because when Dr. M pedaled up on his girly bike, the doof just about wet himself in disbelief.

"What's happening here?"

"Nothing that concerns you," Abrams said.

Dr. M focused on me. I shook my head, not knowing till later that the dweeb had called Mom to tell her I was a no-show at school, on account of which she'd spouted that tired garbage about my suffering formative-wise from not having a testes-wielding role model in the house, which in turn had inspired Dr. M to try and become said role model—after Suzy told him she'd seen me outside 7-11—by getting on his bike and searching for me. And so there I was, on a city street, with Abrams and Dr. M puffing out their chests at each other, vying for the honor of teaching me how people with testes should behave.

"I'll be reporting this abuse to your superiors," Dr. M told Abrams, "and I've little doubt that Ms. Brooks will press charges. Get in," he said to me.

"To what, your bike?"

My phone vibrated, tickling my nethers. It could've been Wilt, Lou or Jeremy, who knows? I unpocketed my burner instead and pretended to check who was calling.

"It's my brother!" I said.

Dr. M, his expression a combination of doubt and teacherly indignation, lunged for the burner, and I've no idea if Abrams had an instinctive reaction to him—like whatever the guy wanted, Abrams wasn't going to let him have it without a fight—or if he didn't doubt Wilt's calls as much as he'd said. But whichever, when I threw the burner in Calvados's direction, Abrams dove after it along with doofus Murray. Calvados saw the old people bearing down on him and decided it was a swell time to utilize his car and get out of the area, flipping me the finger and yelling that he wasn't done with me.

"Noon!" I called to Abrams. "Meet me at the body shop across from my building!"

With the wannabe stepdads still wrestling over the burner, I ran homeward. I had to ensnare Pappas before Calvados found me, before Abrams and Dr. M decided it was more important to rescue me from my own recklessness than to put choke-holds on each other. Which meant that searching the undercarriage of Mom's rental was out. Ditto Lopez's Camry and the Weiss's Buick.

In the lavanderia lot at the end of my block, I scrawled an anonymous note, telling Pappas that silence cost money and he should be in his auto body slum at 11:50 a.m. Wearing Okafur's kitchen gloves, I took one of the death-gadgets from my backpack. I stowed the backpack in some weeds, and as stealth as I'd ever been in my life, I crept into Pappas's building and set the note and death-gadget on the floor outside apartment 1A. On my way out, I banged the lobby door closed a few times to draw the troll from his cave.

48

I've read somewhere that a person spends about a third of his life waiting in lines, at doctors' offices, wherever. A third of life *waiting*: that no-man's land of living and breathing. But in the dark of Pappas's auto body slum, hunkered down behind an old car engine, as far from the door as I could be while still having a clear path to the rotted hole in the wall that was my emergency exit? It seemed more like *two-thirds* of my life would be spent in that no-man's land. Pain was settling in all over my body, my face felt as if it'd been shoved into a working blender, and I had way too much time to psych myself out.

My phone couldn't have vibrated at a better time.

"I've been hoping you'd call," I whispered.

"The stand-off with Security was a bluff," Wilt said. "They couldn't physically stop us, but passing through so many of them *did* slow us down. We've made it to a maze of inner offices that looks like it goes on forever, and we have reason to believe, on good intel, that we'll soon be slowed by assistant assistant managers. Where are you?"

"Final phase. Waiting for Pappas."

Once the guy showed up, I knew, more could go wrong than right. Never mind the whole question of what Wilt and

I'd do if he didn't show up: he would. He had to. Except, "wrong" or "right"? What did those words even mean?

"Remind me again how this is supposed to work," I said. "We don't really think Pappas is going to confess, do we?"

"You'll goad him into something blatantly criminal that Detective Abrams will catch him doing."

Okay. Yeah. So if I succeeded at that, whatever came afterwards, it'd be *right*. All else'd be *wrong*. Still, I was like, *I could've at least brought a weapon*, and I was picking up a hammer when I heard something clink.

"The front gate's being unlocked," I whispered. Hinges whined. "He's coming."

"Don't hang up," Wilt said.

My heart should've been spazzing, my blood pumping at Indy-500 speeds through every vein, but sometimes when I'm nervous about a happening, the second I'm in it, all nervousness leaves me. The garage's front door swung back. I saw Pappas's silhouette and felt calm.

"Hello?" he said. "I'm here."

"Draw him to you," Wilt said. "You're in control."

I clapped a couple hubcaps together to lure Pappas closer. He paused at the bench where his death-gadgets weren't.

"What's this about?" he called. "Hello?"

"Make yourself known," Wilt said.

I moved into view.

"*You?*" Pappas's fat slug of a body sagged, as if he'd figured no way I could be a true threat and relaxed. "This is private property."

"You're rigging tenants' cars with the devices that used to be on the workbench," Wilt said in my ear.

"You're rigging tenants' cars with the death-gadgets that used to be on that workbench," I repeated.

Pappas's denial was textbook. "I have no idea what you're talking about."

"Then why're you here?" I asked.

"Excellent," Wilt said. "Now spook him with Yang."

"Titus Yang isn't pleased," I said.

Pappas flinched. *How'd I know that he and Titus Yang were in any way connected?*

"You think Yang and the rest of the investors are going to do business with a murderer like you?" I said. "The cops found one of your death-gadgets at the site of my brother's crash and they know what it does."

"You have video," Wilt said.

"I have a video that can prove you're responsible," I said.

"Bullshit," Pappas said.

"Maybe. Maybe not."

The guy diddled his belly button worm awhile, seeming far too casual for me to ever rile into criminality. He hadn't changed his clothes from the day before: skanky T-shirt, sweats, flipflops. He'd received a message that could very likely lead to the end of his American Dream and he hadn't even made himself presentable for the negotiation. "This used to be a decent neighborhood," he said.

"Then what, you moved in?" Wilt said in my ear.

"I'd like it to be decent again." Pappas's hand twitched at his gut, as if his belly button worm had bitten him. "Let me see if I understand. I'm supposed to believe that you'd extort the man you accuse of killing your brother?"

"I realize it's not ideal," I said, "but I have to protect

myself and my mom, right? If you pay us enough to get ourselves set up somewhere else—"

"Twenty K," Wilt said.

"—like twenty K, we'll walk away without a word and
let you sell your crap building and get on with your sad life.
Twenty K will hardly cut into what you'll make off the building,
you stupid fat bastard."

"Gratuitous insult," Wilt said. "Nice."

If Pappas asked where this alleged video of mine was, I'd
tell him that I'd left it and the second death-gadget from the
workbench with a friend. I'd say if I didn't meet my friend at a
certain location in half an hour, that friend was going to open a
sealed envelope containing instructions for what to do with the
video and death-gadget. If Pappas asked how he could trust me
not to wring cash out of him in the future—blackmailers not
being renowned for their trustworthiness—I'd tell him that I'd
hand over the video and death-gadget soon as I had the money.
I was prepared for all kinds of dialogue, but the troll didn't
engage, real life not being as verbal as most TV cop shows.

"You want to take the chance that I don't have a video,
lard-brain?" I said.

"Yes, I think I will."

He pulled a length of pipe from his pocket. Wishful thinking. Within half a second, I saw it was a gun. Of course it was a
gun. One had to come into play somewhere in the proceedings.

My heart spazzed. My blood coursed a one-minute mile. I
should've let Abrams drag me to the police station. I should've
trusted him to investigate Wilt's murder from the start. I never
should've worked for Yang or answered Wilt's calls—or no,
since I couldn't have *not* answered the calls, I should've been

happy to just hear his voice and talk about girls and dead merch instead of getting nosy and dramatic about his own demise.

"He has a weapon, doesn't he?" Wilt said in my ear.

"Mm hmm."

"Is Abrams late? He feels kind of late. Not panic-time yet, little brother. Don't worry too much. Although Abrams does need to chop it up, and I'm guessing that right now none of this seems like a wise plan—"

"Never seemed wise, only necessary," I whispered.

"Are you talking to me?" Pappas wanted to know.

"Fair enough," Wilt kept on, "but let's focus on the fact that, if Abrams plays his part, this not-so-wise-but-necessary plan is working. Optimism is our friend."

Except it's hard to feel optimistic when a murderer's aiming a pistol at your face. Doesn't matter if your mom's safe at a police station and your dad is safe downing lunchtime margaritas at Chili's with his wife or his other significant other. Doesn't matter if your friends are safely bored at school and your pseudo-siblings are off safely cleaning a locked apartment. Doesn't matter if the girl you love is safely smoking a Marlboro Light behind an HVAC unit, telling her friends how bad she feels for ashing your heart. It doesn't matter that elsewhere, entire populations are going about their business. When you're in a gun's sights, the whole world doesn't have to be about to end for you to feel like the world's about to end.

Anyway.

Sirens: the soundtrack to this city. At all hours, on most streets, cop cars and fire engines and ambulances blur past you, and it's not usually a cause for personal alarm—sirens approaching close enough to hurt your ears, I mean. Which

I guess is why Pappas didn't move till they were right on us, with car doors opening out front and Abrams calling for me, and me saying the detective's name into my phone even though I wasn't sure Wilt could hear. Crowd noise was again coming through his end of the line.

Pop!

Something flew past my head. I dropped to the floor. Scuffles and crashing sounds broke out around me, junkshop clang on every side.

"Wilt? Wilt!" I yelled, but we'd been disconnected.

I snaked toward the rotted hole in the wall. Another shot cracked loud, ricocheting off cement and steel. My way was blocked by a pair of disgusting, knobbly, hairy feet in flip-flops. I brought my hammer down on one of them. The gun clattered to the floor, Pappas let out this hoarse, strangled howl, and cops tackled him.

49

More than a dozen squad cars, a couple police vans and paramedics' trucks, enough people overall to crowd the sidelines of a football field: Abrams had gone excessive on the backup. He paced, shaking his head at me every so often and sucking on a cigarette like it was the Straw of Life, while I let some EMS guy tend to the cuts and swellings on my face.

"Attempted murder," he said. "Intent to cause grievous bodily harm with a firearm. Resisting arrest. Any and all possible weapons violations. As for more," he meant the death-gadgets, the attempted murder of Mom, the actual murder of my brother, "we'll charge him if and when further evidence warrants it."

Pappas—handcuffed, his hammered foot bandaged—was staring at me from the back of a squad car. No doubt his intent was to intimidate. I showed him my two middle fingers and told Abrams to search the lavanderia lot for the second death-gadget in my backpack. He sent an underling off to get it.

"Judges don't like guns being fired at police," he said, flicking his cigarette stub to the ground.

His partner, who had been ordering cops around in the auto body slum, came over to say something in Abrams' ear.

He shot me a look tons more intimidating than anything Pappas could manage, and before he left to interview "witnesses"—three homeless guys who, I later found out, unsurprisingly said they hadn't seen or heard anything—he leveled another intimidating look at me.

"What's his problem?" I asked.

"You ruined a good thing for him."

The EMS guy had done all he could for my face. My nose was busted, my left eye had completely closed up, but I didn't need stitches. Abrams spilled what I'd already guessed: Yang, Nuñez, and others I'd never heard of had been arrested in a raid. Abrams'd had it out with his partner about working for Nuñez, and the partner, to prove he'd leave off his moonlighting, had mentioned a certain veterinarian. I was like, *Duh. Somebody had to be fixing up the winning dogs after fights.* Seems that if detectives threaten a vet with the loss of his license and worse for lack of cooperation, then offer him immunity from prosecution for his testimony, said vet will spill all kinds of incriminating tidbits about his clients, even one as illustrious as Titus Yang.

"But your video and statement should help," Abrams said.

"You know those anonymous online posts?" I said. "Suzy Painter's responsible for them. Maybe if you convince her it's safe to talk, you'll get a potentially helpful statement from her too."

Safe? Funny, but I figured that both Suzy and I'd be safer if Yang's case didn't make it to court. Because then he'd be more likely to blame the vet for his arrest and everything else. At trial, Suzy and I'd have to give evidence, and I didn't need to be told that unless the system made an example of the billionaire, which I didn't count on, he'd get off lightly. I also didn't need to be told that there was no way to keep Yang from organizing canine death matches in the future. Except I chose to believe he wouldn't—that whatever value he got out of the matches, it wasn't worth the risk, having already been busted once. The system might let Yang slide the first time, but not a second: he was too well-known. They don't let you keep a roomful of toupees and doll collections in prison, not even a country club-type prison, do they?

"What'll happen to all the dogs?"

"They'll be kenneled as evidence for as long as they're needed. After that, those that can be retrained will be put up for adoption. Those that can't . . . "

He left the sentence unfinished.

"You didn't have to tell him that I'd tipped you off," I said, meaning his partner, who was talking to Mr. Lopez in the street.

"No, I suppose I didn't," Abrams said.

"That's Mr. Lopez there. Another tenant. Your guys need to check under his car. The Weisses—the only other tenants in the building—have some kind of Buick, I think. And you know Mom's rental. You need to check them before they're driven again."

He nodded, looking toward Pappas's pock-bricked building when he said, "You do have to come to the station now. Give that statement. Your mother's going to hear about everything and it's probably best if you're on-site to comfort her—as much as you can, looking as you do. Oh, and here."

He tried to hand me my burner phone. I told him to keep it as evidence.

"I guess it's Visit-Your-Mother's-Boyfriend-at-Work-Day, after all," I said.

50

I waited at the front desk while he prepped Mom, not wanting her to freak when she saw me. Which, till she did see me, kind of freaked her out because she had no idea what he was prepping her for. But Abrams'd been clever, telling her to bring a carton's worth of nicotine lozenges to the station, since filling out paperwork for her wrecked car could take an annoyingly long time. I'm saying she could've freaked a lot worse, so.

We met in Abrams' office. As soon as Mom eyed me, the muscles in her face started to jump as if from spasms.

"What happened? What's . . . ?" Her eye-faucets leaked. She pet my shoulders, wanting to touch my face but afraid to. "What happened, hon? Who did this? Somebody'd better tell me what's going on right now. Tom?"

Abrams said she'd understand most things after I gave my statement, which he wanted me to do with her in the room. He sat down at his computer, and with me and Mom in chairs on the other side of his desk—

"You want the version that includes Wilt's calls or one that doesn't?" I asked.

"One that doesn't."

"'Cause I'll be more credible?"

"Yes."

I started with Wilt's stash of money hidden in Mom's nightstand, the phone number I'd found on the $50. Without tagging Wilt's calls, I said what I could about my motivations—how I hadn't believed my brother died accidentally because what had he been doing on St. Benny and where had all his money come from? About my work for Yang and Nuñez, I spilled everything I could remember—from my first meet with Nuñez to my last with Yang, when he interrogated me about the online smear campaign. I told how I'd recorded the St. Benny video and Nuñez's goons had nearly thrown me in a cremation pit. I went over the stuff Abrams already knew, since it was for the official record—about Suzy and Wilt trying to sabotage Yang's op and all that. I told about seeing Pappas with Yang and other moneymen at the beastie fights and in a ground-floor apartment in my building, and how I realized that I'd gotten everything wrong about Wilt's murder and came to suspect Pappas.

Overall, Mom took the story pretty well. Disbelief alternated with worry and she wondered how she could've been so clueless. Near the end, hearing that she—not Wilt—had been Pappas's target, she sobbed out what most parents would: that she'd have changed places with him in a blink.

"But who did that to your face?" she asked.

"That has nothing to do with anything," I said. "It's just something I have to work through at school."

Figuring we could use some private time, Abrams went for coffee, and I don't know about Mom, but I felt like, yeah, obviously we had plenty to hash through, issues-wise, and maybe we always would, but because we weren't going to hash through any of it in a detective's office, there wasn't much for us to talk about.

"I wish there was one thing I could do to make everything better," she said. "Something that would allow us to start over."

Start over from where? From before Wilt died? From when she and Dad were married and we all lived together? From before I'd ever swallowed a single med or—

"I'm doing the best I can," she said.

It wasn't the first time I'd heard her say it, and as always, I had my doubts. "I know, Mom. But I wonder if, especially lately, maybe your best would be better if, you know, you talked to somebody on a regular basis? In therapy, I mean."

She scanned her hard drive of sighs—the breath she eventually let out equal parts acceptance and relief, like whatever problems we had, and despite everything we'd been through, acknowledging that maybe, just maybe, she should see a therapist could be a start to something better.

She motioned at my face. "Do you hurt?"

"Well, yeah."

She got out of her chair and came over to me, asked me to stand. She wasn't usually so formal, which made me a bit uncomfortable, but I did what she asked. She put her arms around me, murmuring, "My baby, my baby," and we stood holding each other till a familiar whiny voice started making itself known in the hall: Dr. M loudly complaining to the department that Abrams was a violent individual who exploited his position in law enforcement, attacking civilians for his own amusement. He, Dr. Murray, had come to press charges, doubting he'd be the only one.

"Look what he did!" he shrieked when he saw me.

"Shut up," I said, which, because he wasn't expecting it, he actually did.

Mom pulled the doofus a little ways down a hall to try and talk him calm, but his agitation infected her and they wound up fighting—the closest to being my father-figure Dr. M had ever been.

"You can't argue with facts!" Dr. M pleaded.

"Your facts are suffocating me," Mom said.

Abrams and I watched them from the door of his office. Re: Yang and Pappas, the detective had only done his job, I knew. Except—doing a job like his probably shouldn't ever be described with "only," as if what he did for work wasn't a huge deal. I wanted to thank him, but that's not what came out.

"I've never met anyone who didn't help a person without thinking about what they'd get from it," I said, "even if it's just them feeling good about themselves."

"And why does that bother you?"

"I don't know, but if everyone's always using everyone else to get stuff they want—as like a possible means of furthering their own agendas—instead of treating other people as *people*? It just seems depressing and wrong somehow."

"There will always be users," he said after chewing the inside of his cheek awhile. "There will always be murderers and thieves and . . . " he nodded toward Dr. M, who was repeating some lame psych mantra, " . . . losers. You can wish things were different, but getting depressed and angry because that wish doesn't come true is a waste of time and energy."

It felt redundant to say, but redundancy was kind of a theme to my life, so. "I'm not sure I can control how I come at things, no matter how much I try to," I told him.

"I understand, believe me."

If anyone had asked, I would've said Detective Abrams was a pretty nice guy. If you liked people.

Mom and lame-o Murray were nearing the end of their fight, having that same hushed back-and-forth the parentals had when they got tired of berating each other.

Eyeing Dr. M, Abrams said, "I need some fresh air. I'm going out to smoke a cigarette."

51

I'd tried texting Wilt probably 1,000 times before he finally called. I didn't know which I wanted more: to tell him what'd happened with Pappas or to hear about his rebellion, but he was too pumped for me to get a word in, explaining how, after he and Claudius and their fellow rebels stormed past a legion of assistant managers, the powers that be sent a delegation to negotiate. Claudius's counselor was in the delegation, along with Wilt's counselor Sean and a general manager. There were more than a few general managers, apparently. During the negotiations, the delegates regularly disappeared to consult with their superiors, but finally it was announced that the Aftermart would be going out of business and every shopper and employee dispersed as pure energy.

"We won!" Wilt said. "Sean, assistant managers, even most of the general managers—they were *all* bored and were on our side the entire time. It was a matter of convincing the higher-ups. I still can't believe it, really. None of us knows how it's going to work—our transition to impersonal energy—or when."

"So this might be the last time we talk, you're saying?

"I think we should assume it is, yeah. And it's your fault."

"Mine?"

"If you hadn't told me to skip therapy and ignore quotas, I wouldn't have gotten the idea to rebel. It sucks—our not talking anymore—but I've got to say, Curtis, I'm grateful to you. More grateful than you can probably ever understand."

I've seen people cry at bread commercials and bawl at the sight of kittens, but just because something brings you to tears doesn't mean it has any special emotional power or depth. It's more about the person crying, I'm saying—what that person sees in the thing. But losing your older brother a second time? For *really* real? It wasn't any bread commercial. And how I felt at that moment? The salty wet on my face? It was probably the reaction Abrams'd been expecting from me in the morgue the night of Wilt's death.

"Anyone else around for me to say goodbye to?" he asked.

Mom left off reorganizing kitchen stuff with Okafur, Narith and Arundhati, and took my phone into the bathroom for privacy. When she and Wilt were done, she opened the door just enough to hand the phone back to me, not coming out of the bathroom herself till long after Wilt and I'd hung up.

In my ear, my brother was all, "Mom said you got Pappas?"

I told him how the last of it had gone down.

"She also said your face was recently used as a punching bag. Rick Calvados, I'm guessing? Because you won Suzy and he didn't?"

Maybe I should've admitted the truth: that between me and Calvados neither of us had won Suzy, that in a way we'd both lost. But I didn't want to let him down. "Yeah," I said.

I could feel our call coming to a close. Since the end was

so near, it was like we both understood that the best thing to do was not put off the inevitable but get it over with as fast as possible.

"Hey, Wilt?" I said. "I love you, you know."

I'd never said that to him before. If he'd lived, no doubt it'd have taken me twenty years to say it, to have felt connected enough to say it—if even then.

"I love you too, Curtis. And thanks."

"You also. Thanks, I mean."

" . . . "

" . . . "

"You hang up first."

"No, you."

"Same time?"

"Okay."

He counted to three. The line went dead and I never heard from him again.

WHAT I KNOW I KNOW

Wilt died because of Pappas's greed and stupidity.

Lots of seriously crap things happen because of greed and stupidity.

WHAT I KNOW I DON'T KNOW

If the original purpose of Wilt's calls was to help save Mom from being killed.

If Wilt's counselor Sean and other higher-ups used Wilt's calls (and me) to help shake up the Afterimant status quo.

If it matters what the original purpose of the calls was.

How well I can deal, in the long term, with seriously crap things happening because of greed and stupidity.

WHAT I DON'T KNOW I DON'T KNOW

???

WHAT I KNOW THAT I DIDN'T KNOW I KNEW

It's possible I'll never be off meds, but so what? Geezers take meds for high blood pressure and whatever else. If I have to swallow pills that make me less angry/depressed, isn't it kind of similar?

52

It's been almost a year since my last call with Wilt. A lot has happened and also nothing. I don't expect that to make sense, it's just how things feel. Except the stuff I'm about to relate? Even though it's factually true, it's still kind of bogus because it'll come off like I'm describing the conclusion of events in my life that don't feel concluded.

So.

Calvados got his scholarship and is off swatting people with his fruit-picker on Duke's behalf. After he exercised his fists against my face the day of Pappas's arrest, he never subjected me to another beating. I don't know if he realized he'd done enough damage or if Suzy had told him to back off, but he basically just ignored me till the school year ended. Whenever kids asked who had worked me over, I told them that I'd run into a door. Repeatedly. I didn't figure they'd believe me, but it kept the Calvados-Brooks-Painter gossip to a minimum.

Suzy and I are online friends. I see her posts and whatnot, but that's it. I don't comment on her stuff, she doesn't comment on mine. It took weeks for us to finish the conversation we'd started on the curb outside 7-11—mostly because I kept scoping her and Calvados together in study and lunch periods and so didn't feel like talking to her or answering her texts. But cleaning out my locker the last day of school, I wasn't paying attention and she ambushed me.

"You've been avoiding me," she said.

"Is it that obvious?"

She knew about Yang's and Pappas's arrests—Abrams had interviewed her—and she'd been wanting to gush all sorts of things about how proud she was of me, of my part in what had gone down, even if my behavior had seemed pretty dim at the time. I got her off topic by telling her that Wilt had wanted me to pass along a message. A final message: *good-bye.* And I explained what the success of his Aftermart rebellion had meant.

Once she finished crying, I couldn't help myself and was like, "It's not that I don't want you to be happy. I just, could you *not* be happy with Calvados at my expense?"

"Rick and I aren't going to see each other anymore in that way," she said. She was leaving for upstate New York as soon as possible, attending Bard in the fall. "There's no point dragging out a romantic relationship I have no intention of continuing after I leave."

The same as it would have been with Wilt or me. There was nothing left to say.

"Promise you'll keep in touch?"

"I promise."

She kissed me, a quick press of her mouth against mine, tight-lipped, and I turned and stared into my locker. I'll always carry a hurt around because of Suzy—or if not always, for a while. But I'm no longer sure she's solely to blame for the hurt. Like she'd said, she never straight up lied about Calvados, right? She just hadn't been super explicit. Besides, just because somebody hurts you doesn't mean you can stop caring about them, even if maybe you should.

Anyway.

I promised to keep in touch but didn't. Or haven't yet. That's the way things go. Except it won't surprise me if one day Suzy and I are friends again. Real friends, I mean. Not virtual.

Dr. M's gross relationship with Mom never recovered from that scene in the police station. He refused to believe that Abrams had helped catch Wilt's murderer and wasn't a violent asshole. Mom called him a loser, said she'd had it, and cut him off. I was worried he'd subject me to a lot of one-on-one sessions at school, but Principal Chu saved me by forcing the doofus to take a leave of absence. I doubt he's ever coming back. Junior year started with Mr. Hearns in his former office.

Mom's been toughing it out in therapy at the free clinic, not as often as she should, but the fact that she's going at all is kind of a miracle. She still has days of impatience, obliviousness, selfishness. Who doesn't? Nicotine patches and lozenges remain a problem. It doesn't help that Abrams now uses both, having finally put down the tobacco sticks. Yeah, Abrams is in the picture. Apparently, he wants more from Mom than she's willing to give, but she says she likes being with him, so.

Jeremy's been admitted to the Gifted & Talented Program at school, and Dad's still with his third wife Maria, though you wouldn't know it from how often he shows up at Chili's with the gopher-lodge hairdo lady. Whatever he does for a living? Why does it matter, so long as he keeps showing up at Chili's, even irregularly?

Evil lard-butt Pappas is stewing in county jail, waiting to stand trial for the murders of Wilton Brooks and Thomas Birch, and for a mess of lesser charges. Yang got six months of house arrest and according to the interwebs spent 500K on creepy dolls to play with during his confinement. Nuñez took the fall for his boss, Abrams told me, and has a couple more years to do in state prison.

But so, Pappas's slum building? It's being unloaded on some new group of investors. Legal stuff is holding up the sale. We still live in it—me, Mom, *and* the pseudo-siblings. You'd think that as Mom gradually regained all the mental equilibrium she's ever likely to have, she'd return the pseudo-siblings to wherever she found them, but no. We've moved into a three-bedroom on the second floor. I have my own room. Mom and Arundhati share. Okafur and Narith also. Word is, since the building will be renovated, not torn down, we'll be allowed to stay, as will the other holdout tenants, the Lopezes and Weisses. Best part is that we don't have to pay rent until the sale of the building goes through.

Narith swears that he came to live with us after Mom rescued him from some restaurant where he worked as slave labor. I once asked Okafur about the "official" channel that brought him under our roof, and he suddenly forgot all the English he's been learning while studying for the G.E.D. I've since seen bona fide adoption papers—the kid is now legally a Brooks—but dates on them are wrong. Like, Okafur was already living here when the adoption process was put in motion. Abrams probably pulled some strings, I figure. Arundhati claims she's an emancipated minor. Whatever. But it's been impossible to get the pseudo-siblings to lay off chores.

"You know you can just hang out and watch TV or something, right?" I say to them.

They bobble their heads *yes* and try for a couple minutes, fidgeting and squirming in front of the TV like that's the real chore. Then Okafur will pull out a rag from somewhere and start dusting a lamp, Arundhati might grab clothes to fold, and pretty soon Narith will give up TV-gawking altogether and go off to scrub the bathtub.

We're starting a business, the four of us, as a way to bring in cash and help Mom with the bills. The business? One World Cleaning Service.

I didn't used to believe in supernatural doings, life after death and all that, and it took Wilt's calls for me to realize how much of a non-believer I'd been. I guess I'd always felt, *What, life isn't challenging/interesting enough, we have to add God, angels, devils, spirits?* Not that I've become a cheerleader for the supernatural or anything. It's just that the unlikeliest-seeming things can happen whether you believe in them or not.

What will I feel in ten years, twenty years—so long after Wilt's death? *My brother died when I was younger,* I'll say. I'll remember that I had a big brother, sure, but will I remember what having a brother *felt* like, when so much of my life will have happened after I *didn't* have one? Living with Wilt wasn't usually a source of up-with-family material, but still. It's weird to think that eighteen years from now, assuming I don't suffer a horrendous accident, I'll have lived longer without a brother than with one. The hardest part of the coming decades will be not surrendering Wilt to memory. To keep that from happening, I have to know that Wilt's been recycled into the universe, that tiny parts of him—quantum-level tiny, I'm talking—are all around, in the rain and sunlight, in the air I breathe, though mostly in me.

ABOUT THE AUTHOR

A New Yorker by birth, Eric Laster lives in Los Angeles. After many years as a *New York Times* best-selling ghostwriter, he is now optimistic that admitting his corporeal existence to the public won't be a bad thing. *Static* is Eric's debut YA novel. Whenever he's not scribing, he records punk rock and presses it to vinyl.

FOLLOW ERIC AT:

 @ericlaster

e_laster

Be part of the Static community
STATICNOVEL.COM